A large, metal door opened, and there before the throngs of kneeling, screaming people, he appeared. Wearing a silver cloak that shimmered blindingly, and a silver turban atop his head, he floated through the air as if carried gently by the wind.

His eyes blazed fiercely as he looked over the people, a malevolent, twisted grin upon his face. In a loud, hollow voice, he addressed them:

"My people, I am Ras-ek Varano," he told them, adopting the name of the once beloved deity of Boranga, "and this is Sekkator, my home. You, and only you, have been chosen to be my kuta. We have been sent to the Other Side for a purpose, and now I have learned what it is. I will take what I wish, when I wish. You cannot stop me. I am to be your ruler, your Master—the almighty . . .

MASTER OF BORANGA

MASTER OF BORANGA

BY MIKE SIROTA

ZEBRA BOOKS

KENSINGTON PUBLISHING CORP.

ZEBRA BOOKS

are published by

KENSINGTON PUBLISHING CORP.
21 East 40th Street
New York, N.Y. 10016

FOR ADAIR,
MY REAL-LIFE HEROINE

FOREWORD

"I am insane . . ."

Thus began a letter that turned up on my desk one morning amidst the trade journals and other routine correspondence that one becomes used to sorting through most every day. My first impression was that some poor, deluded soul had gotten his doctors mixed up, since I was only a general practitioner, not a psychiatrist. The letter was postmarked Honolulu, Hawaii, and the stationery bore the letterhead of the Pacific Hills Medical Center. Hawaii? I had been there briefly during the war, but I did not recall having any acquaintances there. I read on:

Dear Dr. Morrison:

I am insane. At least, that is what the doctors here believe, and would have me believe. However, I am not insane; I assure you, I am not insane! I am as rational now as I was when I last saw you, nearly five years ago. You took care of

7

me through all the various ailments and broken bones of childhood. Do you remember me as one given to wild wanderings of the imagination? Even after the tragedy, a shocking emotional experience, you commented on how well I was able to handle things. No, Doctor, I was not irrational then, and I am not now. I have always admired and respected you, Dr. Morrison, which is why I am writing to you now. I need your help, Doctor, I need it badly. I must get out! I must get back! Please help me, Doctor, please help me!

During the past year, I have been through experiences which no doubt could drive a sane man crazy. I have returned from these encounters badly broken in body, but not in mind. I have actually lived through the horrors that I am going to relate to you. I did not imagine them!

My injuries are practically healed now. I have tried to break out twice, which is their reason for keeping me under restraint. The doctors come to see me nearly every day. I tell them what happened to me and what I now must do, but they won't believe me, they just won't listen. They think I'm insane!

While recovering from my injuries, I wrote down as best I could all that has happened to me. I have sent these pages separately, and I hope that you have already received them. Read them carefully, Dr. Morrison, and believe them. Every word is true. Remember the kind of person that I was. You must help me get out of *here! I must return to Boranga! I must help them! I must save them! I must find her again, my Adara! Help me, Doctor! For God's sake, please help me!*

Respectfully yours,
Roland Summers

Roland Summers. Until I saw the signature, I must admit that I believed I *was* reading the words of a madman. But Roland Summers? Not very likely. I was the Summers' family doctor for years, until the auto accident that killed Roland's parents five years ago. Roland was a fine, intelligent young man, with much athletic ability. He had aspired to win a spot on the United States swimming team and compete in the '48 Olympics, but the tragedy ended that dream. Roland, nearly twenty-one years old at the time, decided to leave school and enlist in the navy. That was the last time that I had seen or heard from Roland Summers. But my memories of him certainly did not fit the image of one who could have penned the words I had just read.

Roland was an above average student. I recall how proud his mother used to be of his scholastic accomplishments. He performed admirably in all sports during his high school days, and even received a basketball scholarship to one of the local universities. But swimming was his first and foremost love, and it was here that his aspirations were the greatest.

The Roland Summers I remembered was a very popular fellow. His friendships reflected his personality, for he avoided the parasitical types who tended to attach themselves to the school sports heroes. He looked for friendships based on mutual respect, this in both men and women. These characteristics were displayed even at a young age, for he never allowed his popularity to go to his head.

After his parents were killed, I personally observed Roland for a time, and I believe that it was his strong will that helped him through this most tragic period in his life. We discussed his decision to leave school and join the navy at great length, and I felt that the choice he made was a rational one. He had planned on enlisting at some future date anyway, and he felt that to get away from home would do him good. I concurred in his decision.

Now Roland Summers was under restraint in a psychiatric ward at a hospital in Hawaii. I could not believe it! Had his mind been affected that greatly over the years? What had brought him to this? I felt that the answer might lie in the pages he had mentioned in his letter. I looked through the rest of that morning's mail, but found no such manuscript. Was there really a manuscript, or was he imagining that, too? With a full slate of patients that day I could not dwell on it for long, but that evening the thought of a young man, a fine, tormented young man, began to haunt me.

The next morning, the manuscipt arrived. With another busy day scheduled, I was unable to read the pages until that evening. I asked one of my associates to cover my calls so that I could read it undisturbed.

My colleague was to cover many calls for me that week, as I became caught up in one of the strangest occurrences one could possibly imagine. You will shortly understand why. I present to you, in his own words, Roland Summers' story of his unbelievable experiences on Boranga.

CHAPTER ONE

THE FOG

I have always loved the sea; the sea, with her beauty and mystery, her gentleness and raging fury. I can see the waves from here in my room, but somehow it does not look quite the same through the bars. I imagine that it is because of the sea that I am here today. However, I cannot blame her. My only wish is to ride her waves once more, to seek out that which I know to be.

It is difficult to say why I have decided to put down on paper the events of the past few months. Perhaps I do it to relieve the long, monotonous hours that I spend recovering from the injuries. Perhaps it is to reassure myself that it really did happen, or maybe to convince myself that it did not. But it *did* happen, I know that it did! Maybe that is why I am relating this story now, in the hope that someone will believe what I say, and help me.

To tell this story properly, I suppose I should go back just a bit. I had served in the navy since 1948, and the last fifteen months of my hitch were spent in and around Hawaii. I received my discharge about two years ago, and I decided to stay in Honolulu for the time being. I really loved the islands, which were still somewhat free of the over-commercialism that far-seeing planners were predicting. Having finished my education while I was in the navy, I was qualified to teach physical education to young children, and was fortunate to find a job doing this in Honolulu. I also found a part-time position as a deckhand on one of the chartered fishing boats, this more for enjoyment than pay, for I never tired of journeying amidst the islands.

Denny McVey became my close friend during the time we served together on a destroyer. Denny, who worked in the engine room, was an absolute whiz when it came to anything mechanical. When his hitch was up, not long after mine, he too decided to stay in Hawaii, and he found a job in an auto repair shop. Denny was a year younger than me, and we had a great deal in common. We shared an apartment together, and, when not working, we shared lots of other things, including a mutual appreciation of the beautiful island maidens that abounded everywhere. Denny was quite adept with the ladies, and I usually got to go along for the ride.

We spent much time speculating on the day when we could venture into business for ourselves, and overwhelm the islands with our keen business acumen. Somehow, we never seemed to decide just what kind of business we would start, but we enjoyed the vision nonetheless. We did not know then how close we were to realizing the dream.

One evening, Denny arrived home after work in a most agitated state. Our apartment was on the second floor, twenty-four steps up, and when there was some moderately exciting news he usually covered the stairway in twelve steps. That night, I counted eight footfalls. The door burst open, and Denny flew in, breathless.

"Rollie, it's happened!" he managed to blurt out while trying to catch his breath. "We won't have to wait any longer, do you understand? We won't have to wait!"

"Now whoa, slow down and tell me what you're talking about," I said as I grabbed his shoulders and sat him down.

"A boat, Rollie, a fishing boat!" he replied. "We can have our own fishing boat. I saw it today. It's the chance we've been waiting for!"

"And what makes you think that we would be able to buy our own fishing boat?" I asked. "We don't have that kind of money."

"You don't understand!" Denny exclaimed. "I ran across a fellow today who wants to get rid of an old boat for practically nothing. It's a beauty, Rollie, it really is! Of course, it needs a little work—"

"Of course," I countered. "Just a *little* work."

"But it *is* serviceable," he replied. "I'm sure of that. And the price is right. Listen, tomorrow is Saturday, and neither of us has to work. At least come down with me in the morning and take a look at it."

I finally agreed to look at the boat, if for no other reason but to calm Denny down. However, he spent most of the evening talking excitedly about all the things we could do with such a prize. I must admit that, after an hour or so, I became caught up in his enthusiasm and began to look forward to seeing the object of his praise.

The next morning I became half owner of the *Maui Queen*, though I daresay she looked anything but royal. The *Maui Queen*, some thirty feet long, certainly appeared to have outlived her usefulness. Most all of her paint had been chipped off, and the wood was rotted in places. Barnacles clung in great masses just below the water line. All the visible hardware was rusted, and one of the wheelhouse windows was conspicuous by its absence. But the unregal outward appearance of the *Queen* was easily matched by the disaster in the engine room. The engine, a conglomeration of rusted parts, had apparently been taken apart and put back together again without success. Many parts were left over, and these were scattered here and there all over the floor. Scurrying sounds foretold of other occupants below-decks, not only in the engine room but in the seedy cabin. The price was right, however, as Denny had reported, and with his assurance that the *Maui Queen* was salvageable, we happily made our purchase.

For the next two months, we spent nearly all of our free time working on her. Both of us toiled on the outside of the boat, replacing rotted wood and hardware that could not be cleaned, caulking the seams, painting, and installing a new wheelhouse window. We had the *Queen* hauled into dry-dock after evicting the vermin, and I was able to scrape all the barnacles from her. Soon the *Queen* had once again taken on the regal appearance that must surely have been hers in the past.

Down below, things were not quite as simple. Denny made the engine room his private domain, spending hour after hour with the badly abused engine. While I considered him the master of all things mechanical, I doubted whether anyone short of a miracle worker could coax life from that pile of junk. But Denny would not give up. I busied myself by making the cabin habitable, while he continued his seemingly impossible task. When the day finally came that Denny allowed me to set foot in the engine room again, I was overwhelmed by what I saw.

"Why, the thing looks as good as new!" I exclaimed. "Will it run?"

Looking somewhat hurt, Denny replied: "Will it run? I've done everything one could possibly do to an engine, and some things that aren't usually attempted. I've talked to this engine, babied it, nursed it. It has feelings, you know. It won't let me down; you'll see."

So with little ceremony, the *Maui Queen* was once again returned to the sea. On Denny's signal I started her up: once, twice, nothing. The third time the engine turned over and, in Denny's own words, began to purr like a kitten. Denny ran up on deck, and we pounded each other on the back. Together we jumped up and down gleefully, shouting like a couple of kids. We had ourselves a great ship. Her maiden voyage around Honolulu Harbor pushed us to the zenith of euphoria.

In the following months, we took the *Maui Queen*

out every weekend. Sometimes we went for fun, exploring the bays and hidden lagoons. On other occasions, we took out fishing parties. But the venture that proved most lucrative for us was the capturing of rare and exotic fish, which were purchased by brokers for shipment to collectors and universities in the States. We had bought some diving gear which we used for this, and were fortunate to locate some previously untapped areas that abounded in these specimens. We were never at a loss for deckhands, as the docks were full of eager young fellows anxious to earn a few dollars. One lad named Kim proved quite capable, and he accompanied us on most of our voyages.

Soon the few runs that we were able to make each month were proving to be most profitable. We began to weigh the pros and cons of attempting it on a full-time basis. True, our jobs were steady, and helped to provide us with the necessities of life. But we both loved what we were doing, and somehow believed that the future was bright. With the adventurous spirit of youth, we quit our jobs and undertook the operation of the *Maui Queen* with great fervor. We continued taking out fishing parties now and then, but most of our time was spent in gathering rare fish and coral, as well as anything else that the buyers happened to be interested in at the time. To save money, we moved our meager belongings into the cabin of the *Maui Queen* and gave up the apartment. The *Queen* was now our home in every sense of the word.

Things went better than we expected for a while. We put Kim to work for us full-time, and he accompanied us nearly every day. He learned to handle almost anything that we could, including some of the diving. On Denny's suggestion we even learned the skill of catching live porpoises, which always seemed to be in demand from research laboratories or marine parks. Catching the mammals was risky and time consuming, but it was fun and most rewarding.

Then came the day that I will likely never forget. It was a Tuesday morning, and we had given Kim the day off, since the previous day's run had taken us much longer than expected. We left the harbor about five-thirty that morning after fueling up. Our destination was the tiny island of Moku Manu, just off the northeast coast of Oahu. Weather conditions were ideal, and we arrived near mid-morning without incident. I was breaking out the gear for the first dive, which I was to make, when I heard Denny shouting from the bow.

"Porpoises, a large school of them, about two or three miles north-northeast!" he yelled, his binoculars trained on them.

"Well, the man from Hilo was by the other day," I replied. "They could really use a couple of them as soon as possible. Let's give it a try."

"Do you think the two of us will be able to handle it?"

"We'll never find out by standing around here. Let's get going!"

Denny set the *Maui Queen* in motion and aimed her toward the school, while I rode the bow in order to keep them in sight. The porpoises, with only slight variation, maintained their speed. We were trying to get close enough to attract their attention, because we knew that these fun-loving creatures enjoyed romping alongside a fast-moving boat. After pursuing them for about ten miles, we had narrowed the gap considerably, when the engine, Denny's beloved engine, sputtered and died.

"Well, you must have jilted her or something," I quipped. "Looks like the love affair is over."

"Impossible!" Denny roared. "There should be no reason for it to go out. It was working perfectly. I'll go down and check her."

Denny disappeared below, and I began gathering up our gear from the deck, anticipating the possibility that we would not be getting any work done that day. About ten minutes had passed when I noticed that we were drifting into a very light fog. Concerned, I called Denny back up on deck.

"Did you find out what's wrong with it?" I asked.

"There's nothing wrong with it," he replied.

"What do you mean there's nothing wrong? It isn't working, is it?"

"That's just it, Rollie. It *should* be working. I checked it over from top to bottom and can't find a thing wrong with it. It just—stopped!" He leaned over the railing, his head down.

"Denny," I said, slightly annoyed, "you're a mechanic. You know that a machine just—"

"My god, Rollie! What's that in the water?"

I ran to the railing and peered over the side, where the reason for Denny's agitation was clear. The water had turned white!

"What do you make of that?" he asked.

"I don't know, but I intend to find out!"

I raced to the bow, where I saw that the white water was a broad strip about twenty feet wide. The *Maui Queen* was riding right down the middle of it. Up ahead, the gleaming ribbon stretched as far as I could see.

"Rollie, do you realize that we're moving?" Denny asked, as he joined me. "Is this thing some kind of current?"

"I've never *seen* a current before," I replied, "and yes, I guess we are drifting."

"No, Rollie, not drifting. We seem to be riding on top of this thing. If we were drifting, we'd be bounced around like a cork. And notice the speed. We're moving faster every minute."

I did notice the speed of the *Queen* now, and it *was* increasing. I also realized that the light fog of a few minutes past was now quite thick. We decided that our next course of action was to radio for help, and together we ran to the wheelhouse. Denny sat down at the set and switched it on. The radio was dead! Coincidence? Not likely. I believe that the radio went out at the same time the engine did. I looked at my watch, noting that it too had stopped. And our compass? It was spinning uncontrollably. Was this some kind of magnetic field? Or . . . ?

Denny relayed his thoughts to me. "Rollie, I'm scared. I don't know what the devil's happening. When I dive, I run into sharks, and that doesn't frighten me as much because I can see them. But this? I don't understand it."

"I'm as confused as you are, my friend," I told him. "I guess we have no choice but to ride this thing out, and see where it's taking us."

"You can stay topside if you want, but I'm going down to the engine room and see if I can't get that baby going again. Maybe we can pull ourselves out of this thing."

Denny went below again, and I did not try to stop him. I'm sure he realized, as I did, the futility of attempting to repair anything mechanical on the *Queen*, but I understood why he at least had to try. I sat down at the radio and tinkered with it for a while, but soon gave this up.

Hours, or what seemed like hours, had passed since the engine stopped. Denny was still below with his pride and joy. I stood on the bow of the *Queen*, trying vainly to see where we were. The fog enshrouded the *Queen* now, a cold, clammy fog that somehow portended evil. We were moving even more rapidly than before, just how fast I had no way of telling. I realized that I was shivering from the cold, and decided to join Denny below.

Suddenly, I noticed something. It was hard to distinguish at first, but I believed it to be . . . yes, it was! I could *see* the ribbon of white water, or whatever it was that we were riding on. But how was this possible? I was not even able to see the deck of the *Maui Queen* below my feet through the fog; but the ribbon was becoming visible! First dimly, then brighter, even brighter. It glowed with an eerie phosphorescence that pierced the dense shroud encircling it. I called Denny up to have a look at it.

"What, in heaven's name, do you make of that?" he asked.

"I don't know, but I have this strange feeling that the journey is coming to its conclusion. Anything to report about the engine?"

"Nothing. I've taken it apart, and put it back together again. You just can't repair something that isn't broken. I think—Rollie, am I crazy, or are we slowing down?"

Denny was right; we were moving slower. I looked over the railing again, and the ribbon was even brighter. During the next hour or so the glow increased in intensity, while the *Queen* continued to slow down gradually. The light became so bright that we were unable to look directly at it. All the while the denseness of the encompassing mist remained unchanged.

The glowing strip on which we rode now widened to cover a vast expanse of ocean. Soon the *Queen* sat in what appeared to be the center of this sphere, where it stopped moving.

"I think that we're here," I stated.

"Yes, but where the devil is *here?*" Denny replied.

The *Maui Queen* began to spin, slowly at first, very slowly; then faster, like a carousel. Between the motion and the brightness I felt myself growing dizzy, and I noticed that Denny was already staggering.

"Grab onto the railing," I shouted at him, "and hold on for your life!"

We both wrapped our arms around the metal as the *Queen* gyrated faster and faster. I began to feel a kind of sinking sensation, almost as if we were falling. The fog was lifting now, only to be replaced by the dazzling whiteness which rose up along the sides of the *Queen* and completely encircled us. Denny let go of the railing and slumped to the deck, unconscious.

23

I crawled over to him to see if I could help. The *Queen* continued to spin, the speed now beyond reason, while the sinking feeling continued. I fell to the deck beside my friend and remembered no more.

CHAPTER TWO

STRANGERS IN THE HEAVENS

The air was cool and invigorating; the *Maui Queen* rocked gently, peacefully, on a calm sea. Darkness surrounded me, although the first hints of dawn were beginning to appear on the horizon. I felt relaxed, almost euphoric, and I believed that I could lay there like that forever. Forever . . .

No! I had to snap myself out of this! The horrors of what we had endured flashed before me in rapid sequence. Such thoughts were not easily replaced by euphoria. Was it all over, or had it just been a prelude of more to come? Whatever it was, I knew that I could not lie on the deck of the *Queen* idly. I had to fight that feeling! I had to get up!

I crawled toward the railing, straining with every movement. Finally I reached it, and slowly, painfully, I pulled myself up. My head began to throb, as if a thousand hammers were striking it from all directions. A terrible thirst overwhelmed me. My mouth and throat were dry, impossibly dry, as though I had swallowed sand.

I looked back to where Denny was lying, noting that he too was beginning to stir. I had to go to him and help him, but I couldn't! The unrelenting thirst had to be quenched. I had to have water! I staggered in the direction of the wheelhouse, where we kept a canteen hanging right next to the radio. Yes, it was still there. I removed the top and held it to my lips. Slowly, slowly, I kept telling myself. Don't pour it down. Sip it slowly, a little at a time.

I picked up the chair, which had toppled over, and sat down, trying to regroup my thoughts. The water had wrought miracles, for the burning thirst was nearly gone, and the pain in my head had subsided. Two or three minutes later I felt well enough to rise. At that moment I remembered Denny. Was he experiencing similar sensations? No matter, for I had to help him. Taking the still half-full canteen with me, I walked slowly onto the deck of the *Queen*. Denny was in the same spot where I had last seen him. He had risen to one knee, and was holding his head in his hands. As I reached him, I called his name. He raised his head and stared at me uncomprehendingly, his face reflecting his anguish.

"Water! Give me water!" he pleaded. "I need water! I'm so thirsty!"

I gently laid Denny on the deck, supporting his head with one hand, and I raised the canteen to his mouth with the other. I limited him to small sips, although he vainly struggled with me for larger swallows. Satisfied that he had had enough, I dragged him a few yards and propped his back up against the outside of the wheelhouse. Fetching a towel from the cabin below, I drenched it in water and applied it to his head. It did not take long to revive him.

"What a hangover I've got this morning!" Denny exclaimed. "Was I plied with *sake* or something last night?"

"You mean you don't remember what we've been through?"

"Yeah, I guess I do, although it still seems like some kind of frightful nightmare. Where the devil are we?"

"I haven't the slightest idea, but everything appears normal again. I'm going to try the engine. Maybe we can get out of here."

"Wait, I'll go with you." He started to rise.

"Are you sure you're up to it?" I asked.

"Don't worry about me. I want to get going worse than you do."

We entered the wheelhouse together, and Denny tried to start the engine. It was still dead. The radio was also silent. Everything was as it had been.

"Well, what now?" Denny asked. "No means of propulsion, no way to contact anyone. Where do we go from here?"

"We let the *Queen* take us, and hope that we run into somebody, or vice-versa. We have no means of rigging up a sail. So we drift, and at least one of us keeps an eye open at all times. If our stores haven't been damaged, we should have enough food and water to last for a while."

I left Denny on deck and descended to the cabin to

check on our food and water. We had examined the *Maui Queen* as thoroughly as possible topside, but found no visible damage. Below, all of the water kegs had been knocked loose from their supports, but only one of them had cracked open, its contents soaking the floor. I replaced the good kegs in the makeshift rack that Denny had built for them, using extra rope to make doubly sure they would not break loose again. I then mopped up what water I could from the floor. Our food supply, mostly all in cans, was intact. We had installed a bolt lock on the cupboard door, and this had held.

I began to check the rest of the *Queen* belowdecks for signs of damage. Although many loose odds and ends had been thrown around, all seemed to be in good shape. I was completing my inspection of the engine room when I heard Denny calling for me to come up on deck. I closed the engine room door behind me and started up.

"What's doing?" I asked, joining him. "Have you spotted something already?"

"Not a chance," he said. "I just noticed something unusual. How long has the sun been up this morning?"

"About an hour, maybe an hour and a half. Why?"

"Take a good look at it. Anything strike you as strange?"

I looked toward the sun. "Other than the fact that it's red, and certainly makes for an inspiring sunrise, I don't notice a thing out of place."

"That's just it," he said. "It's at least an hour or more over the horizon already. Why should it appear red after all that time? Also, it seems to be larger than usual."

"Denny, you've observed the sun come up many times over the ocean. All sunrises are beautiful and different in their own way. This just happens to be a most unique one. Can't you see that?"

"No!" he snapped. "There's something else. Don't you feel it?"

"Feel what?"

"The heat, man, the excessive heat! It feels like it's a hundred degrees already, and it's only six or seven in the morning. Doesn't *that* seem unusual to you?"

Denny couldn't have been more right. Sweat was pouring from every part of his body. His clothes were soaked through. I had just begun to notice the heat, and I felt the perspiration pour from me, too.

"Rollie, where are we?" His tone was almost pleading. "Where, in the name of heaven, are we?"

I tried to answer him with as much conviction as I could muster. "We're adrift somewhere off the coast of Oahu on a boat where nothing works, on an exceptionally hot late summer morning. That's it, nothing more. What other explanation could there be?"

"I can't accept that, and I don't think that you can either. That glowing maelstrom we went through last night wasn't anything we could explain; neither is this. Something's wrong here, Rollie. Something is very wrong!"

I did not reply, for I had no answer. We both stared at the sea, searching in vain for something that would clear up this mystery, but whatever we were looking for was not there. The *Maui Queen* continued to drift aimlessly over the calm sea. The strange red sun climbed higher in the sky. It became hotter and hotter, until we finally found it impossible to remain on deck without some kind of protection. The wheelhouse became a furnace, causing us to rig a makeshift umbrella from our bedsheets to use on the deck, as our vigil had to be maintained at all time.

At what we approximated to be noon, the malignant orb beat down on us mercilessly. It appeared larger than I could ever remember seeing it, as if it were there solely for our torture. We had no means of telling how hot it was. I had once been to Death Valley, and I believed that this heat far surpassed what I had encountered there. We dove into the water in an attempt to cool off, staying as close as possible to the *Queen* for whatever shade she could provide. The water was not cold, but it was refreshing. We feared attack from sharks, but saw none.

For the rest of that long afternoon we did everything possible to counteract the effects of the heat. Denny, totally exhausted, fell asleep for a few hours, quite mercifully. I readjusted the umbrella to divert the sun's rays from him and settled down to keep watch. In my mind, I tried to reconstruct all that had occurred since our fateful pursuit of the porpoises, but as far as an answer was concerned, I kept coming up blank. I did believe that we had been carried a great distance out to sea, and although I wished it differently, I felt that it would be a long time before we would sight any body of land. Was it to be like this every day? If so, could we endure it? The water supply was fair, but it would have to be rationed, especially under this intense heat. Food did not appear to be a problem, since neither of us had shown much of an appetite that day, but I felt that it was important to keep our strength up. I hoped that we would feel more like eating after the fiery sun had set.

When Denny finally awakened, I gave him a couple of swallows of water. He reported feeling much refreshed, and suggested that I attempt to sleep for a short time. At first I rebuffed the suggestion, but finally, fatigued from the heat and everything else that had occurred, I too found slumber.

I was still under the umbrella when I woke, and I noticed that it felt much cooler. When I emerged from beneath it, I saw Denny standing on the bow. The sun was rapidly disappearing over the horizon.

"How are you feeling?" he asked.

"Almost like a new man," I replied. "I've even got the slightest pangs of hunger. How about you?"

"I hadn't really thought of food, but now that you mention it, I guess I am hungry."

"It's reassuring to know that we at least get a respite in the evening. I'll go below and whip something up for us."

I got a fire going in the small wood-burning stove, upon which I heated a can of beans and some dried beef jerky. With water a precious commodity, I measured out just enough for two cups of coffee. Soon we were having our first meal in what seemed like an eternity. The murderous sun, now our avowed enemy, had fallen completely below the horizon by this time.

"I guess I was hungrier than I thought," said

Denny, eagerly wolfing down his food. "It sure has cooled down, hasn't it? Why, I'm almost cold."

"Perish the thought," I replied. "I don't think that I could ever be cold again after today. But you're right, it is getting cooler."

"Now that it's nightfall, do you think the moon will have any surprises for us?"

"Bite your tongue! I've had enough surprises to last me for years. Look, I can see it now, just peering over the horizon."

We sat in silence, our eyes glued to the half-full moon. It rose fairly rapidly, and there did not appear to be anything unusual about it. Satisfied, I turned to Denny and smiled.

"You see?" I said. "It looks perfectly normal. There's nothing to concern ourselves with. Do you agree?"

"I guess so," he answered, "but that still doesn't explain what happened today. Maybe—no! Rollie, look!"

Denny had gotten to his feet to stretch, for neither of us had moved from the spot in more than a half hour, so intent were we on watching the moonrise. Now he stood there frozen, staring incredulously toward the northwest. I turned quickly to view the source of his trepidation, and my reaction to what I saw was no different. Hanging majestically, just over the horizon, was *another moon!* This one was nearly full, and appeared to be twice the size of the first. We gazed at it for a few moments, not wishing to believe what we were seeing. Finally, Denny spoke.

"Rollie, since yesterday we have seen things that just don't correspond to the laws of nature. Something is wrong here, very wrong. I know you believe the same thing that I do. Say it, please! Say it, so that I won't have to."

"I believe that we passed through a doorway of some kind, a warp. I have no idea what we passed into. It could be a space warp, a time warp, or—even something else."

"What's that?" he asked.

"A dimensional warp. There has been much speculation and theory over the possibility of other-dimensional worlds co-existing on a parallel with our own. Those who believe in this concept have been ridiculed, their theories left to gather dust in desk drawers. A professor of mine formulated some ideas about other-dimensional worlds. He seemed to discount the space warp-time warp theories, and was most convinced of what he believed. The other students thought him a bit mad, not to mention his colleagues. But I felt him to be sincere, and he, sensing this, took me into his confidence. We spoke for hours on the matter, with me doing most of the listening. I did not think him to be a fool then, and I don't now."

"What exactly were his ideas?" asked Denny, interested.

"He believed that these other-dimensional worlds were very similar to our own, with possibly some physical variations and some differences in evolution. Aside from this, he felt that these worlds would be much like ours, even right down to the languages. To travel between these worlds, much as man one day hopes to travel between planets and even galaxies, he conceived of a dimensional doorway, or warp, as he called it. He said that these existed, and cited instances where ships have vanished without a trace in relatively calm seas, some disappearing minutes after routinely contacting a port or another ship. This has happened a few times in the Sea of Japan, and also off the coast of Florida. These doorways appear infrequently, usually in vast, isolated areas. He called this a safety valve, a means to assure that any travel between these worlds is limited. I may be a million miles off base, but if we're not on Earth, then I'd have to say that a parallel world is my next choice."

"What about the ribbon of white water that we traveled on?"

"A runway of sorts, or maybe a path. When the warp opens, I would guess that there are many paths extending out from it, much like spokes from the hub of a wheel."

"Then if all this is as you say, our only hope of getting back to where we came from is to find another one of these doorways on this side and return through it, true?"

"That would be the only way," I answered. "I don't know about you, but I sure wouldn't like to face the prospect of going through that thing again."

"Maybe not, but if it's the only way home, I'm all for it. What're our chances of finding another one?"

"Not very good. According to the professor, the safety valve would work both ways. Few doorways would open out of here either. We could drift for weeks, months, and not locate one. Our best bet now is to find land. Maybe then we'll be able to have some questions answered."

We talked for a little while longer, and finally I convinced Denny, as agitated as he seemed to be, to go below and get some sleep. He gave in and retreated to the cabin, where I doubt that it took him very long to doze off. I remained on deck to keep watch, doing my best to ward off the chilled night air. Alone, I re-examined my thoughts and began to wonder if maybe I was a bit crazy, along with my former professor. Did I actually believe the things that I had just told Denny? Could we be in another dimension, another world? Were we still on Earth, and was it undergoing some incredible changes in nature? Were we on another planet? No, that was only for the real dreamers. I hoped that we would soon find land. Maybe then we would solve the enigma. But did I really want to know the answers? I wondered . . .

Such were my thoughts far into the night. When Denny came back on deck, I had nearly dozed off. With almost nothing said between us, I went below to the cabin. I found slumber in seconds, and slept a deep, dreamless sleep.

CHAPTER THREE

DEATH OF A ROYAL LADY

Our second day upon this strange sea varied little from the first, nor were any of the four subsequent days to provide us with much change. The red sun rose each morning, dispersing the chill night air even with its first faint glow. By mid-morning, its unbearable radiance had forced us to shelter under our makeshift umbrella. Here we remained throughout most of the terrible day, alternating between quick dips off the side of the *Queen* and short naps. Evening gave us a chance to eat, sleep comfortably, and prepare ourselves for much the same the next day. The two moons did offer us a fascinating diversion as they hurtled through the heavens in different directions, both disappearing long before dawn. The water supply, while still holding up, was beginning to cause me concern by the morning of the sixth day. At the rate we had been using it, I estimated that it might last for perhaps four or five more days.

During the six days, the sea remained calm as it gently rocked the *Maui Queen* over its vast expanse without any apparent purpose in mind. We did not sight any land, nor did we see any signs of life, except for one incident on the fourth day while Denny was swimming off the side of the vessel. I looked over the railing to ask him what his preference was for dinner that evening. Far below him I saw a shape, and although I could not make out what it was, I knew as it glided by that it was enormous. I ordered Denny to leave the water quickly, and when he joined me on deck, he too saw it. A minute or so later it was gone. We agreed that henceforth any swimming would be done under the watchful eye of the one on deck.

During the afternoon of the sixth day, I began to sense something different. A breeze, albeit a warm breeze, started to blow from the east. The normally calm sea was showing signs of agitation. Whitecaps appeared at the tops of the waves that now rocked the *Maui Queen* less gently than before. Denny and I began removing any loose items from the deck, preparing for the possibility of a storm. While we might have been in a strange and different place, we both knew that the sea was an unpredictable creature under any circumstances.

About two hours before sunset the wind, cooler now, had risen in intensity. The waves were also higher, some depositing water on the deck. It was difficult to maintain footing on the *Queen* under these conditions. As a precaution, I started to break out the emergency gear. The inflatable life raft was stored in a locker on deck, as were the knapsacks.

These three sacks contained, among other things, extra food, water, a first aid kit, and various tools. I decided to change the water in the canteens, and I took them below to the main barrels. I had just finished filling the third one when I heard Denny, who had remained on deck to watch, shouting.

"Land! Rollie, get up here quick; it's land!" he screamed. "Off to the starboard side!"

I joined Denny on deck, and the two of us clasped hands joyfully. The land he had sighted, apparently a large island, was about five miles distant, and the storm seemed to be taking us right toward it.

"Let's hope that we find a nice, sandy beach to get blown onto," I said, "although with this storm carrying us, and the *Queen* with no power, I guess we don't have much say in the matter. We'll just have to wait and see what happens. In the meantime, I'm going to finish preparing the emergency gear just in case."

During the next hour, the island loomed closer and closer. We could now make out what looked like sheer rock cliffs rising hundreds of feet in the air. I began to wonder if there would be a beach to land on at all. The storm raged now, its waves completely engulfing the *Maui Queen*, tossing her like an insignificant cork. Clouds appeared for the first time, obliterating the red sun which had been floating atop the horizon. Rain started to fall, slowly at first, then in blinding sheets. I cursed the luck that had brought us this tempest so close to the land we sought.

Closer now, much closer. At the base of the cliffs I could make out what looked like a small strip of sandy beach, this indicating that we might be able to land after all. But an immense wave suddenly lifted us high atop its crest, and for an instant I could see huge rocks looming throughout the water, blocking any hope we might have had of safely beaching the *Maui Queen*. I shouted the news to Denny, and he echoed my despair. We each donned a knapsack, and then inflated the raft. We hastily tied the third knapsack to the inside of the rubber raft. Then, futilely hoping that the *Queen* might make it through, we returned to the starboard railing to keep watch.

The first outcropping appeared about twenty feet off the stern, a second only ten feet from our bow. Visibility was limited, and we still had to fight to keep our footing on deck. We passed two other stone sentinels before our luck finally ran out. A cluster of rocks, the largest standing about five feet out of the water, appeared in front of us and slightly to the left. We were sure that we would strike it, and accordingly we returned for the life raft which we bore to the stern. As we neared the barrier, a huge wave spilled over the deck. I grabbed the railing and held fast, but Denny, caught unawares in his haste, was knocked forward on his face. The side of his head struck the winch, which was bolted to the deck. He moaned softly, and then was still.

I reached Denny just as soon as I could maintain my balance, noting that he was barely breathing. A large gash was bleeding profusely on the side of his head. As I started to open his knapsack for the first aid kit, I heard a sickening crunch, and I was thrown against the railing. The *Queen* had struck the rocks on her starboard side near the bow. I knew I had little time to spare. I snatched up the life raft and dropped it into the raging sea. I then picked up Denny and, holding him under his arms, I deposited him as gently as possible under the circumstances into the raft.

Assuring myself that there was nothing more I could do aboard the *Queen*, I started to climb the railing so that I might join Denny in the raft. But once again the *Queen* struck the pile of rocks, the impact throwing me to the deck, where I sat stunned for a moment. In that instant the raft had begun to drift, and by the time I had negotiated the railing again it was some ten feet distant. The *Queen* was now breaking up, and with no alternative I dove into the churning water. Struggling with the gear on my back, I struck out in pursuit of the raft and its helpless passenger, but found myself barely able to move. My only chance was to get rid of the knapsack, which I did. A few long strokes and I was able to grab hold of the bobbing boat just as the next wave hit. The raft rode the crest of the wave for a few feet before settling down, but I managed to hang on to it.

With my strength nearly gone, I hauled myself into the raft. Denny was still unconscious, his breathing shallow. I quickly bailed out the water that had gathered in the bottom of the raft with cupped hands; then I sank down, exhausted. I looked back in time to see the *Maui Queen*, or what was left of her, sink slowly beneath the violent waves. Pieces of her were floating everywhere I looked. The *Maui Queen*, our beloved *Queen*, was gone!

I now turned my attention to the maze of rocks all around us. As each wave carried us further inland, I felt sure that we would be smashed against one of these outcroppings. How we avoided them was nothing short of miraculous, but somehow we got past them all with no mishap. Now there were only about a hundred yards of open water to the shore. The waves had begun to subside, and I felt confident that we would make it.

While bailing out what little water remained in the raft, I happened to look down into the sea. Once again I discerned the huge shape that had stalked us at sea just two days earlier, and my heart sank. We had come so far, and were now so close. Was this horror, whatever it was, to deny us our chance? No, I had to do something! We had to get to that beach! I untied the small, two-piece oar and put it together. I then began paddling with whatever strength I was able to summon. The shape glided right under the raft, deep at first, but soon rising higher and higher until it was only a few feet below. Still I could not see what it was. I thought it to be a matter of moments before we would be capsized, when suddenly it was gone. I continued paddling for a few more seconds, but it did not reappear. It was then I realized why: I could now see the ocean floor, for we were very close to the beach. The creature, as enormous as it must be, could not remain submerged this close to land, as it apparently wished to.

A couple of minutes later I was pulling the raft up on the strand. Noting by the water line that the tide was now at its highest, I pulled the raft back far enough to prevent it from returning to the sea. I dragged Denny toward the base of the sea wall and placed him in a hollowed-out, cave-like depression.

Night was falling, and the smaller of the two moons must have been making its appearance, but I was unable to see it because of the high cliffs.

Denny's knapsack contained a small kerosene lantern and some waterproof matches. Although shaking from the cold I was able to light it, and the small amount of heat that it provided was comforting. I then cleansed the gash on his head, daubed it with antiseptic, and bandaged it. After a few anxious moments his breathing became less labored, and a more natural color appeared on his face.

With my friend now resting comfortably, I left him lying near the lantern and went out to see just where we were. By the dim light remaining I was able to see that to my left, about fifty yards, the shoreline ended where the water met the sea wall. I decided to explore in the other direction, because the beach seemed to extend that way. I traversed the strand for about a quarter of a mile, but found the same thing to be true at the other end. I was chagrined. Unless there was some way either over or through the cliffs, it looked like we had arrived at a dead end.

I began my trip back to the cave since I was anxious to look after Denny. My progress was slow, for I was more exhausted than I had thought. The night air was chilling. Slowly, more slowly, I plodded along. Less than two hundred yards from the cave, I decided that I had to stop and rest, only for a moment. I found a couple of rocks near the base of the sea wall and sank down between them, out of the chill. Only for a few minutes though; I would rest only for a few minutes. I had to get back to the cave. Only for a few minutes . . .

When I awoke the sun was already high, the heat oppressive. Fortunately, by staying close to the base of the sea cliffs, I was shielded from the sun's deadly rays. I cursed my stupidity for leaving Denny alone the night before. Why had I not waited until the morning to explore? Now I ran the final two hundred yards, unmindful of the heat. As I neared the cave I called his name, but received no answer. I dashed into the depression and looked around. Realizing what had happened, I slumped to the sand on one knee in disbelief.

Denny was gone!

CHAPTER FOUR

THE GUARDIAN

The waves broke gently on the soft, sandy beach.
The sea was calm, as calm as it had been during the
time we had drifted on it. I surveyed the scene from
the mouth of the cave, where I had been trying to
gather my thoughts. The water could not possibly
reach the cave, so it was unlikely that Denny could
have been carried out by the tide. If he had gotten up
on his own, then he must have regained consciousness. Yes, that had to be it! He must be all right! How
else could he have moved, unless—no, that was
impossible! Even if this island were inhabited, I had
seen no means of ingress, nor any place where it
appeared safe to scale the high cliffs. Denny must
have arisen earlier than I and walked down the beach
looking for me. I felt sure that by retracing my steps I
would find him.

I emerged from the cave into the blazing heat. In

the sand I noticed footprints, just one pair. So Denny *had* gotten up on his own. The footprints led to the spot where we had left the raft. I glanced in that direction, but I saw that the life raft was gone! Could he have set out to sea again? No, not likely. I hurried down to the spot, eyeing the footprints along the way. Ten feet short of it I discovered something else, something that made my blood run cold. Denny's footprints were now intermingled with many other sets of footprints. I could make out three, no, four sets, the impressions indicating that they had been made by some kind of flat sandals. From this spot they appeared as if they all walked down to the raft, but here the signs became muddled. I guessed that they had dragged the raft behind them to the water. But where had they come from? Was there another beach just around the sea wall, one that allowed for easy access inland? If so, how would I be able to get there?

The tracks made by the raft in tow along the sand ended where the sea met the cliff. It was high tide, just as it was when we had first landed. They must have set out around the cliff; it was the only answer. I decided to check again at low tide to see if there was any indication of a boat being dragged ashore, leaving an impression in the hard-packed sand. As unlikely as this seemed, it was all I could think of at the moment. My mind was spinning from this strange turn of events. Denny was missing, apparently taken by others. His knapsack and the lantern were gone, as was our life raft. The other knapsack was still in the raft. This left me with nothing but a hunting knife, all I had taken with me the night before. No food, no water.

Determined not to make this small beach my final resting place, I began to retrace my steps along the sand. Perhaps in the daylight I would discover something that I had missed the previous night. In my anxiety to sort out the mystery on the beach I had forgotten about the sun, and now I realized that my skin was ablaze, nearly blistering in some spots. I returned to the base of the sea wall and the minimal protection that it offered. There, I began to re-examine every foot of the cliff for some means of passage to the interior. For hours I explored every possibility, only to come up with nothing again and again. Once more I reached the far end, where I turned around and started back along the wall. For the first time that morning I realized that I was thirsty. Without water I knew that my tenure on this beach, alive at least, would be of short duration. I hastened my efforts.

Halfway back, I glanced down to the shoreline. The tide had been receding steadily, and on the wet sand I could make out some small objects. Although I feared exposing myself to the sun, I knew that I must investigate. Removing my shirt, I tied it turban-style around my head and walked slowly, deter-minedly, toward the sea.

The objects I had spotted lay scattered for about seventy-five or a hundred yards. They consisted mostly of bits of wood, wreckage from the *Maui Queen*. The *Queen!* With all that had occurred, I had not even given her a second thought since she went down the previous night. Now the sight of her remains added to my depression.

I went on almost mechanically, checking over each piece, not really caring any more. Suddenly, no more than ten feet in front of me, I saw a knapsack, unquestionably the one that I had, of necessity, discarded during my swim for life. I picked it up and examined it. The outside was torn, shredded, as if something had . . . had bitten through it. I checked its contents. There was a hand ax, two cans of C-rations, and, thank heavens, a canteen of water. The other items had apparently fallen out. I unscrewed the cap and quickly downed a few swallows of the precious fluid.

The water gave me the renewed strength to continue my search. I stuck the hand ax in my belt, then attached the canteen to it. Once out of the sun, I ate one of the small cans of food, putting the other in my pocket. After discarding the now useless knapsack, I resumed my trek. The afternoon was passing quickly, and still the sea wall had not seen fit to reveal any of its secrets to me. As I neared the cave where I had first left Denny, a feeling of despair once again overwhelmed me. Was I to spend another night on this shore? Would I too be taken in the dark hours? I was determined not to let this happen.

I went to the spot where Denny must have encountered the others. Though I didn't know what I expected to find there, I had run out of alternatives. I followed the footprints again, hoping for some sort of clue. It was low tide now, and at the base of the sea wall was a small adit, previously concealed by the water. I hastened to it and peered within, but the darkness prevented me from seeing very far. However, this *had* to be the answer! The cave, though little more than three feet in height, could accommodate men on their hands and knees, and was certainly wide enough, at least at the mouth, to fit the raft through.

Without any hesitation, I entered the cave. To delay would have been pointless. Even the fatigue I felt was not enough to stop me. I moved slowly but made progress, my eyes eventually becoming used to the dark. The tunnel offered little variance for some distance. The floor was solid rock, smoothed by the constant flow of water over it. In some places it was slippery, and here the going was difficult. A small curve to the right widened the tunnel, but the height varied little. Another slight curve to the left, followed by a sharp turn to the right, brought the sound of rushing water to my ears. It grew louder as I crawled along, and within minutes I had emerged into a chamber containing an underground river. Perched a few feet above it, I could see that my choice of direction was limited. To the right, the water was escaping through a narrow opening in the rock, probably returning to the sea at a point in the cliff far below the surface. Realizing that the tunnel would be filled when the tide came in, I quickly made my decision, lowering myself into the river. The current was strong, but the water was only a couple of feet deep, enabling me to keep my balance. The chamber was narrow, and I was able to support myself as I moved along by pushing against the walls with both hands.

Ten minutes of slow progress finally brought me to a point where the chamber widened, as did the river. The going was easier now, the current slackening considerably, and I did not have to hold on. The water was slightly deeper, but offered no handicap, while the ceiling of the chamber rose to about fifteen feet. I had a chance to examine the chamber as I walked through it, and I was fascinated by the fact that the walls were impregnated with something that glistened in the darkness. I was no geologist, but I swore that I was looking at rich veins of gold. There must have been a fortune there. A lot of good it would do me now. Funny how greed has become an inbred part of the human animal. For me to even think of it just then was ample proof of that.

A ledge now appeared to my left, a narrow strip at first, but one that continued to widen as I progressed. The water had remained shallow all this time, giving me a false confidence that nearly proved my undoing. While studying the ceiling and walls, I took a step and discovered that there was no bottom. After the initial surprise, it was a simple matter to swim for the ledge. In a few seconds I had reached it, and I paused for a moment before hauling myself up.

Suddenly I felt a sharp pain in my ankle, and I hurriedly pulled myself onto the ledge. There on my leg, its teeth sunk in deeply, was a river rat. Its size was not unusual; as rats go, this one might even have been considered small. I shuddered nonetheless. Rats were not among my favorite creatures, especially one that was attacking me. I lifted my leg and smashed it hard against the rock wall, crushing the beast. It squealed loudly and relinquished its hold, falling into the water. As it struggled frantically in its death throes, I became aware of many small shapes in the water. The dying rodent was surrounded; within minutes it was being devoured by its own kind.

The sight disgusted me, and I turned away. While catching my breath, I bled the small punctures where the rat had bitten. After cleansing the wound as best I could, I tore off a strip from my shirt and bound it tightly, halting the flow of blood. I now knew that I could not re-enter the river. If Denny and his abductors had come through here, they most probably had a small boat of some kind, not to mention our life raft. My only hope was that this ledge widened further along. I prayed that the rats preferred to remain submerged.

For what seemed like hours, I moved slowly along the narrow ledge. It showed no signs of widening, and in a few places it narrowed even more, making passage more difficult. Whenever I chanced to look down I discerned the small, furry bodies swimming just under the surface. They seemed to be awaiting my one misstep. Sometimes they broke the surface, three or four at a time, their squeals echoing throughout the chamber. This unnerved me greatly. I hastened my efforts, although my leg was now beginning to throb painfully.

Finally, the ledge widened. Now it was no longer a narrow shelf, but a broad strip of land that sloped gently down to the river's edge. Small rats lined the bank. I hesitated, but they scurried away into the river, squealing and hissing. Emboldened, I quickened my step. The river was much wider now than at any time before, and a bank appeared on the opposite side. Above, the ceiling of the chamber rose another couple of yards. The movement of the river seemed to be quickening, and again I thought I heard a roar in the distance. I hurried along the bank for another three hundred yards, but now there was no question about what I had heard. The river surged seaward in a raging torrent, the roar almost deafening. It reminded me of the time I had first seen the Colorado River as it raced through the Grand Canyon on its way to the Gulf of California. I hoped that there would be enough bank to allow me passage.

Along the way, I made a discovery that convinced me I was on the right path. Sitting on the opposite bank was the raft, and next to it the lantern and extra knapsack. The raft had most likely been abandoned at this point because of the raging water, but I had to wonder why Denny's captors hadn't carried it along until it could be used again. I could only assume that the rest of the way along the tributary's edge would offer no barriers, and I hoped that this was true. Though I would have liked to retrieve the equipment, I knew that to cross the river would have been suicide.

The torrent curved to the left, and I continued to follow it. Then it widened into a larger body of water, this the size of a small lake. Now I understood what had caused the rapids. The lake occupied an enromous chamber, and was completely encircled by narrow ledges. In the distance, I could see where the river emptied into the lake. I could discern something else, too. It looked like—yes, there could be no mistake: it was a shaft of light! I had reached the end of this accursed tunnel. I simply had to traverse the most accessible ledge, and I would be free.

With my eyes riveted forward, I did not see the object on the ground, and I tumbled headlong as my toe struck it. I quickly regained my feet and glanced downward. There, leering up at me, was a human skull! Caution and fear now replaced the exhilaration I had felt only moments before. Gingerly I stepped over the skull and approached the nearest ledge, which was not as narrow as the other I had traversed. I exercised a great deal of care, however, for I was forced to continually step over heaps of human bones that blocked my way. Was this some kind of burial chamber, I wondered? Whatever the case, it was terrifying!

Halfway around, I chanced to peer into the lake. Far below the surface I made out a shape. I stared in disbelief. Its outlines were the same as the creature that had stalked us under the *Queen*, and later in the life raft. Was it here by coincidence, or did it have some sinister purpose? In any case, I prayed that it chose to remain below.

I did not have far to go, and I felt sure that I was going to make it when I stumbled and nearly fell on another shattered skull. I quickly caught myself, but the skull rolled toward the edge and fell over, hitting the water with a splash that, to me, sounded like a gunshot. The creature, agitated by the disturbance, began to ascend. With the ax in one hand, the hunting knife in the other, I placed my back against the wall and prepared to meet the unknown horror.

Water flew as the huge head, this sitting atop a thick, snake-like neck, broke the surface of the lake. The mouth emitted a horrible sound, a bestial roar intermingled with choking and sputtering. For an instant unspeakable nocturnal visions from my childhood flashed in front of my mind. But this, unfortunately, was no nightmare.

Its head was covered with coarse, dark green scales, these piled high and extending for a foot or so down its neck, like some sort of hideous crown. The small, red eyes were the essence of malevolence. Its snout was pushed flat against its face, the large caverns that were its nostrils flaring obscenely as it breathed. Just above its snout protruded two horns, each two feet in length. Its wide mouth opened and closed as it voiced its cry, showing powerful jaws containing many rows of sharp teeth, foremost of which were two upper cuspids, these larger than the others. All of this sat atop eight or nine feet of neck, this extending from the lake and swivelling around like a broken periscope as it sought the source of the disturbance.

Now the wicked eyes rested on me, and the slow-thinking brain reacted to my presence. The head bore down upon me, the beast gurgling and sputtering, its mouth snapping open and shut. It reached for me, and I fell to the ledge, its jaws closing just inches above my head. I could scent its fetid breath as it passed, the stench overwhelming me. The neck seemed to move uncontrollably in short, spasmodic jerks, forcing the head back toward the center of the lake. I regained my feet and prepared myself for the next charge, which was not long in coming. The beast's head, apparently at the mercy of the spastic neck, gyrated slowly toward me. This time I stood my ground until the last possible second, and as the beast neared I struck at the snout with my knife just as I fell. The beast recoiled, roaring and coughing. But the wound I had inflicted was slight, and I knew that it would not hesitate to charge again.

I was aware that I had to do something quickly, for the falls that I had been forced to take had reactivated the pain in my leg, leaving me nearly blinded with agony. The head began to work its way toward me again. I staggered to my feet and switched the weapons in my hands, the ax held as far behind my head as I could. The beast drew closer, now only a few feet from me. I threw the ax with all the strength that I could summon forth.

It lodged deep in its snout, an area that I knew was vulnerable. Once again it recoiled, this time emitting hideous screams along with its roaring. The shrieks echoed off the cavern walls, creating an unbearable symphony of horror. Its neck began to swivel, slowly drawing the head down toward the lake. As the monstrosity disappeared below the surface, the hideous noises stopped. The cavern was as a tomb once more.

Ignoring the pain, I sped toward the shaft of light in the distant tunnel. I knew that the beast was merely tending its wounds, and would return shortly. I hated to lose the ax, but it was a small price to pay to escape this place. Skulls and other bones flew wildly in my path, for stealth was a luxury now. Finally I reached the far side. The lake narrowed, and was now a river once more, no more than a couple of feet deep. Twenty yards into the tunnel, the pain began to slow me down again. From behind I heard the Guardian, as I dubbed him, roaring and choking. There was no way he could reach me now. His power was limited to the expanses of the underground lake. In spite of my pain, I moved forward with a feeling of pride, for I had made my first conquest on this strange world: I had defeated the Guardian! With head high I made my way to the shaft of light, now only a few hundred feet away.

Ever since we had entered this world, it seemed that triumphant or pleasant moments were short-lived. The current situation that I found myself in proved to be no exception. As I approached the shaft of light, I saw that it was beaming down through a nearly circular hole in the roof of the chamber, some twenty feet or so above my head. I peered through the hole, but instead of seeing the sky, or even the accursed sun, which I might have welcomed at that moment, I saw only an extension of the cavern. The ceiling rose to a height of seventy-five feet or more above where I stood, its surface covered with something that emitted a dazzling flourescence. I could not tell just what this was, but the shaft of light was now explainable.

Dejected, and in much pain, I limped down the tunnel. I had thought for sure that this part of my journey was over, but such was not the case. As I made my way alongside the river I noticed more light up ahead. Determined not to get excited until it had been investigated, I approached slowly. What I found was the same thing I had seen in the overhead chamber, only now I was able to examine it more closely. It appeared to be some kind of phosphorescent fungus, the shapes varied but in most cases almost circular. They grew in clusters, about eight or nine in each bunch, the largest about twelve inches in diameter. The strange light that they gave off was baffling. When I tried to remove one, it clung tenaciously. In some places they completely blocked out the walls.

I stopped once to rest my leg, which was now swollen around the ankle. Despite being tired, I had no desire to fall asleep down here, not knowing what to expect next. I resumed my trek, soon noticing that the strange fungus on the walls was beginning to thin. Eventually there were none of the discs, and the tunnel was dark once again. Now the river began to zigzag, first to the left, then to the right, then left once more. After straightening out for a hundred feet or so, it turned sharply to the right. As I turned with it, I noticed something that was most exhilarating: Air— cool, fresh night air!

I had reached the end of the tunnel. What a fool I had been, looking for light to mark the end. When I had entered, it had been late in the afternoon: I had been down here for many hours, and it was the middle of the night.

I decided to follow the river for a while before stopping to rest. The pain in my leg was excruciating, and I would not be able to go on for long. In the darkness I could make out little on either side of the river. I stumbled on and on, until I realized that I was dragging myself along the ground. I was practically delirious, for I imagined that I saw a small fire burning a short distance in front of me. I crawled toward it. As I drew nearer, I believed that I saw a man squatting next to it. I caught the scent of something cooking; it smelled good. Was I really suffering from delusions? The man looked in my direction. He jumped up quickly, apparently grabbing something, and came toward me.

I remembered no more.

CHAPTER FIVE

TER-EK

The fire was out when I awakened. I was still near the river, upon a mat of woven straw. It was daylight, but a dense cloud cover hung overhead, blocking the sun's rays and creating a most agreeable temperature. A man was kneeling at the edge of the river, his back turned toward me. As I was about to hail him I happened to glance at my left leg. Attached to my ankle was a small, quivering creature about the size of a man's fist. Its color was brownish-gray. I shook my leg, but it held tenaciously. With an exclamation I grabbed the handiest rock I could find and was about to smash the creature with it when the stranger, hearing the commotion, raced toward me and grabbed my wrist.

"I placed the *suva* on your wound to suck out the poison," he stated. "Do not destroy the suva. Soon it will die and fall off by itself. Then the poison will be gone." The language was very similar to one of the Polynesian dialects that Denny and I had picked up around the islands, and I found that, except for a few strange words, I was able to understand him.

"Who are you?" I asked.

"I am Ter-ek, a warrior in the service of Lar-ek, ruler of the Homarus and true king of Boranga. It is the time of the *satong*, and it is that which I seek, so that I may place its head at the feet of my king before seventeen darknesses have fallen. I have tended your wounds and your fever for a night and a day and a night now, and I lose the time that I need to finish my hunt. You are of the Mogars, of course. When the suva dies, you will be well enough to return to your people. You will tell them that a Homaru saved your life and let you go in peace. The Homarus have always wished peace with the Mogars, although your queen tells your people otherwise." He spoke these words in a monotone that betrayed no emotion, no anger because of his delay, or fear because he faced a supposed enemy. That he saved my life was not a boast, just a fact.

"I wish to thank you, Ter-ek, for what you've done, and I apologize for any inconvenience I might have caused you. I am not a Mogar, nor have I ever heard of the Mogars. I do not know where Boranga is, for I have never been there."

"I do not understand your words," said Ter-ek. "This is Boranga; everywhere is Boranga. You can be from no other place. And you must be a Mogar. You cannot be Homaru, or I would know you. You must be of the Mogars, unless you are one of the outcasts."

"I assure you I'm not one of them," I told him. "I

58

came from the other side of that mountain—"

"You came from the—*other side?*" His voice displayed the first hint of emotion.

"Yes, I—"

An unexpected change now came over Ter-ek. He dropped to his knees, cringing at my feet. His head was practically buried in the sand, and he quivered much like the suva on my leg.

"Forgive me, *Kuta*, how was I to know?" he pleaded. "I have always served the Master well, as have my people. He knows this, as I'm sure you do, Kuta. Please, Kuta, spare me! Forgive the manner in which I spoke to you. My intentions to heal you were good. Please, Kuta, spare me!"

Shocked by this turnaround, I said: "Now wait a minute, Ter-ek; I came from the other side of that mountain over there, along a lengthy underground river, and emerged not far from here. I was pursuing a group that took my friend with them. Now, please get to your feet."

"I will do whatever you say, Kuta," said Ter-ek, rising.

"And please don't call me Kuta," I implored. "My name is Roland. Who is Kuta, anyway?"

"A kuta is a Holy One," he explained. "Did you truly come by the underground river, Ro-lan?"

I liked his pronunciation of my name, and decided not to bother correcting it. "I came through the tunnel, as I said. I found an opening when the tide was low. It was the only way that I could find to get through the sea wall."

"How came you to that side?" he asked.

"I started to explain before," I said. "Our boat was

destroyed on some rocks during a storm. We landed on the beach in a small raft. My friend was taken in the night. I followed the next day, and now here I am. It's as simple as that."

"I know of no boat that has tried to sail around Boranga," Ter-ek replied. "Why did you wish to sail there?"

"I am not from Boranga," I explained.

"There is only Boranga and the sea, Ro-lan." The statement was to the point.

I tried to explain to Ter-ek about all the things that now seemed so distant to me. The United States, Hawaii, ocean liners, airplanes; our journey through the dimensional warp. I told him of our sun, of the single moon at night. He listened attentively, but I sensed that my efforts were futile.

"You are a teller of fine stories, Ro-lan. I believe that you are no kuta. I wish to find out some day from where on Boranga you have sprung. Before I continue my pursuit of the satong, I must know of one other thing. You say that you came through the tunnel, along the underground river. What did you encounter on your journey?"

"I saw rich gold deposits, strange glowing fungus, numerous rats, and—oh yes, the Guardian."

Ter-ek shook his head. "Many of your words are strange to me. The guar . . . what was it you last said?"

"The Guardian? That's the name I gave it. It was an overgrown lizard that I ran into in a lake." I guess I tried to sound a little cocky about it.

"*Tomo Raka?* You met Tomo Raka and lived? If this is true, then surely you are more than a man."

His tone was now one of awe and respect.

"I lost a good ax in his snout for my trouble," I assured him. "But surely this is no great feat. At least five men passed that way not long before I did. Surely I would have found some sign that they had been killed. All the bones I saw appeared to be old."

"If those who took your friend were of the Mogars, they would not have come that way. There is another passage, known only to them. You passed by it, but could not have seen it. It leads safely and quickly out of the tunnel. The Mogars send many of their prisoners and old ones to Tomo Raka for sacrifice."

"That accounts for the raft lying where I saw it," I replied.

"See! The suva has died," Ter-ek announced suddenly. "The poison is gone now."

I looked at my ankle and saw the horrid thing lying in the dirt next to my foot. "When will I be able to walk?" I asked.

"If the suva has done its work well, you should be able to walk now."

I rose slowly to my feet, fearful of putting any pressure on my left leg. I need not have worried, however, for the suva had succeeded. Except for some slight discoloration around the wound where the creature had attached itself, the leg felt as good as new. I walked a few paces to test it, realizing as I did that I was still weak from the events of the past few days. I returned to the straw mat and sat down. Ter-ek brought me a variety of fruits and nuts, along with some kind of dried meat that proved to be very palatable. I was famished, as I had not eaten in days, and I wolfed down nearly everything.

As I ate, I had a chance to study Ter-ek, who was busying himself with his gear. He was a fine looking fellow, perhaps a couple of years younger than myself. His height was a bit over six feet, and he was proportionately well muscled. In Hawaii he would not have warranted a second glance, so much did he look like a descendent of those who first inhabited the islands many hundreds of years past. His face denoted intensity, determination, though it was not an unkindly countenance. His clothing was plain, consisting of an animal skin wrapped loosely around his middle. A wide, belt-like leather strap held the garment to his body. Plain leather sandals, wrapped securely around his feet and ankles with thongs, completed the scanty wardrobe.

Ter-ek had gathered all his belongings into a large pouch which now hung over his shoulder from a thin strip of leather. There was one item that he did not place in the pouch, sticking it instead in his belt. It was a large, well-honed knife, the blade of which was about a foot long. To complement this, he hefted a vicious-looking spear which stood six or eight inches taller than himself. The shaft was carved from a smooth, polished hardwood, and the sharp point was surrounded by five barbs, each a few inches long. Not until later, when I saw it in action, did I realize just what a formidable weapon this was.

As he sat down next to me, Ter-ek said: "Now that you are well, I must delay no longer. I must find a satong and kill it, or be killed by it. I wish that I could learn more of you, Ro-lan, because, although you are a strange man, I believe you to be both honest

62

and brave."

"I desire to learn more of you and of Boranga," I said. "My prime concern, though, is to find my friend. Since I know nothing of Boranga, I could not even guess where to begin looking. I feel stronger now, and I'm sure that I can travel. I propose that we journey together. We can learn much this way. I can help you hunt down this satong that you seek, and afterwards you can help me find Denny."

"If you are able to travel, then I would be honored to have you accompany me," said Ter-ek. "But you must be warned that the killing of the satong and the presentation of the head are sacred rites among the Homarus. This must be carried out by the hunter only. Even should I be in danger of death, you must not interfere. If you did, and I lived, I would only be forced to destroy myself. Is this understood?"

"I would find it hard to stand by while a friend was being killed, but I will try to abide by what you ask. Will you be able to help me find Denny, should you succeed?"

"Before we reach the place of the satong, I will tell you how to reach Mogara, for it is there that you will find your friend. If I am killed, you will know where to go. Should I survive, I will take you there and assist in his rescue."

"That is fair enough, Ter-ek," I said. "Let us leave."

Besides the torn clothes on my body, my possessions had dwindled down to only my hunting knife and the canteen. The last can of C-rations must have fallen out of my pocket in the cave. I felt lost on this strange island that Ter-ek had called Boranga, but the confidence that I had in this serious young fellow offset my fears, and I believed that with his help I would soon find Denny again. Ter-ek had already begun his march, and I hastened to catch up with him. We were on our way to find a satong, and although I had no idea what a satong was, I felt certain that this was not going to be any kind of a pleasure trip. How right I was.

CHAPTER SIX

A SATONG HUNT

We traveled in silence for an hour or so, although I had much to ask Ter-ek. I felt surprisingly strong, and was able to maintain the brisk pace that he kept. The landscape of Boranga proved to be less than fascinating. We had followed the river for about fifteen minutes or so before finding a shallow spot where it could be crossed. Heading away from the river toward the northeast, we crossed a wide, barren plain that was sparsely dotted with small brown shrubs. It went on like this endlessly, though at no time could I see for more than a mile in any direction because of the low-hanging fog. The temperature was comfortable, even slightly cool. Nowhere was there any sign of fauna.

Ter-ek finally broke the silence. "By nightfall tomorrow, we will reach the forest surrounding the hills that the satongs occupy. We will camp on the plain before entering the forest, for to be attacked by a satong at night would mean death. Only when you can see them seconds before they attack do you have a chance of killing them. During the day they seldom wander from the hills, but at night there is always that chance. When we stop tomorrow, I will tell you how to reach Mogara. We will enter the forest when the first light of morning appears, and we must proceed with great caution and in silence. By the end of the afternoon we will reach the hills and, if I am fortunate, I will locate and kill one quickly. Even so, the chances of our retreating through the forest and reaching the plain before dark are not good. We shall therefore camp near the hills, in the very midst of the satongs. As dangerous as this sounds, it will at least give us a fighting chance should they attack, more than we would have deep in the forest."

"Ter-ek," I said, "before we undertake this, I wish you would tell me just what a satong is."

Surprised, he answered: "A satong is . . . a satong! I don't know what else to say. It is a beast, but it is not a beast. It is a man, but then again it is not. It is . . . a satong. For as long as anyone can remember, the Homarus have hunted them. Once the satongs roamed across all of Boranga, killing and destroying. They favored the taste of human flesh, and their appetites were always insatiable. Then it was that Dor-ek, great warrior-king of the Homarus and ancestor of Lar-ek, led his people against the satongs. Many were killed, and the rest were driven across the length and breadth of Boranga, until they finally sought refuge in the hills. As a tribute to Dor-ek, each warrior laid the head of a satong that he had killed at the great one's feet. Now we present the head not only as a tribute to our king, but as a test of our own courage. Four times in our lifetime we must kill a satong and return with the head in less than seventeen days, this being the number of days in which Dor-ek and his people destroyed most of the satongs. This is my second hunt.

"Recently, the Mogars have attempted to frighten our people by spreading the rumor that the satongs were actually children of the Master, and that to kill one was an unheard of act of sacrilege. Some of our people believed these stories and joined the Mogars, lest the Master strike them down. Some have even attempted to stop the Homarus from their quest against the satongs by ambushing a lone warrior along the way. We countered this by altering the path that a warrior must travel to reach the hills, and it is very seldom that the Mogars find us. We know that the satongs cannot be children of the Master, for the satongs have been on Boranga long before the time of the Master, and many heads have been taken since then. Surely he would have struck many down by now."

"Ever since you mistook me for a kuta of the Master," I said, "I have meant to ask you who or what the Master is. Is that what you call the deity you worship?"

Ter-ek suddenly stopped and stared at me, his eyes widening in disbelief. He looked around furtively before speaking.

"I could almost believe that you are not of Boranga, as you claim," he said icily, "to speak the words that you just did. You invite death not only to yourself, but to one who walks with you. Never again speak such words! The Master hears all; the Master knows all!" He dropped to his knees and faced toward the north. *"Noma Kuto Boranga!"* he chanted, rocking from side to side. *"Noma Kuto Boranga, Noma Kuto Boranga!"*

Although I did not understand the reason for his reaction, I knew by his agitation that I had better change the subject. I would have liked to find out more about this Master, for my curiosity was aroused, but this was not the time for it. Could the concept of a deity have such a terrifying effect on a man with the courage of Ter-ek? As he arose I made my apologies, and with a grunt of acknowledgement from him we continued our march. The afternoon passed slowly as we walked. It was warmer now, although the sun remained hidden. I still had much to ask of Ter-ek, and I planned to select what I felt would be a safe subject. That night, while camped on the plain, I learned more of this world that I had unwillingly been deposited upon.

"Ter-ek," I asked, "tell me about the people of Boranga."

"Long ago, the people of Boranga were all one," he began. "This was after the time of Dor-ek. The Homarus were prosperous, and most were happy, but not all. Led by a malcontent named Mogar, one faction craved only the opportunity to do battle with other men. As there was no one else to fight on Boranga, this group journeyed east and established their own city, Mogara. Since then, these people have always been at war with the Homarus, first under Mogar and then his offspring. Many times we have made overtures of peace to them, but they have been bred only to fight.

"The second faction consisted of those who suffered from some inherent madness. The Homarus had tolerated these people for years, had even attempted to help them, but they were hopelessly insane. When their numbers became such that their presence constituted a danger to our people, they were driven away, far to the north. It was to these people that the Master came, blessing them and taking them as his own. They are the Holy Ones, the kuta of the Master. To this day they dwell with him on the Other Side and serve him."

I would have loved to try and pursue his last words, but thought better of it. Instead, I asked: "Ter-ek, what of your own people?"

"The Homarus live in Var-Dor, a walled city in the forest far to the west. We live a simple life. Mostly we are farmers, shepherds, and artisans. Warriors, like myself, are needed to do battle with the Mogars when they attack. We stay in training constantly. If not for the Mogars, our role would be useless, as there is little crime in Var-Dor. The people are all satisfied with their way of life. We do not question anything outside our own sphere. Once there were those among us, the Thinkers, who did search for more knowledge, but pressure from the kings eventually eliminated this element. I sometimes feel that maybe their way had some merit, but . . . no; please, Ro-lan! Forget what I said. I am most happy with our simple life in Var-Dor."

"Then it is only the fighting men who are required to hunt the satongs," I stated.

"*All* Homaru males, regardless of what they are, must perform this duty to the king," he replied forcefully. "It is the custom. Few are ill-trained, however."

I heard no more from Ter-ek that night, for both of us were fatigued, and sleep came quickly. Early the next morning we resumed our journey in silence. The long day's trek seemed interminable, and the unchanging tundra, shrouded in fog, began to grow monotonous.

Around late afternoon, I noticed that the clouds that had hung so close to the ground all day were beginning to rise. Soon I was able to see ahead for miles. The forest that Ter-ek had spoken of was now plainly visible. Another hour's march would put us at its edge. I was thankful, for the journey was taking its toll, and I would be more than happy to rest. Curious that the sun had not broken through the clouds since he found me, I asked Ter-ek if this was usual, or if we were just fortunate.

"*Ama* (this is what he called the orb) would destroy all; her fires boil the waters and sear the flesh. This is why I doubted that you had come here from the sea, as you told me. On Boranga, the clouds protect those who walk in the open from the fires of Ama. In the forests, the trees protect us. Even at the Cliffs of Mogar, where you entered the tunnel, there is some shelter. On all of Boranga you are safe from Ama's fire, except for one place. This area is known as the Sands of Fire. I have never been there, but I have heard much spoken. These sands stretch for miles before reaching the sea. There is no protection from Ama, and because of this, the sands have turned to

70

liquid, bubbling and churning during the day. Even when Ama has disappeared for the night, the hot sands continue to bubble, and those who would be foolish enough to walk upon them are pulled down to their death. From the edge of the plain did my own father witness the death of a friend in the Sands of Fire, and he has warned me always to stay away from them."

I was intrigued by Ter-ek's story of the Sands of Fire, and I dwelled upon it in silence as we walked. Soon we had reached the edge of the forest. Ter-ek's sense of timing had proved impeccable. Darkness was just starting to fall. I began building a small fire about fifty feet from the closest trees while Ter-ek unpacked his pouch. He offered me his straw mat to sleep on as he had the night before, but I thanked him and refused. As tired as I was I knew that even the hard earth would feel like a featherbed that night. Being the perfect host, Ter-ek felt obliged to walk over to the forest and gather up an armful of large fronds. Later that evening, I discovered that these broad leaves made one of the most comfortable mattresses that I ever had the pleasure of lying on.

Our dinner consisted of the fruit and dried meat that I had partaken of a few times since yesterday. When I asked Ter-ek what kind of animal this meat was taken from he described a domesticated animal that the Homarus raised, called a *wurra*. His description led me to believe that it was similar to a sheep, only a good deal larger. I asked him about other animals on Boranga, mentioning the fact that we had not seen a living creature in two days.

"All the animals on Boranga that are left, save

those that we raise, take refuge deep in the forests. Before the time of the Master, Boranga abounded in game. However, animals tend to fear that which they do not understand. It was apparently the will of the Master that many of them would perish. Those who escaped the plains unharmed, the hardier ones, entered the forests of Boranga. Not many are left. We try to leave them alone, killing only to defend ourselves. The Mogars, though, hunt them for sport, usually leaving the carcasses to rot."

"Tell me more about these Mogars," I asked. "Why are you so sure that they took Denny?"

"Had it happened anywhere else on Boranga, I would have guessed that it was the Mogars," he answered, "for it is their way. That it happened by the Cliffs of Mogar assures me that it was indeed them, for no one else would have cause to journey there."

"Of what significance is this place to the Mogars?"

"To understand this, you must first know more of the Mogars. Each king has been a descendent of the original Mogar, and one has always been as ruthless as the other. The last, named Amogar, took to wife a woman named Ophira, a she-devil whose evil manner transcended even her own people. As warriors, the Mogars usually dispatched of their enemies with merciful speed. Ophira, however, was dissatisfied with this, and she initiated unspeakable tortures, resulting in excruciatingly slow deaths. Some among the Mogars took pleasure in her mad ways, and a following developed. The majority remained loyal to Amogar, who was sickened by the methods of Ophira.

"Ophira hated her husband, considering him a coward. Indeed, Amogar had begun to hint at the possibilities of discussing peace with the Homarus, for Ophira's bloodthirsty ways had left him with little desire for violence. She denounced him as a weakling for this, and won more followers among the Mogars. Soon her power was equal to his. Ophira had given birth to a daughter shortly after they were wed, but she now refused Amogar a son to be his heir. She chose instead to raise her daughter, Oleesha by name, with her own insane ideas, so that her kind of leadership would persist even after she died. In this, I assure you, she has succeeded well.

"Amogar, meanwhile, had fallen in love with a woman of the city, and this woman bore him a son. As the woman was unwed, she was forced to raise the child in secret, lest Ophira's followers learn of it. For a while all went well; but one day, about six months after the child was born, both the woman and baby disappeared. No one knew if Ophira had found out, but Amogar secretly sent search parties out every day for months. No trace of the two was ever found. Amogar grieved in silence.

"Thus the two ruled the Mogars for more than twenty years, all the while hating each other. The two factions existed side by side, neither one daring to overthrow the other, lest the strength of the Mogars be weakened. Oleesha grew up to become exactly the kind of she-witch that her mother wished her to be. It is said by some that she is even worse than her mother. In her twentieth year she poisoned Amogar. Taught well by Ophira, she saw to it that his death came slowly, and he suffered greatly. His people placed him in the Boat of the Final Journey, to follow all the kings before him. This boat, according to custom, is taken to the base of the Cliffs of Mogar and, ablaze, set out to sea.

"Before he died, Amogar wished a chance to continue the rift between his followers and those of Ophira. He called his people around him and spoke thus: 'My people, tonight I go to join my ancestors in the Final Place, below the burning sea. The Master has seen fit that in my last hour with you I should leave you a message. Never bend to the will of Ophira. Remain loyal to your ideals, just as you have remained loyal to me through all these years. If you wish something to give you faith, then I offer you this: twenty years ago I had a son by the woman Osara. As a baby, both he and his mother disappeared. This child is the true heir, and only he is fit to rule you. As I lay here in the Boat of the Final Journey, I swear that he will return one day to resume his rightful place among you. Watch the forest around the city for a sign of him. Most importantly, visit the Cliffs of Mogar during the dark hours. If in the journeys that lie before me I find him, I will send him to you. When he comes, you will know him. Take him to Mogara and proclaim to all that the true heir, Omogar by name, has returned. Many will rejoice, and Ophira's power will be no more. Never give up this hope, my people. With my dying words, I promise you his return.'

"That night, Amogar's body was sent to sea on the Boat of the Final Journey, but his words had served their purpose. Many of the Mogars remained loyal to him, and the balance of power among the people did not change. For years they have faithfully kept watch for Omogar. This has infuriated Ophira, but her power has been kept in check. Even the few assassinations that she has carried out against her late husband's most trusted people have not dimmed their hopes. In death he had managed to win a great victory from her."

"The story you have just told me is astonishing, Ter-ek," I told him. "I have also started to put two and two together, and I think I know why you are so certain that the Mogars took Denny. Could they have mistaken him for Omogar?"

"It is what I have been thinking," Ter-ek admitted.

"But Denny will deny that he is Omogar," I insisted. "What would happen to him then?"

"If your friend plays at the game, then he will most likely be killed by Ophira or her spawn. If he denies it, then he will be killed by Amogar's followers to save face."

"Any way you look at it, Denny is in trouble," I said angrily.

"Should things go well for us tomorrow, then we will discover the fate of your friend soon enough," said Ter-ek. "Now I will tell you how to find Mogara, should I be unable to take you there."

Ter-ek proceeded to give me the route to the Mogar city. He seemed resigned to whatever fate the satong hunt of the next day had in store for him, though my feelings were not the same. I was hoping that we would both survive, that he would accomplish what he had come for. The prospect of traversing this strange land alone did not excite me. Though troubled by all that had occurred, I nonetheless slept soundly that night. Even the odd noises that came from the nearby forest did little to disturb me.

At the first sign of light Ter-ek woke me, and after a quick breakfast of the usual fare we broke camp and entered the verdant jungle. Although early in the morning, the forest was hot and steamy. The trees grew tall and close together, blocking out all the sun's glare. Lengthy grass and dense bushes covered nearly every inch of ground. The going would surely have been difficult had it not been for Ter-ek, who passed through the jungle as if a path had already been hewn for him. I guessed that the Homarus knew the way well, since many had sought the satong. There were still no animals to be seen, though during the course of the morning we were constantly surrounded by a myriad of sounds. Birds called to each other from high in the trees. From behind us I heard a throaty roar; ahead, the sounds of scurrying through the foliage. I asked nothing of Ter-ek, for he had cautioned me to silence.

The monotony of the forest trek remained unchanged for hours. Finally we approached a clearing, where Ter-ek told me that we would find a water hole. As we peered through the bushes, I was afforded my first look at Borangan wildlife. As it was with the wild beasts of my own world, the water hole seemed to be a place of truce, for natural enemies shared it together in peace. There were two adult leopards and a cub, assorted monkeys and birds, a strange, reddish-colored beast that looked like a small rhinoceros, two dog-like creatures, possibly wolves, some gentle antelope, and two animals that were quite unique. Their paws and torso resembled that of a bear, but their necks and heads were much like an ostrich.

Suddenly, the tranquil scene was shattered by a hideous scream. The animals, startled, broke for the foliage in all directions. To our left the bushes shook, and from them emerged the source of the sound. Without even a glance at Ter-ek, I knew that I was witnessing my first satong. It stood upright, and had two normal looking hands, but there its similarity to man ended. Its feet resembled those of a large cat, with long, protruding claws digging into the ground. Its legs, arms, and upper torso were covered with brown, shaggy hair. The head, like its hands, was hairless, and sat directly on the shoulders, no neck in evidence. The skull was twice that of a normal human's, with blue and red veins visible on every inch of it. The face was the final atrocity. Its left eye, wide open and bloodshot, was higher than the right one, which was half closed and listless. The bulbous nose was interrupted by two tiny holes, which were its nostrils. Its mouth was a gaping slash that showed a mouthful of broken, rotted teeth. Two small ears sat atop the horror, which stood nearly seven feet tall.

One of the antelope that was escaping from the water hole passed near the satong. With surprising agility for a beast of its size, it leaped toward the deer and grabbed it by the neck. Three times it lifted the creature in the air and brought it down on the ground with a thud. Assured that it was dead, the satong flung the antelope over its shoulder and carried it to the water, depositing it on the bank while it drank its fill. It made a horrid hissing noise, as if it were sucking the water in.

With a curt gesture, Ter-ek motioned me to remain where I was. He deposited his pouch on the ground, and with his right hand he drew the long knife from his belt. With the spear in his other hand he emerged silently from the bushes and approached the beast from behind. Closer, closer he drew. Suddenly the satong whirled, and, raising itself to its full height, began to scream and roar. Ter-ek, without a moment's hesitation, threw his knife with uncanny accuracy into its left eye. It shrieked even louder, grabbing at the knife with its hands and charging wildly. Ter-ek grabbed the end of his long spear, and as the beast neared him he drove it deep into the middle of the stomach. He appeared to know exactly the spot he wanted, and I guessed that this was where its heart lay. The satong froze in its tracks, and Ter-ek twisted the spear around and around. The reason for the barbs was evident; the beast was torn up inside, and with a final cry it fell, lifeless.

Ter-ek, calm throughout the battle, now sank to his knees and repeated the chant that I had heard two days earlier: *"Noma Kuto Boranga. Noma Kuto Boranga,"* he said over and over in a quiet tone. When he was finished, and had regained his feet, he motioned me forward.

"We are fortunate, Ro-lan. I have killed my satong. The quest ends here. We need not risk a night in the hills. By nightfall tomorrow we can reach Mogara. I still have time before I must return to my people, so I will help you. We have water, and, thanks to the satong, fresh meat. But I have one more thing to do before we leave," he added.

Ter-ek removed the tightly wedged spear from the

body of the satong and placed it on the ground. He then withdrew the knife from the beast's eye and calmly proceeded to sever the head from the shoulders. Not having the stomach for this, I turned toward the forest, just in time to see another of the horrors emerge from the bushes. It eyed me immediately and came at me, shrieking and roaring. I yelled to Ter-ek, at the same time grabbing the knife from my belt. As it neared, I hurled the blade at its face and dove to one side. Ter-ek flashed past me with his spear, and within seconds the satong was dispatched.

Brushing myself off, I strode toward the fallen beast. Ter-ek was removing his spear from its body. My knife was wedged firmly in the center of the beast's good eye, in this case the lower right orb.

"Your aim was excellent, Ro-lan," said Ter-ek. "Without blinding him first, it is nearly impossible to kill a satong."

"Be assured that luck had a great part to play in it. Under the circumstances, I was fortunate to hit the beast at all. I admire the courage you show in facing these devils. Now you've got two heads to present to your king."

Ter-ek shook his head. "I may kill five of them on this journey, but with only the head of the first may I return. It is the custom. On my first hunt for the satong I went all the way to the hills, and I slew three. Still, only the first head must be returned for each of the four hunts."

Ter-ek returned to his grisly task while I busied myself gathering his gear from the bushes. This time I kept a wary eye, lest we be attacked again. When his task was done and the blood drained, Ter-ek wrapped the trophy in a specially treated oil-cloth that he carried in his pouch. After placing it in the sack, he cut strips of meat from the antelope, taking only as much as we would need for a few days. I filled up my canteen and his water pouch and, leaving the bodies of the two satongs for the scavengers, we headed south to Mogara, the city of the Mogars.

CHAPTER SEVEN

KING OF THE MOGARS

For the remainder of the long day we marched in silence through the steamy jungle, stopping but once for rest and refreshment. As I watched Ter-ek's pouch swinging at his side, I thought back to the spectacle that I had witnessed earlier. Had he made the slightest error, the satong would have caught and crushed him, so great was the speed and strength of the thing. To Ter-ek, the simple fact that 'It is the custom' was more than enough reason to risk his life in such a manner. I looked forward to meeting the Homarus who, if Ter-ek was representative, must be a courageous and noble people, though perhaps inclined to dwell in the ways of the past.

One incident occurred during the otherwise uneventful journey. We had stopped to rest, and were lunching on some fruits and berries that Ter-ek had gathered. Something in the bushes to our left caught my eye, and I decided to investigate. The foliage was exceptionally dense for about ten or fifteen yards, but I finally reached my objective. The narrowest beam of sunlight filtered down through the trees, and it glinted off some object that lay partially hidden under bits of branches and shrubs. Thoughtlessly I reached for the object and caught the thin ray on the back of my hand. I had momentarily forgotten the intensity of the Borangan sun and, concentrated as it was in this pencil-thin beam, it was especially painful. I quickly withdrew my hand. After making sure that the burn wasn't serious, I approached the thing more carefully. Brushing the branches aside, I saw that the object was an egg; in fact, there were three eggs. They were large, about three or four times the size of an average chicken egg, and their shells were impregnated with what looked like tiny bits of crystal. I removed one from the nest and began to retrace my steps to show it to Ter-ek.

Suddenly, amidst much cracking and trampling of bushes, the strange, ostrich-like creature which I had first seen at the water hole emerged. It stood no more than ten feet from me, its head and neck so grotesquely inappropriate atop its immense body. It quickly surveyed the situation and, seeing one of its precious eggs in my hand, began to hop up and down, all the while making no sound. The sight of this ungainly creature hopping, as well as the long neck moving in circles, would almost have struck me funny had I not been so scared. Its claws looked formidable enough, and I was sure it could do a lot of damage, as angry as it was. I retreated slowly as the animal continued its weird dance. Back, back I went, right into the bole of a tree.

Here was a fine mess! I did not wish to take my eyes off the creature, lest it charge. With one hand behind me, I began to feel my way around the tree. The thing now stopped its dance and strode toward me with purpose. Fearing that it might overtake me with superior speed, I turned quickly and scrambled up the huge tree. The egg in my hand made climbing awkward, but after negotiating a few branches I now sat about fifteen feet above the ground. I hoped that the beast was not arboreal.

The strange thing reached the base of the tree and stood directly below. Once again it began hopping up and down, its silence unnerving. Six, seven times, before it stopped. It then moved to the tree and began to climb! Completely shaken, I yelled for Ter-ek. He responded, and I heard him crash through the bushes. As he neared the spot and saw my predicament, the look of concern left his face, and for the first time since I had met him, he cracked a broad grin. In seconds he was roaring with laughter.

"You've picked a fine time to show me that you have a sense of humor!" I shouted angrily. "Get this devil away from me, will you?"

"You have one of the *ghoma's* eggs?" Ter-ek asked, composing himself.

"Yes, I do," I told him, holding up the shiny thing.

"Throw it to me," he instructed.

He caught the egg and held it high in the air for the ghoma to see. The beast stopped its ascent and leaped to the ground, facing Ter-ek. Once again it began its ritualistic hopping.

"Ro-lan, point to the nest," he shouted.

From the tree I could see the other eggs, and I indicated the general direction. Turning his back on the beast, he strode unconcernedly to the nest and placed the egg back in. The ghoma began to move toward him, but he gave the beast a wide berth and returned to the base of the tree while the thing continued in a straight line toward its nest. Assured that all its eggs were there it faced us, hopped in the air three times, and then settled itself into what appeared to be a sitting position.

"You may come down now, Ro-lan," Ter-ek laughed. "The ghoma will no longer chase you. It is a gentle and inoffensive beast. However, like any other mother, it will fight to protect its young. Henceforth, you must avoid the temptation."

I descended the tree quickly. In a moment I stood at Ter-ek's side, grinning sheepishly. The ghoma sat calmly and motionlessly over its eggs, eyeing us.

"I still have much to learn of your world, Ter-ek," I said. "If a creature like that is gentle, then I imagine that the rabbits and squirrels are carnivorous."

He looked at me questioningly. "I do not understand what you mean, Ro-lan."

"Never mind," I said, trying to suppress another grin. "Let's get out of here."

We traveled until it was nearly dark, finally stopping to rest for the night in the middle of a large clearing. Each of us took turns on guard, but while the forest abounded in nocturnal noises, our camp was undisturbed. We resumed the journey in the morning, Ter-ek walking a couple of paces ahead of me. I was still amazed by the ease with which he found his way through foliage that seemed inaccessible in many places.

Hours passed, and although the heat and humidity of this steamy forest was beginning to have its effect on both of us, we pushed on. Many were the animals we heard along the way, but they were most adept at concealment. Some of them scurried through the bushes only a few feet from us but managed to stay hidden. Dusk was approaching, and we were anxious to reach Mogara before the shadows of night had descended fully. Ter-ek had told me that the Mogars protect themselves well from the prowling satongs; hence we would be less likely to encounter one if we were within the sphere of the city.

Soon we ran into a small, rapidly running stream. Ter-ek was pleased, for it meant that we were near the city. It was the landmark that he had been seeking. This stream, he told me, was a tributary of the larger river, the Otongo, that I had followed under the mountains. Dense foliage lined both sides, in some places hanging over and completely obliterating it. We followed the tributary for about half a mile, then veered away from it about ten yards. Ter-ek motioned me to stop, then got down on his hands and knees. He told me to remain on my feet and follow closely in his path. Presuming that he knew what he was doing, I complied. Ter-ek crawled slowly, as darkness had now engulfed us. He moved in a straight line, always intent on the ground in front of him. Once he motioned me back, himself retreating about three feet. Turning to the left, he crawled another ten feet, then turned right again and examined the ground cautiously. Satisfied, he continued forward. On we went, the procedure being repeated a number of times. But finally, the glow of fires and the hushed murmur of voices told us that we had reached our destination. The stream that we had originally followed now emerged from the foliage into a clearing and continued toward the base of a large hill far in the distance, though not before first paralleling Mogara.

Ter-ek regained his feet, and together we peered through the bushes at the 'city' of his enemies. Two sentries were visible, although I was sure that there were more. They patrolled along the edge of the forest, one of them passing no more than fifteen feet from the spot where we were hidden. When he had passed I concentrated on the city, which was brightly lit by many large fires located along the main thoroughfare, as well as numerous torches hanging over the doorways of the dwellings. There were many hundreds of these small huts, all placed somewhat unevenly in eight rows. Little room existed between them, but the rows were separated by avenues of a sort, the widest one running through the middle of the city. The shanties varied little in size, obviously designed for no more than utilitarian purposes. They were built from what looked like thick bamboo stems, which were lashed together with strips of leather. The roofs were of similar construction, with a few scattered fronds for added protection.

In the center of the city, on the primary road, stood an obelisk. It was nearly twenty feet tall, and in the flickering firelight it glowed a brilliant crimson. At its base was something that I was unable to identify. Past the cryptic tower, near the hill, were two larger huts, similar in construction to the others but four times the size. In front of these huts stood two large chairs, each on top of a separate dais about three feet off the ground. Various skins and furs covered both chairs.

The absence of dogs or any other domesticated animals in the city puzzled me. I learned later from Ter-ek that the Mogars considered all animals a nuisance, only worthy of being hunted for game or sport. There were people wandering about the city, and I strained to witness their activities. The men closely resembled Ter-ek in their features. They too wore skins around their middles, but these were different from the Homaru's, in that they were ornamented by what looked like bits of fur. Some of these men strolled through the streets, stopping to kneel at the obelisk if they happened to pass it. Others sat idly in front of their huts, eating dinner and conversing with their women.

I now had my first look at the women of Boranga, and I daresay I was not disappointed. From where I stood, they appeared incredibly beautiful. All displayed long black hair that hung far below their shoulders, while the contours of their bodies were accentuated by the tight-fitting, brightly-colored sheaths that they wore. Their dark skins enhanced the sensuality of their faces, which were highlighted by full, crimson lips. They swayed naturally, albeit enticingly, as they walked, their movements almost hypnotic. Some were barefoot, though most were shod in slim, utilitarian sandals. There were few that could have been thought of as less than alluring.

Eventually I loosed my mind from the spell cast by these Mogar beauties, my primary concern being for

Denny. I wondered where he could be. Was he still alive, or had they disposed of him quickly? Was he even in Mogara, or could Ter-ek have been mistaken? As I pondered on this, I neglected to watch the sentry, who was returning along the edge of the forest. Terek had dropped to cover, and was now tugging at my leg, trying to force me to do the same. In the instant that it took me to react, I realized that the guard was no more than ten feet away from us, a small torch in his hand held high as he gazed suspiciously in our direction. As I fell to the ground I accidently rustled the bushes with a noise that, to me, sounded like the dropping of a bomb. The sentry reacted immediately.

"You there, stand up so that I may see who you are!" he demanded.

All caution was forgotten now. "Ter-ek, let's get out of here!" I shouted, racing back into the forest.

"Ro-lan, wait!" he snapped as he followed at my heels. "You will be killed!"

The Mogar sentry shouted the alarm to his fellows, at the same time taking up the pursuit. I could hear him crashing through the bushes behind us. Ter-ek seemed intent on stopping me, but I wished to put some distance between ourselves and the now aroused Mogars. However, after only twenty yards or so, the reason for Ter-ek's concern became evident. Suddenly there was no ground below my feet, and I felt myself falling. The brush had given way and revealed a deep pit. But because of the density of the foliage, I had a split second to react as it gave way, and I grabbed hold of the edge with my fingers. I knew that I could maintain this for only seconds, and was most thankful when Ter-ek reached the pit and grasped my wrists.

"It is a satong trap," he told me, hauling me out of danger. "Mogara is surrounded by them. It was the reason for the caution taken in approaching the city."

"Now you tell me," I replied breathlessly. "Ter-ek, look out!"

The first of the Mogar guardsmen had reached us. Ter-ek's back was toward him, his spear discarded in order to help me. The Mogar lifted his own javelin, intent on thrusting it into Ter-ek's spine. I managed to shove Ter-ek to one side just as the weapon was lowered, and it became embedded harmlessly in the ground. Before the Mogar could remove it, I struck him full in the face. He staggered for a moment, and then fell forward into the pit. The brief scream that emerged from below was horrible.

Ter-ek regained his feet and hurried to retrieve his weapon, but it was too late. Three, four, five Mogars now surrounded us, their spears waving menacingly. As we stood near the edge of the pit, one Mogar held his torch downwards. There, at the bottom of the nearly fifteen foot deep hole, lay the body of the first guardsman, impaled on a bed of long, sharpened spikes, which covered the entire floor. I shuddered as I witnessed the grim spectacle.

"Gorog is dead," the Mogar with the torch announced to his fellows. "It will not go well with these two, for he was a favorite of the princess, one of her own guard. Here, let's have a look at them!"

He waved his torch at Ter-ek, deliberately scalding his body as he examined him. Ter-ek winced, but made no outcry, the two spears held against his back, restraining him. Then the Mogar repeated his cruelties with me, and I too remained silent, despite the pain. Satisfied that he had seen enough, he stopped his torture.

"We have among us a Homaru," he told the others as he strutted around us. "He is probably on his way to mate with a satong, whom we all know are the brothers of the Homarus. How honored we are by his visit!" The others laughed. Encouraged, he continued: "And here we have another bearded one, his clothing strange to me. Could it be that Omogar has returned to us a second time? What will the dolts believe now? I should throw him in the pit, so that there will be no more foolishness. Of course, this will not be acceptable to your father, will it, Dovan?"

"Be assured it will not, Droom," a voice to my rear replied. The pressure of the spear in my back abated. "These prisoners should be taken before the Council to be judged. No harm will come to them beforehand, of this I will make sure."

"The Council, bah!" Droom spat. "Your father and his bunch are fools, just as you are, Dovan. The queen will pass judgement on these two, or perhaps she will allow her 'son' to do so."

"The queen's justice is known to all of us," Dovan replied angrily. "Come, let us return them to the city, and hope that sanity will prevail for a change."

Our hands were bound behind us with leather thongs, and we were marched back to Mogara, Droom walking ahead with the torch. Ter-ek walked proudly and silently, prodded by spear points along the way. One Mogar walked behind me, also jabbing me occasionally. The one called Dovan paralleled me, a few feet away. I glanced over at him once, but he quickly averted his eyes to the ground. He was a young man, perhaps eighteen or so, and was splendidly built. All these Mogars appeared to be well-muscled fighting men, though Dovan lacked the cruelties of the others. I hoped that I would get a chance to know him better.

We emerged from the forest and walked directly down the main thoroughfare. The city had been alerted, and thousands lined the way to get a good look at us. Some taunts were thrown, but most were just curious. I overheard comments regarding myself and my beard, which I now realized had become shaggy. Droom took full advantage of the situation, making sure that all knew who engineered the capture. He did not quiet down until we passed the strange, crimson obelisk in the center of the city. He fell to his knees, head bowing up and down, and repeated over and over the chant that I first heard Ter-ek intone: *"Noma Kuto Boranga!"* All now genuflected, including Ter-ek. I was forced down by a sharp spear, where I attempted some sort of mimicry to satisfy my captors. As they chanted, I had a chance to study that which I was unable to make out before. At the base of the obelisk, also painted bright red, was a large trap door, two gold rings its only ornamentation. It seemed an incongruous place for a door to be located. I wondered just what was below.

When the ceremony ended, we regained our feet and resumed the march toward the two large huts. Our captors stopped us at the base of the two chairs, and once again forced us to our knees. From the corner of my eye I saw Dovan slip away from the party

91

and move toward the crowd, where he met with a gray-haired man, the two of them becoming involved in a heated discussion. Meanwhile, Droom approached the chair on the left, and from its side he removed an object that looked like an animal's horn. Putting it to his lips, he sounded four long blasts. The noise resounded off the surrounding hills, and the forest became alive with the cries of animals, all agitated by this strange noise. From deep within the jungle I discerned the horrid scream of a satong.

The last echo faded away, and all became deathly still. Droom returned the horn to its place and took his position at the head of the guard. He stood next to me, and before falling to his knees he could not resist placing a foot squarely in my ribs. I stared at his sadistically smiling face, and I swore that he would pay for his treatment of Ter-ek and myself. I considered making this vow known to him, when suddenly the curtains over the doorway of one of the huts parted, and four cringing servants emerged. Two held the curtains to either side, while the others bowed in the dirt, defining the boundaries of an imaginary pathway to the thrones.

A young woman stepped forward from the dwelling, and slowly, purposefully, she passed between the groveling retainers. She was tall, with the lengthiest ebon hair of any female that I had yet observed in Mogara. Her body was sleek, sensuous, the fine curves displayed to perfection by a tight black sheath studded with shimmering stones. Her long, bronzed legs tapered down to disproportionately small feet, which were encased in fine slippers. She possessed fiery, crimson lips, these parted to reveal gleaming, perfect teeth. Though my head was bowed, I found that I could not take my eyes off her. I wanted to believe that she was the most beautiful woman I had ever seen in my life, but something was wrong. As I continued to stare, I realized what it was: her eyes! They were not soft, like those of the island beauties I had known, or of the Mogar woman I had seen here. These enigmatic azure flecks burned with the fires of malevolence, boring deep into one's soul. They were the quintessence of evil, and I could understand why all were staring at the ground as they genuflected; for none wished to meet her gaze. I found myself unable to avert my own eyes, and as she approached, I realized that she was staring at me. Thus was my first sight of Oleesha, princess of the Mogars, daughter of Ophira and Amogar.

As Oleesha neared to within a few feet of the thrones, she turned and faced the other hut. The spell was now broken, and I quickly averted my eyes downward. Still, I found myself sneaking glances at this incredible woman, and I feared that I would become ensnared again. With her back toward me, she raised her hands in the air and clapped twice before again facing the people. This time, I returned my gaze to the dirt and kept it there.

"Omogar!" I heard her intone in a strong, lilting voice.

"Omogar, Omogar!" the people repeated. "Omogar, Omogar!"

I was aware of a figure emerging from the other hut and walking toward Oleesha. The chanting became louder, until soon they were screaming the name. I wanted to observe this, but I dared not look. The two figures met, and together they approached the chairs.

93

With the help of servants, they ascended the platforms and sat down. The intonations were now at a fever pitch, the people in a frenzy.

Suddenly, all became still. For what seemed like hours, but could not have been more than a minute, silence reigned, broken only once by the shrill call of a bird in the forest. Finally, Oleesha spoke: "Droom, to my feet!" she ordered.

Droom rose and approached the princess, bowing as he walked. When he reached the throne, he again fell to his knees.

"Stand, Droom," she ordered, "and tell me why I am disturbed only moments after partaking of my evening meal. What do you find so important?"

I took some solace in knowing that this bully was being reduced to a quivering bowl of gelatin. He responded in a timid, quaking voice:

"Two men, Princess; I captured two men who were sneaking about the city. One is a Homaru, the other a stranger. They killed Gorog, Princess, your very own guard."

"Bring them to me!" she demanded.

Droom turned and barked orders to his men. We were prodded to our feet and urged forward. At the foot of the platform, we again knelt.

"Have them stand and face us, Droom," Oleesha ordered.

Apparently Droom had been looking forward to this, for he took the opportunity to kick Ter-ek in the stomach. Ter-ek bared his teeth, but again restrained himself and stood up. As Droom approached me, evidently to repeat his cruelty, I determined that, regardless of the consequences, I would not let this bully have his way again. As his foot came up I rolled to one side, this causing him to fall backwards and land on his head. Subdued laughter could be heard all around me as the enraged Droom regained his feet. Before he had a chance to react I also rose and, running toward him, deposited a drop kick squarely on his chin. As he fell backwards again, he struck his head on the platform. He crumpled in a heap, unconscious, at the feet of his beloved princess.

I laid on the ground, breathless, six spears probing at various parts of my body. Three men carried the dazed Droom away from the platform, and I watched them until they disappeared into the crowd. If I was going to die, I at least had some satisfaction.

Once again I heard Oleesha speak: "Let him rise," she ordered her men. "You, foolish one, approach so that I might see you."

I walked toward the platform, my escorts close at hand. For the first time since the Mogar royalty opened court, I was afforded a close look at those on the dais. The flickering light from the torches that were held by the servants added an eerie quality to Oleesha's eyes as they bore through me, but even these mesmerizing flecks could not keep me from seeing that which I had hoped for. Seated on one of the thrones, decked out in the trappings of a Borangan monarch, was *Denny McVey!* He looked none the worse for wear, and his bearing was certainly that of a king. His beard, which was as long as mine but trimmer, enhanced this image. Apparently he had taken to the part well, and the bewildered Mogars had not yet decided what to make of him. I glanced quickly at Ter-ek. He had seen my face and understood, but a curt shake of the head told me not to display any outward signs of recognition. I wanted to jump up on the dais and pound my friend on the back, but I knew that this would jeopardize all of us so, with much difficulty, I held back all the emotions I felt. Denny was having fewer problems, for I noted that he was examining Ter-ek and I with idle curiosity, even boredom.

I returned my gaze to Oleesha, and saw that she was looking at Ter-ek. He stood frozen, defenseless against her gaze. Even though she was not looking at me, I could still feel the strange power in those wicked eyes.

"You, Homaru, your name!" she snapped.

"It is Ter-ek," he replied, trying to shake off the spell.

"You have been sent to spy on us, have you not, Homaru?" she accused. "Perhaps you wish to murder many of us, as you did with Gorog."

"*I* killed Gorog as he attempted to put a spear in Ter-ek's back!" I shouted. My efforts were rewarded with a spear shaft across my neck.

"Silence, foolish one!" the princess spat. "I did not address you. You will have your time to speak." She turned back to Ter-ek. "You have not answered my question, Homaru."

"I have entered the forest to hunt the satong, nothing more."

"You lie!" she screamed. "The hills of the satongs lie far to the north."

"As I entered the forest, I saw a satong moving in this direction," Ter-ek lied. "Wishing to avoid the hills, I trailed him. Only a short distance from

96

Mogara I lost him."

"The Homarus hunt the satongs alone," she replied. "Why are you not alone?"

"I found this stranger in the forest nearby. He was injured. I assisted him, thereby losing the trail of the beast."

"And who is this stranger?" she queried.

"Who knows?" Ter-ek answered. "Perhaps he is your Omogar returning to you."

A gasp arose from the assembled multitude. Denny leaped up from his seat and glared at Ter-ek, his twisted face a mask of anger. Oleesha stood up and faced Denny. In silence she stared at him for a few seconds, then pointed to the throne. Subdued, he resumed his seat. Oleesha turned and faced the people, her hands raised. Murmuring was audible throughout the crowd.

"Be silent!" she ordered them. They complied. Taking her seat, she screamed at Ter-ek: "Your mere presence here is already your acceptance of death. To speak such lies before the true Omogar will just lengthen the duration of your demise, making it more painful. I will speak with this stranger now."

Before she had a chance to ask her first question, a bell rang loudly. The curtains of Oleesha's hut parted, and again a number of servants emerged, this time crawling on their bellies. The bell tolled a second time, and as one the crowd fell to the ground, flat on their stomachs. Ter-ek and I were forced to this position also, while Oleesha and Denny dropped to one knee. Minutes passed, and I was unable to see anything from this position. I heard the slow, steady crunch of feet on the hard ground. Soon this stopped, and Oleesha spoke: "Arise, and behold the splendor of your queen!" she announced.

I obeyed, once again prodded by the tips of a few spears. Ophira, the queen, had been carried from the hut on a sedan chair, which had been placed directly between and in front of the two daises. As I looked at her, I saw a vision of Oleesha about thirty years hence. It was obvious that she was the mother of the princess, for their features varied little. Her hair was also lengthy, though not as long as that of her daughter, and it appeared to be in the final stages of graying. The visible skin on her body was dry and pock-marked. Her face, surely once as beautiful as any among the Mogars, was twisted grotesquely, reflecting her years of hatreds and jealousies. The heavy make-up she wore did little to cover this. Her eyes, though not comparable to those of Oleesha, burned with their own kind of evil, and were also hard to look into too deeply. A bright green sarong completed the not-too-pretty picture of Ophira, queen of the Mogars.

She studied me carefully for a moment, and then examined Ter-ek. Satisfied, she called her daughter to her side and conferred with her for a few minutes. Although I stood close by, I was unable to hear any of the conversation. Denny remained apart from the two, and I gazed at him, until I finally caught his eye. As he stared at me, I could not detect the slightest hint of recognition in his face. Surely he was overplaying his part, but maybe it was better that way.

Finally, their discussion concluded, Ophira faced me once more. "You, come close!" she screeched, pointing a long fingernail at me. I obeyed. "What are you called?" she asked.

"My name is Ro-lan," I answered.

"You are not a Homaru, and you are not a Mogar. Where are you from?"

"I am not of Boranga," I told her, deciding to have a try at the truth, but with few details. "I came here from across the sea. Not knowing Boranga I became lost, and I injured my leg. Ter-ek found me and helped me, as he said before. He was in pursuit of a satong. That is all."

This revelation started a new uproar among the Mogars. The two women held a brief discussion, while the guards exerted a bit more pressure with their spears against my body. Ophira then silenced the throng.

"You and the Homaru have spoken nothing but lies in the presence of the highest of the Mogars," she sneered. "You have killed a member of the princess' guard, and have injured Droom, who is of my own retinue. All that is left is to pass judgement on you. I leave this sentence to the son of our late, beloved Amogar, who was so miraculously returned to us from the sea only recently to rule his people." Her tone was mocking. "I give you Omogar, king of the Mogars!"

Denny rose from his throne, amidst cheers and shouts from the Mogars. The people began to chant: "Omogar! Omogar!" Denny walked to the front of the platform and signaled for his servants. They helped him to the ground, and he approached Ter-ek. Standing directly in front of him, he examined the Homaru from head to toe, finally slapping him hard across each cheek. Ter-ek, humiliated, still held his ground. While the chants grew in intensity, my best friend then turned to me. As he stood in front of me, I could see a piece of cloth secured on his head, covering the gash that he had received before we abandoned the *Maui Queen*. He began to study me, and I could take it no longer. I had to talk to him.

"Denny, for God's sake, what's going on?" I implored, quietly.

He jumped back startled. For a moment he stared at me and then, in a violent rage, he smacked me in the face with the palm of his hand. I fell to the ground, stunned.

"Silence, you scum!" he shrieked. "You dare talk to Omogar before he has commanded you to speak?" To the guards he screamed: "Pick him up!"

My heart sank, for I now realized that this was not an act. The two women leered at me, one young, one old, both possessed of unquestioned evil. I thought that I would go mad. The chanting was now deafening, but Denny seemed to revel in it. He returned to his platform, where he faced the people and raised his hands. They became silent. He looked at Ophira and Oleesha, then at Ter-ek, then me. Finally, his proclamation came in a voice that was Denny's, yet at the same time was not, for it seemed that someone, something else, now dwelt within his shell.

"To these prisoners, who have affronted your princess, your queen, and now your Omogar, there is but one judgement to be made: Death! The *Slow Death*, to commence immediately!"

CHAPTER EIGHT

THE COUNCIL

The fires of Mogara flickered and danced in the moonlit night of Boranga. Flames reached high into the air, then returned to earth as others rose and fell. Such were the things I noticed in the instant following Denny's proclamation. Did it strike me immediately that my best friend in the world—for that matter in two worlds—had just decreed my death? No, it could not be! I refused to believe it! Soon this damned nightmare would be over . . .

All around me people were screaming and dancing, their hands raised in the air. On the platform stood Omogar, grinning wickedly. Two women, one in black, one in green, writhed and twisted obscenely in some kind of mock dance, at the same time nodding their approval. If there was a Hell, then surely this must be it; but what could I have done to be here, and what could have brought such a noble soul as Ter-ek?

Ter-ek! For the moment I had forgotten him. I glanced in his direction and saw him engaged with four of the Mogars. Even against such odds, and with his hands tied behind him, he was giving an admirable account of himself. I felt proud to have such an ally, and I grieved as I realized that I might be responsible for his death. I decided that I would emulate this worthy and not give up without a fight. But while I was able to place the heel of my foot into the faces of two guards, I was quickly overwhelmed by numbers. Six of the Mogars brought me to the ground, removed the bonds from my wrists and spread-eagled me. I was then fastened firmly to the ground by four large, staple-like pieces of metal that were driven in with mallets. When I was secure, they arose. A quick glance advised me that Ter-ek had also lost his battle.

The screaming crowd, now caught up in the frenzy of their leaders, was spitting at us and trying to kick us. Had the guards not been able to ward them off, we surely would have been trampled to death, for we were helpless.

Denny now climbed to the top of Ophira's sedan chair and screamed at the populace. "The Honor!" he yelled insanely. "Who desires the Honor?"

Shouts and screams went up as one after another volunteered. Fights broke out among the crowd. Apparently this honor was desired by all. Denny leaped to and fro on the sedan, anxious to decide, but the decision was soon made for him. From the rear of the crowd rose an ear-splitting voice, heard by all:

"The Honor is mine, and mine alone! I captured

them, and I have been humiliated by one of them! Please, Omogar, allow me this Honor!"

The voice was very familiar, and as the crowd parted to let him through I saw that it was Droom! He had made a quick recovery, and now he bellowed like a wounded elephant.

Denny looked pleased. "The Honor is claimed by Droom," he told the people. "What say you to this?"

As one, the Mogars voiced their approval. I shuddered to think of what this honor must be for such as Droom to desire it so, and I was not long in finding out. From the rear of the platforms came a servant carrying one of the long Borangan knives, its tip glowing red hot. It had apparently been in the fire for some time. That it was anticipated probably meant that death was the standard welcome for guests of the Mogars. The servant handed it to Droom, who ceremoniously raised it first to Ophira, then her daughter, then Denny.

"Your pleasure, Omogar?" Droom roared.

"The Homaru first," he replied maliciously. "The two small toes!"

Droom grinned wickedly. The crowd screamed louder and louder. The bully approached Ter-ek slowly, wishing to prolong the event. Ophira and Oleesha were beside themselves with ecstasy; Denny leaped gleefully on the sedan. Droom now straddled Ter-ek's right leg. The Homaru fought futilely to free himself. Droom lowered the point of the red-hot knife toward Ter-ek's foot. Closer, closer it came, until it was only inches away.

Seconds later, Droom trembled in his death throes. A barbed Borangan spear, thrown from somewhere in the crowd, was embedded deeply in his throat. The now forgotten knife lay at Ter-ek's feet. Droom grasped the shaft of the spear and staggered about, his eyes glazed. As he fell forward, the momentum pushed the spear upward at an angle, directly into his brain, while the other end took hold in the ground, preventing him from toppling forward. With a final shudder, Droom expired. The sight of him standing upright, his eyes bulging, a spear shaft protruding from his neck, was grotesque. If this action was perpetrated with a purpose in mind, then it had succeeded, for with the spell broken the crowd became silent.

"Who dares to interfere with the orders of Omogar?" the frenzied Ophira screamed.

A figure emerged from the crowd and strode with purpose toward us. Stopping between Ter-ek and myself, he stared defiantly at the rulers. It was the young sentry, Dovan, who had opposed Droom's treatment of us when we had first been captured.

"As torture and death are all that you and your kind understand, Ophira," he announced solemnly, "then the killing of this beast will assure me of your attention. Yes, I killed him, because the method by which you choose to treat your prisoners is cruel, and does not represent the wishes of all the Mogars. The Council has not been consulted in this matter, which defies Mogar law."

"The Council, bah!" Ophira spat. "Amogar, my husband, forced the Council on us before he died. Your bunch of doddering old men is useless now, for Omogar has returned to rule us! It was your own people that brought him here and proclaimed him

Omogar. Do you deny this?"

"No sooner had we brought him here, did he fall under the spell of your spawn," he replied, pointing at Oleesha, who lay spent on the dais, her wicked eyes glazed. "He could not be the true son, for Omogar would not allow this to happen to him."

"You found him in the place of your own prophecy, did you not?" she gloated.

"The prophecy also told us to watch the forest," said Dovan. "Perhaps this one is the true Omogar." He indicated me. "Did he not appear from the forest?"

"He lies, he lies!" Denny screamed. "I am the true Omogar! Only I shall rule the Mogars! I, and no one else!" He shook his fist at Dovan.

"You see, Dovan," Ophira leered, "the true Omogar has spoken. The Slow Death shall continue. You shall be punished for the murder of Droom. Guards, take him!"

Dovan leaped to the lifeless body of Droom and tore the spear from him. Six guards approached as he stood ready to defend himself. But a group of about fifteen armed Mogars emerged from the crowd and surrounded the would-be attackers. Nearly half of them were older men. Prominent among them was the one that Dovan had conferred with earlier.

"Kill him! Kill him!" Denny screamed at the guards.

"The first one who moves toward my son will be slain instantly," the older man announced in a calm, authoritative voice. The guards backed off.

Denny had descended from the sedan to stand next to Ophira. Oleesha, now revived, stood on the other side of her mother. The three presented an intense picture of hatred as they glared at the old man. They seemed powerless.

"The prisoners will be placed in a guarded hut tonight," the old man continued. "Tomorrow the Council shall meet to discuss this Omogar. We shall also decide the fate of the prisoners. When Ama gives way to darkness, we shall communicate our decisions to you. The madness of this evening shall stop! Return to your huts with your spawn, Ophira."

The three of them were now consumed by rage. I admired this man, who had the temerity to face them in such a manner. Surely Dovan came from fine stock. Ophira dove into her sedan chair, pulling the curtains about her. The bearers grabbed the poles and whisked her into the hut. Oleesha leaped from her platform, declining any help, and disappeared in the wake of her parent. Denny was the last to leave, shaking both fists in our direction before he entered his dwelling. As I watched him, a wave of emotions swept over me. Would I be able to save him before these people tore him to pieces? Even if I did, would I be able to help him? His mind had apparently been wrested from him by the young she-devil. I felt utterly helpless.

The crowd, which had been slowly dispersing ever since Droom had been killed, was now non-existent. Only Dovan, his father, their people, and the guards remained. The large fires continued to burn brightly, but the torches that lit the front of many of the huts had been extinguished, for the hour was late. Following the man's instructions, the guards pulled the shackles from the ground. We were led, a bit more gently this time, to an empty hut. No words were spoken, and we asked no questions.

In the hut, our hands and feet were bound. We were given water, then allowed to lie down. Guards were posted in front of the doorway. I glanced at Ter-ek, and he smiled at me. Moments later he was asleep, his breathing regular. I thanked God that he was alive and well, and that, for the time being at least, his blood was not on my hands. It took only a few seconds more for me to join him in the depths of slumber.

When we awakened the next morning, we found Dovan and his father in the hut. They had brought us water and various fruits, and they untied our hands so that we could help ourselves. Starved, we eagerly devoured the fruits, while the two of them sat silently and waited for us to finish. When we were done, the older man spoke: "I am Heran, elder of the Mogar Council. This is my son, Dovan." His voice was strong, well modulated.

"I wish to thank the both of you for what you did last night," I replied. Ter-ek nodded his assent.

"We would do as much for anyone to prevent the shame that has befallen our people," said Heran. "If things were not worse before, we have now added to our woes by bringing this Omogar to Mogara."

"He is not Omogar; he is my friend," I told them.

As one, Heran and Dovan leaped to their feet. Dovan came at me angrily, but Heran grabbed him and held him back.

"You heard him, Father!" Dovan shouted, struggling. "They are his friends! For such as this I risked my life!"

"Please, it's not as you think! He was not like this before. Hear my story so that you will understand."

"Dovan, he would not admit friendship to that monster so readily without a reason," said Heran calmly. "Let us hear what he has to say before we pass judgement."

With Dovan subdued, they resumed their seats. I believed that these were men I could trust, so I decided to tell them everything. They listened in silence, their emotions not betraying them. When I was done, they conferred in whispers. Then Heran addressed Ter-ek.

"Homaru, do you believe this story that your friend tells us?"

"All that he described from the time that I met him is the truth," Ter-ek answered. "As for the rest, I will say this: I too find it difficult to believe. We of the Homarus never question anything beyond our own sphere. However, in the time that I have known him, I have found Ro-lan to be a brave man, and an honest one. I do not believe that he would have reason to lie to me. His first thought was to find his friend, who had been injured. I found him at the place where the Otongo journeys underground. He had been bitten by the evil small ones who dwell only in the depths. He described the *morf*, which grows only on the tunnel walls. He saw Tomo Raka and lived. He could not have passed any other way, for is it not true that only the Mogars know of the other passage?

"Finally, Heran, there is something else about him that makes me believe he is not of Boranga. He knows not of . . . of holy things. He questions that which

108

should not be questioned. He is no fool. I am almost convinced that he does not know. You have lived long, Heran. Have you ever known of one without knowledge of the holy things?"

"I have not, Ter-ek," he replied, "although I still cannot begin to understand. What else could there be other than Boranga? To travel on the sea when Ama is strongest could only mean death. Surely there is nothing else."

"Since I have met Ro-lan, his words have danced often through my head," said Ter-ek. "I began to wonder if perhaps the teachings of the ages could not be flawed in some way. There is no proof that there are other worlds, but there is also no evidence that there are not. The Homarus pride themselves on intelligence, yet we never question that which has been passed on to us. Unless we some day learn to the contrary, I choose to believe what Ro-lan has told me."

"I was among those who found Omogar that night by the Cliffs of Mogar," Dovan offered. "If you followed us through the cave, then you saw what was left near the secret passage. What was it?"

"You left our life raft, a lantern, and an emergency knapsack," I answered.

Although some of the words were strange to him, Dovan knew that I was not lying. He looked at Heran. "He is right, Father." To me: "Please accept my apologies, Ro-lan. We must go immediately and reveal the identity of the false Omogar."

"No, you mustn't do that!" I pleaded. "Once he is of no value to Ophira, she will have him killed!"

"If he continues his mad ways, the people will

109

destroy him," Heran replied.

"It will be up to you to make sure that they don't kill him," I told them. "I want to help him, but I must get him away from here first. This will be the only way to insure keeping him alive. You must do this for me. He is sick, believe me. Please tell me all that has occurred since you found him."

"I can tell you this," said Dovan. "Each night, when the water permits it, four of us journey to the Cliffs of Mogar to maintain our vigil, in keeping with the late Amogar's wishes. Always we are disappointed, as are those who watch the forest. One night, we emerge from the tunnel shortly after the last drop of water has emptied. No sooner do the sandals of the last man strike the sand when a moaning sound is heard. Fearfully, we raise our torches. Staggering down the sands toward us, a strange bundle in his hands, we see him. 'Here, I am here,' is what he says. This is the message we have waited for these many years. The son of Amogar has come to us! We run to meet him. He staggers and falls, but we catch him. He is returned triumphantly to Mogara. Oleesha is summoned to aid him for, as she has the power to destroy, so also does she possess the means to heal. For days she tends to him alone, letting no one near. We inquire as to his health, but always the answer is the same: 'He is well, but in a deep sleep. Soon your Omogar will come to you.' This is what she tells us. You saw him as we did, for the first time. If this be your friend, then surely she has worked evil on him. All the people who have clung for years to the hope that their Omogar would return will now follow him; save a few. Our dream of peace and sanity is gone."

"If Ophira knew that the support of the people would all be hers, then how were you able to get away with what you did last night?" I asked them.

"As I was shocked last night," Heran answered, "so was I sure that many of the people were. They have not yet rallied to Omogar. Dovan's act made them even more hesitant. It will take time, but they will accept him. Ophira will make certain of that. Do not fear, Ro-lan. We will not expose your friend. No one would believe such a story as yours, even if we did. We would be ridiculed, and this would strengthen them."

"Why have you and others of the Council not been killed over the years?" I asked.

"Some were assassinated by Ophira shortly after Amogar died," said Heran, "but even her own people warned against this. We are not a numerous people, and even with internal struggles we have desisted from killing each other in order to maintain our strength. With the forces evenly balanced, as they have been over the years, this has not been difficult. Now, with the power in the hands of Ophira, it is hard to tell what will happen. It has been inbred in us not to kill another Mogar. For now it will remain so, but I doubt that it will last for long."

"Tell me about the Council," I asked.

"The Council was so decreed by Amogar on his deathbed," Heran answered. "It consisted of those of us, eighteen in number, who were closest to him. With him, we too grew tired of the wars with the Homarus, the killings, Ophira's senseless tortures, the hunting of helpless beasts. He charged us with

111

the task of preserving some sanity among the Mogars, in the hope that some day a new leader would emerge to rule with tolerance. We of the Council all wished peace with the Homarus, and we still do. For this ideal did Amogar meet his death at the hands of Ophira's spawn. Three of our number were killed; the other fifteen still survive. There are others who believe as we do, but it is us, along with our wives, sons, and daughters, that keep the hope alive. Many others feared Amogar, and through this fear we have maintained their allegiance over the years, although we have not shared many of our thoughts. Now even these will be lost to the false Omogar.

"Last night, I conceived a plan in which the two of you may help us establish peace among the Mogars, and also between the Mogars and Homarus. At the same time, we will see to it that your friend is returned safely to you, Ro-lan. Today the Council is to meet. Late in the day, we intend to inform Ophira that a decision regarding your fate has not yet been reached, that we will need another day. She will not like it, but she will accede. Later, after Ama has long since passed, we will help you to escape. Return to the Homarus, bringing my wish for peace to Lar-ek, your king. Gather your forces and return here in exactly forty days. Approach the city from all directions, shortly before Ama disappears. Do not fear the satong traps. We will see to it that they are covered. At this time, the Council will begin an internal revolt. Ophira and Oleesha will be destroyed; the false Omogar held for you. Without them, their followers will hesitate. When it is known

112

that the forces of the Homarus surround them, they will capitulate. Little blood will be shed. This is our hope."

Ter-ek looked at me, and I nodded my assent. "You speak fine words, Heran," said Ter-ek, obviously moved. "I am sure that Lar-ek will agree to your plan."

"Be cautious," Dovan warned, "for although we feel that we can survive the forty days, we cannot be certain just how quickly Ophira's strength will grow. I will try and warn you beforehand if problems are anticipated. Now, until tonight we must rebind your hands. I'm sure you understand."

Before we were tied up again the four of us clasped hands, a sign of peace and friendship in almost any world. Dovan assured us that he would guide us past the traps, and Ter-ek advised him that he would be able to find the way from there. Before they left, I asked Dovan about the bundle that Denny was carrying when they found him. He told me that it had been taken with him into the hut, and he assumed that it was still there. I guessed that it was Denny's knapsack, and I wished that I could get my hands on it before we left. Dovan warned me that this would be impossible, so I abandoned the thought.

The long day passed slowly. It was warm in the hut, the single opening providing little ventilation. The surly guards looked in on us every hour or so, but said nothing. Ter-ek and I spent the day making plans. He was most pleased about our meeting with Heran.

"For many years we have sought peace with the Mogars," he told me. "We could have achieved it by force, but this is not our way. Even if it was, we share the same reluctancy as the Mogars to lose our people. Heran's alternative is a fine one. Bloodshed will be avoided as much as possible. Oh, there will be some Mogars who will find the prospect abhorrent, and they will fight until they are killed. However, most of them will accede."

Darkness began to fall, and we eagerly awaited our liberation. Dovan had stopped in during the afternoon to bring us food and water. Now he entered the hut once again.

"I am now one of your guards," he informed us, "along with another whose allegiance lies with Ophira. Heran has already informed the queen of the Council's deadlock. All will be quiet tonight. When the city is asleep, I will enter the hut on the pretext of checking your bonds. After I cut you free I will call for the other guard and feign unconsciousness. He will enter and see me on the floor. You must stun him quickly, so that he cannot give the alarm. Do not kill him, for he must confirm my story of your escape. I will then lead you past the satong traps into the forest. When I return, one of the Council will render me unconscious on the floor of the hut. This must be done in order to divert suspicion from myself and the Council."

"Your plan is a fine one, Dovan," I said, "but what of the sentries?"

"The sentry patrolling the north boundary is one of us," he stated. "There will be no trouble."

"Dovan," I told him, "silence will be a valuable commodity tonight, and we may not get a chance to speak. I would like to thank you for all that you have

114

done for us. We owe you our lives."

"Ro-lan speaks for me also," Ter-ek offered.

"The anticipation of peace with the Homarus, and the death of those she-monsters, is more than worth any risk taken," Dovan replied. "Let us say no more. I advise you to get some rest before the appointed time."

Dovan left us, but neither of us desired to sleep. We had been confined all day, and were anxious to depart. From our hut, we were able to hear the clamor of the city as the people went about the business of the evening. For hours we listened, and eventually the sounds diminished. Soon all that could be heard were the noises of the forest. Monkeys chattered, birds screeched, a leopard roared. We were sure that the time was near.

Suddenly the jungle noises ceased, and all became deathly still. Perhaps a satong was on the prowl. What else could cause that? Ter-ek became rigidly alert as he strained to hear the slightest sound, while his eyes darted to and fro. For at least a minute there was nothing. Then, from the faintest recesses of my mind, I thought I heard a faint humming. Was it real, or was the ghostly silence getting to me? I looked at Ter-ek, and it was apparent that he heard it also. He sat frozen, his eyes widened in terror.

"No, no, it cannot be!" he cried. "Not now, not here! *No, it cannot be!*"

"Ter-ek, what the devil is it?" I asked, disturbed.

"It is the *Hour!*" he screamed. "I must get out of here! Please! I must get out!" He began struggling madly with his bonds.

From outside, it sounded like all Hell had broken

gently this time, to an empty hut. No words were spoken, and we asked no questions.

loose. I heard the pounding of running feet; Mogars were screaming and shouting. As Ter-ek continued his struggles the curtains on our door parted, admitting Dovan and the other guard. Both faces were masks of terror. The guard looked at Dovan.

"It is the Hour!" he announced, terrified. "Before we descend, they must be killed!"

"Yes," Dovan replied, glassy-eyed. "They must be killed. It is the Hour!"

I stared at the youth, horrified. What kind of madness was this? The humming sound had intensified now, permeating the hut. Dovan and the other approached us, their spears poised for thrusting. Ter-ek continued to struggle with his bonds, oblivious to their actions. The second guard now stood over Ter-ek, ready to strike. Suddenly Dovan turned, and with great force he drove his spear into the other's heart. Without a word he drew his knife and cut my bonds. Then he turned to Ter-ek and, before freeing him, slapped him twice across the face. I went to stop him, but he warned me away.

"This must be done, Ro-lan," he stated, trancelike. "It is the Hour. Ter-ek understands. You must escape through the forest. In this condition he would be useless, and you would surely be killed. I cannot help you further, for I must descend. While I still have some reason left I beg of you, Ro-lan: Please return in forty days, as we planned. The Council awaits you. That is all, for I must go."

Dovan cut Ter-ek's bonds and dashed out of the hut, dropping his spear. From outside, the frenzied noises continued. Ter-ek stood up and addressed me. "I am sorry that you saw what you did, Ro-lan," he

116

apologized. "It is the Hour! We must leave here immediately!"

"But the streets are full of Mogars! How will we get past them?"

"Fear not. They will make no attempt to stop us. Come, we must leave!" He leaned over and scooped up the abandoned spears, handing me one of them. We raced outside, where I witnessed an uncanny spectacle. People ran madly from all directions, converging on the obelisk in the center of the city. The large door was raised, revealing a lengthy stairway that disappeared into the blackness below. The Mogars fought among themselves to descend. Men shoved women out of the way; women kicked children from their paths. All their faces were frozen in fear. The humming sound had reached ear-shattering proportions, adding to the already incomprehensible scene. Warriors and guardsmen ran right by us, not even giving us a second glance. Only one thought dominated the minds of the Mogars, and that was to reach the stairway.

I saw Oleesha and her vile parent running toward the obelisk. In her frenzy, Ophira had disdained the use of the sedan chair, or perhaps there were no servants left to carry it. In her mad dash, Oleesha was kicking people from her path. These regained their feet and followed in her wake, some even overtaking her. No one cleared a path for them on the stairway. Like everyone else, they had to fight to descend. Apparently this insanity recognized no royalty.

Denny emerged from his hut, his arms waving wildly. "The Hour! The Hour!" he screamed as he ran along the street. "It is the Hour!"

I ran to him and intercepted him. I grabbed him by the shoulders and shook him. "Denny, it's me, Rollie!" I shouted. "For God's sake, snap out of it! It's Rollie!"

He stared at me for a moment, terrified, and then struck me full on the chin. I went down.

"Fool! I must pass!" he shrieked. "It is the Hour!"

Denny continued his mad flight. I got up quickly and started after him, but Ter-ek grabbed me by the arm. His face was beginning to show increased signs of fear.

"Let him go, Ro-lan," he implored. "We must get out of here *now!* Time is short!"

He started to run, and I followed in his path. The direction that we traveled in took us near Denny's hut, which gave me an idea. I was about to shout to Ter-ek when he halted.

"Ro-lan, we must go back! In my haste, I ran in this direction. We must leave the city to the north!"

"We are near Denny's hut. I must stop for a moment."

"No, Ro-lan, no! You must not stop!" he pleaded. "We must leave! Please, follow me!"

"Go on ahead," I told him. "What I must do will take but a few seconds. I will catch up with you."

"Ro-lan, wait—!" he yelled, but I was already on my way. I covered the few yards to the entrance in moments. The floor of the unoccupied dwelling was covered with fur and skins. It took only a second to locate what I sought. There, in the far corner, was Denny's knapsack. With no time to examine its contents, I flung it over my shoulder and emerged from the hut. Ter-ek, although terrified, had remained where I left him. Together we retraced our steps through the city, which was now entirely deserted. The last of the Mogars had reached the stairway, and the door had begun to close. The obelisk pulsated with crimson light, as if it were alive. The humming stopped, and Mogara was silent again.

I had the foresight to grab a torch as we raced through the streets, and I handed it to Ter-ek as soon as I caught up with him. The path that led to the scene of our initial capture was easy to follow, and in minutes we stood at the edge of the satong trap. The body of Gorog still resided at the bottom of the pit, this showing an apparent laxity on the part of the Mogars to retrieve their fellow. Ter-ek strode purposefully to a clump of bushes, and from it he withdrew his leather pouch. The head of the satong, his prize, was safe. I had completely forgotten about it, but he must have tossed it there before the guards overcame us. Even now, in his terror, it was apparent just how much he cherished the grisly thing.

The forest was quiet all around us. Suddenly, from the direction of Mogara, I heard a soft moan. At first I thought it to be the wind, but I could feel no breeze at all. The air was very still. It grew louder, soon sounding more like the pathetic wail of a woman in mourning. Ter-ek had heard it too, and his eyes became glassy. Draping the pouch over his shoulder, he leaped to his feet.

"No, no!" he screamed, waving the torch frantically over his head. "The Hour is here! *It is here now!* Run, run!"

He leaped over the satong trap and raced madly

through the foliage. Unable to grab him, I followed in his path. I could barely see him, so I followed the light of the torch.

"Ter-ek, stop!" I screamed. "You'll be killed! There are traps everywhere!"

He continued his insane rush, oblivious to my warnings. I knew that I would be safe by following directly in his path, so I did my best to keep my eyes on the wildly swaying flame. The moaning continued, though as we fled from the city its intensity seemed to diminish. It was an eerie, unnerving noise, and mingled intermittently with it was something that sounded vaguely like—laughter! I was glad that we were leaving it behind.

Onward ran Ter-ek, heedless of everything, save his own insane desire to flee Mogara as quickly as possible. How he managed to avoid disaster for so long was nothing short of a miracle, but inevitably his luck ran out.

The torch disappeared from sight. I heard a scream, then nothing. We were now far from the city, and the silence was ominous. My heart sank as I reached the spot where I had last seen the torch. There, before me, was the open maw of a satong trap. Resignedly I peered down into it. By the light of the torch which lay on the floor of the pit, I saw Ter-ek, shaken but apparently unharmed, rising to his feet. There were no stakes in this pit. I guessed that the Mogars preferred to catch a live satong every so often to taunt and torture it with impunity from above. For the first time, I thanked the Mogars for their cruelties.

With the help of a thick vine that I found nearby, I assisted Ter-ek from the pit. He was subdued now, and again apologized for his actions. Whatever happened back there to turn brave men like Dovan and Ter-ek into glassy-eyed cowards must indeed be terrible. I hoped that some day I would learn the secret. For now, I was content with putting distance between us and the accursed city. Moving cautiously, we reached the stream near the spot where Ter-ek had first taken to his knees. We were out of danger temporarily, and we hastened our steps into the dark Borangan forest.

CHAPTER NINE

ACROSS BORANGA

The first signs of dawn became evident through the dense Borangan forest. We had been journeying for about four hours since our hasty departure from Mogara. Ter-ek had been concerned about nocturnal travel through the jungle, but fortunately we encountered no difficulties. With the potential danger now past, he motioned me to stop to rest, and I willingly complied. The stream, which we had been following, offered us plenty of water. Ter-ek started to scout around for food while I took the opportunity to examine the knapsack.

I was surprised to discover just how good it felt to hold a familiar object in my hands again. Other than the debris washed up on the beach and the items left in the tunnel, this knapsack represented the last link with my own world, a world that now seemed so far out of reach. I loosened the straps and poured the contents on the ground in front of me. There were a half dozen cans of C-rations, a compact first aid kit, a canteen, yards of thin but strong rope, salt tablets, two spoons, two forks and, most important, a hand ax and a hunting knife. I hefted the ax in my hand, relishing its feel. Ever since the encounter with the Guardian I had favored this weapon, and I was glad to have another one.

I called to Ter-ek, who was exploring the foliage nearby. As he emerged from the bushes, I saw that he was carrying some kind of fruit. He expressed curiosity about the contents of the knapsack, and as we ate the tasty fruit I explained each unfamiliar item to him. He became especially enamored of the hunting knife, which was encased in a fine leather sheath. I made him a gift of it, for which he was grateful. He fondled it with pride, and then attached it to his belt.

The C-rations fascinated Ter-ek. He turned one of the metal cans over and over in his hand, trying to understand how there could be food in such a solid object. I opened two of the cans, handing him one which contained a mixture of beef and beans. Ter-ek thought it to be a culinary delight, and he relished every spoonful. I must admit that even I found the taste pleasing, for I was hungry.

As we ate, I reflected on this strange world in general, and on the island of Boranga in particular. These people were similar in many respects to the Polynesians of my own world. Their language was nearly the same, varying only slightly. The Borangan forest fit all the descriptions I had ever heard of the African or South American jungles. Many of the animals that I had seen were identical to those of my world, with a few exceptions. How close was our world to this one? The only thing I did know was that the whole thing was beyond my ken. Perhaps when I got back, I would find someone who might explain it to me. Did I say *when* I got back? Wishful thinking, most likely.

What about the rest of this world? Surely Boranga could not be the only populated area. If a parallel existed for Polynesia, then what about one for New York, for California, for Japan or England? Did this enigmatic killer sun prevent life anywhere else, or have other civilizations learned to protect themselves from it, perhaps even to use it to their benefit? Even if there were advanced peoples, could they have developed technologically in a world where all things mechanical seemed unable to work? Maybe it was the elements of the warp that froze all the devices on the *Maui Queen*. Perhaps anything developed on this world could indeed function. I would have to ask Denny if he . . .

Denny McVey, my best friend and partner. Partner? Partner of what? Our investment was smashed to hundreds of pieces. My best friend had become a raving madman. What power did the terrible Oleesha hold over him? He was an intelligent, strong-willed individual. I doubted that the superstitions and fears of these primitive people could be forced upon him. Could it have been the blow on his head? Perhaps his memory suffered from it. When he came to in the hut, he knew nothing. Oleesha, realizing that the people awaited their Omogar, took every advantage of the situation to implant in

Denny's mind the will of her mother and herself. Yes, that must be the answer! Perhaps some day I would know. Perhaps, if I was able to get him away from Mogara—alive.

Forty days! Not for this long would we return to Mogara. Should I return to the city right now on my own and attempt a rescue? What chance would I have alone? Could I count on any more help from the Council? I doubted it, since any foolish move on my part could jeopardize their hope for peace. No, this way was best. Although reluctant to leave Denny, I knew that I must return with Ter-ek to his people and carry out the plan of the Council.

With these thoughts swimming through my brain, we resumed our journey. But as I glanced at the serious Ter-ek, it occurred to me that I had forgotten his original purpose, that of killing a satong and returning the head to his king. I remembered that the task must be accomplished in a certain number of days, and I hoped that I had not fouled things for him.

"Ter-ek, how long will it take us to reach Var-Dor?" I inquired.

"Five days of steady travel with no interference will bring us there."

"Will you return in time to present the head of the satong to Lar-ek?"

"It has been nine days since I left my home. My task must be completed in seventeen days."

I was relieved by this information, for I had caused Ter-ek enough trouble since he had found me by the river. In my mind, I echoed his hope that the journey to Var-Dor would be uneventful. I was still troubled by the events of the previous night and, although I should have known better, I decided to question him.

"Ter-ek, since I have been with you, strange things have occurred. Many were self-explanatory; others you have explained. Some things you have merely hinted at, saying that they must not be spoken of. I respect your wishes in this regard. Perhaps some day I will find out about them for myself. However, last night I was witness to, no, I was part of, an extraordinary occurrence. I know what I saw, even though I am still having a difficult time reconciling myself to the fact that it really happened. There is no precedent for it in my world. Could you offer me some clue as to what we encountered in Mogara?"

Ter-ek halted, and once again began looking furtively around. I had upset him once more, and I regretted it, but I could not stand being kept in the dark. With a look of anger on his face, Ter-ek spoke: "I have saved your life, and you have saved mine. The bond between us is strong. However, you again exceed the limits of our friendship, no, our brotherhood. I am firmly convinced now that you are not of this world. It is because you are not that you will most likely discover the answers some day, and I fear that they will not be to your liking. Listen to me, Rolan; I will explain all to you that I can, all that seems strange to you as we travel, but holy things must not be spoken of out loud. Be thankful that you are ignorant of this knowledge. Your friend knows, though he has been here but a short time, and you saw what it has done to him, did you not? I have said too much already."

He dropped to his knees and repeated the ritual

that I realized was common to all on Boranga. Facing north, he rocked from side to side chanting: *"Noma Kuto Boranga, Noma Kuto Boranga!"* over and over. This time he kept it up for many minutes, while I sat by the stream and waited patiently for him. I dwelled on his strange words until he was finished. After a few more glances around, Ter-ek indicated that he was ready, and the journey continued.

We followed the stream the entire day, though at times the foliage was so dense we could not even see it. Ter-ek seemed to have a natural sense of direction, and was always able to find it again. We saw many animals that had come there to drink, but in most cases they fled as we approached. Once a large leopard threatened us, but it too retreated as Ter-ek strode purposefully toward it, never straying from his path. Another time, when the stream had temporarily disappeared, we encountered two gho-mas. They watched us silently as we neared, but showed no sign of giving ground. They were probably guarding a nest, so we gave them a wide berth.

The day dragged on, the hot, steamy forest wearing us down. With but a few short breaks we had been traveling since long before sunrise, and although Mogara had been deep in the forest, Ter-ek was certain that we would reach the plains before nightfall. He assured me that this was the most difficult part of our journey, that we would be able to pace ourselves better once out of the foliage.

As we walked, I began to notice a change. The heat was lessening, although the humidity remained. Within minutes we were encircled by dense fog, and this, along with the heavy brush, made the going even more difficult. Fortunately it did not last long, for we soon reached the end of the jungle. The now familiar plains lay ahead of us. Ter-ek expressed his satisfaction in our reaching the tundra, and he suggested that we put a little more distance between ourselves and the forest, since it was still light. I nodded my agreement, and we continued on for another hour or so.

Finally, the fog began to lift. The sun had set, and the first of the two Borangan moons appeared. We camped on the edge of the stream, where once again, to Ter-ek's delight, we partook of the C-rations. By the light of a very small fire we discussed the events of the past few days, although I was careful to omit any reference to 'holy things.' In regard to our newly found allies among the Mogars, Ter-ek assured me that I had become the party to an historic event. For as long as anyone could remember, the Homarus have sought a means to end the long conflict with the Mogars, but only after the Mogars had witnessed the cruelties of such as Ophira did they finally see the light. Ter-ek relished the proposed peace, and was sure that his people would concur. I trusted in Heran, just as Ter-ek did, and I eagerly anticipated the march to Mogara for more than one reason.

I slept well that night, for the long day's trek had proven tiring. The next morning, quite refreshed, we set out again. We journeyed at a leisurely pace across the sparse plains, and by late afternoon the small stream that had served as our guide since leaving Mogara terminated, for we had once again reached the Otongo. We were close to the spot where Ter-ek had first found me, the familiar mountains looming on our left. After fording the river, we set up camp on its west bank, shortly before dusk.

Ter-ek was quite proficient in the use of the barbed spear, and during our journey he attempted to impart some of his skills to me. I had thrown the javelin a number of times in college, and I was able to get some distance on the Borangan weapon. My accuracy, however, left much to be desired, but after a couple of days in the hands of a master, even that improved considerably. It was possible that some day my life would depend on how well I could handle the spear, so I took my lessons seriously. I also practiced my accuracy in throwing the hand ax. I was more comfortable with this weapon, and exhibited a greater proficiency.

The Borangan spear had other uses besides fighting, and before dark Ter-ek gave me a demonstration of one. He walked down to the Otongo and waded into it. With the spear poised, he peered into the water, taking slow, deliberate steps. Finding what he looked for, he stopped and thrust the barbed point into the water, but he came up with nothing. He repeated his motions, and on the second thrust he brought up a large, wriggling fish, which he removed and tossed at my feet. It resembled a trout, and it must have weighed at least five or six pounds. After a few more fruitless attempts Ter-ek landed another one, nearly the same size. I was never a great fish fancier back home, but I must admit that our dinner that evening was superb, and a welcome change of pace.

*　　　*　　　*

During the night, I once again battled the Guardian, only the outcome did not look too promising this time, for the ax merely glanced off his snout and enraged him. Both my legs were injured; I was weaponless, defenseless, and he lifted me in his jaws far above the lake. It was odd that his teeth, although razor sharp in appearance, caused me no pain. He began to descend, dragging me toward the water. I must not let him take me under! Closer, closer he brought me to his submerged world. I must hold my breath! I cannot drown! I'm completely submerged now! He has taken me into the lake . . .

When I awoke I was soaking wet, and I realized that it was pouring. I don't ever recall seeing rain fall this hard. The quiet Otongo had become a raging torrent, threatening to rise above its banks. Ter-ek, now on his feet, shouted at me to gather my gear and follow him. Within seconds, I was hard on his heels. Soon I understood the need for haste. The Otongo was overflowing, and the land surrounding it began to resemble a lake. High in the mountains, the base of which was less than two hundred yards from our camp, water had begun to gather. Now it was flowing down the side of one peak, soon to join the flood from the swollen river. We could not have selected a worse location for our camp, though at the time I doubt that Ter-ek had even considered a deluge such as this.

Ter-ek ran exceptionally fast as we veered away from both the river and the mountains, but I was able to stay with him. Glancing quickly behind us, I saw the first rush of water from the mountain reach the base, where it merged with the flood from the swollen river. Propelled by this new force, the water spread out across the land. We were still far ahead of it, but I was growing concerned, for I was unable to spot any higher ground. Ter-ek seemed to be running with purpose, so I thought it best to leave it to him.

Soon the ground began to incline ever so slightly, and in less than a minute we were climbing a steep hill. Water was pouring down the slope, but it offered no hazard. The swirling flood was only about a hundred yards behind us. On we ran until we were halted by a vast outcropping of rocks, the crown of the hill. The boulders rose upward, twenty feet above where we stood. I gazed down, noting that the water had reached the base of the slope.

"What do you think, Ter-ek?" I asked hurriedly. "Can it reach us up here?"

"I have seen this before," he replied. "Nowhere are you safe near the river when the rains come. What a fool I am! We must ascend these rocks and hope that they are high enough!"

I took the flexible hemp out of my knapsack and tied it to my spear, testing it to make sure it was fastened securely. I then heaved the spear up as high as I could into the rocks above. I reeled in the rope, hoping that the spear would wedge itself into something, but it did not. It fell to the ground at my feet. Two more tosses proved futile, but the fourth time it caught and held. Ter-ek motioned me to remove my gear and scale the rocks first. As I climbed, I looked at the water, which had now risen halfway up the hill, showing no signs of abating. I knew I must act quickly, and once on top I immediately shouted to Ter-ek to toss up the gear. First came his spear, which clattered harmlessly behind me, then the knapsack, my canteen, and his water pouch. But quite stubbornly, he refused to throw the pouch containing his prize up to me. Returning it to his shoulder, he attempted to pull himself up, but he was unable to negotiate the rope. The pouch proved to be a great hinderance.

"Ter-ek!" I screamed. "The water is almost upon you! Throw the pouch up to me, quickly!"

Reluctantly, he let go of the rope and dropped to the ground. He removed the pouch from around his shoulder and held it in his hands for a brief instant, hesitant to let it go. Finally he heaved the thing up to me, but his obsession with it apparently affected his aim, for although I stretched as far as I could, I was unable to reach it. The pouch hit the rocks and rebounded toward Ter-ek. It hit the ground a little to his left and rolled past him down the slope.

His own safety far from his mind, Ter-ek turned and pursued his precious parcel down the hill. The flood waters were only yards away now. "Ter-ek, leave the blasted thing and get up the rope!" I screamed, but to no avail. The pouch finally stopped rolling, and he pounced on it. He hurriedly draped it over his right shoulder and turned to retrace his steps up the hill, but he was too late. The water swirled around him, knocking him off his feet. He splashed futilely, apparently unable to swim.

It took me only moments to descend. Ter-ek was still in sight, but the force of the water was moving him further away. I dove into the water and swam toward him. The current continually changed direction and made the going difficult, but I was able to shorten the distance between us. My years of training and preparation did not seem as wasted now as it did so long ago.

Finally I reached him, and I latched onto him tightly. He was nearly unconscious, and was gasping for air. Swimming now became more difficult, but a fortunate change in current carried us back toward the rocks. The end of the rope, afloat in the water, was within reach, and I managed to grab onto it with my free hand. The swift current was pushing us toward the boulders, but I extended my leg and prevented us from being dashed against them. Removing the pouch from his shoulder, I hung it over mine. I took the slack out of the rope and implored him to climb it. He was still weak, but after a few tenuous minutes he hauled himself to the top. I followed him up, immediately falling exhausted at his side.

After catching my breath, I examined Ter-ek. He was overwhelmed by fatigue, and breathing very hard. I made him as comfortable as possible under the circumstances, and then hauled up the invaluable rope. As I did this, I saw that the water had risen halfway up the rocks and was still climbing rapidly. I hoped that we were high enough to avoid it, though this seemed doubtful.

I went back to check on Ter-ek, at the same time realizing that it had stopped raining. I hoped that this was a good sign. Ter-ek was breathing more evenly than before, and this also was encouraging. I had left his precious pouch by his side, and even in his state of semi-consciousness he clutched it possessively. Once again I had to wonder at the minds of men who placed such importance on this ritual that they would risk their lives, perhaps even forfeit them, in order to accomplish their goals. Surely the Homaru king would understand if unforeseen circumstances such as this flood, a Mogar ambush, or numerous other occurrences would prevent a warrior from returning with the head of a satong. There would be no shame in this, and the man would certainly deserve another chance.

The water continued to rise, although not as rapidly as before. It now swirled only four feet from our aerie. There was nowhere else for us to climb, so I sat down next to Ter-ek and resigned myself to our fate. If the waters were to reach us, I would have to swim for it. Alone, I might be able to stay afloat for a while, though eventually the strong current and my own fatigue would likely win out. With Ter-ek, however, it would be another matter. I would try my best to help him, but his trophy would have to be sacrificed, for it would be a definite hindrance.

Fortunately, this choice did not have to be made. The water ceased rising, maintaining its level for about an hour or so. Finally it began to recede, albeit very slowly. Reassured, I was able to fall into a fitful sleep, not awakening again until daybreak. The initial sight that greeted me when I opened my eyes was the smiling face of Ter-ek, quite recovered.

"We seen to be destined to assist one another in the avoidance of dangerous situations," he said cheerfully. "Once again I owe you my life, Ro-lan."

"And if I save yours a couple of more times then perhaps we'll be even," I replied jokingly. "Forget it, Ter-ek. You're alive, and your prize is safe."

"There is an unspoken question on your lips, Rolan," said Ter-ek, as he gazed longingly at the pouch. "I vowed that I would answer anything I could. You wonder why the head of the satong is so important to me; why, unable to swim, I risked the flood waters to save it. I have only days left within which to lay the head at Lar-ek's feet. Should I return with no head, or should I return with it after the seventeenth day, I would be banished from Var-Dor for three hundred days. I must live by myself, and have no contact with any other Homaru. If this occurs a second time, the penalty is death. We are a peace-loving people, but this tradition of paying honor to Dor-ek, our great warrior-king, is strong.

"As a Homaru, I am not afraid of death. But Aleen, she whom I love, awaits me. We were to be bound in marriage, when the second call came. Should I be banished, I would not be able to see her, and would find this unbearable. Even after I returned, it would be possible that she would not wish to see me again, for banishment is shame. Perhaps someone braver than I would win her. No, I could not face this. I would have preferred to drown than return empty-handed. When one does not return at all, it is presumed that he died at the hands of the satong, and his memory is honored."

"Have many returned empty-handed a second time?" I asked.

"Some of the Homarus, bound by the customs of our people, have done so. They were beheaded by the sacred sword of Dor-ek, the head being offered at the feet of Lar-ek in place of the satong. In this way, their memory also becomes honored. There were many who, having failed for the second time, chose permanent banishment over honorable death. They wander all over Boranga, friendless until they die. Sometimes they are seen, and the false honors that had been bestowed upon them are removed. Their names are unspoken from then on."

"Suddenly I have this desire to see you and your prize safely returned to Var-Dor," I replied. "Can we get going?"

"The waters have receded almost completely," he reported, "though the Otongo is still greatly swollen. Fortunately we do not have to cross it again. I was a fool to let us camp so near to where the river skirts the mountains, for floods like this are not uncommon. Perhaps it was because I had not seen a storm for many hundreds of days that my caution was lax. I apologize, Ro-lan. We can leave now."

Before we descended, I surveyed the terrain from our lofty perch. To the east, I saw the swollen Otongo rushing toward the underground passageway through the mountains. To the west, north, and south I saw nothing but hills. We had entered a blind canyon, and had we not made it to the top of this outcropping, we surely would have had no chance.

We reached the bottom of the hill and exited the canyon. Our route along the base of the mountains guided us once again in a westerly direction toward Var-Dor. For two full days the landscape remained unchanged, although far to the north I discerned an increased number of trees. Their density was nowhere near that of the eastern jungle, but they were a refreshing sight.

On the morning of the fifth day, we arose early. We

had met with no incidents since the flood, and Ter-ek advised me that we should reach Var-Dor by late afternoon. By mid-morning the mountains on our left fell away, and after a few miles of sparse plains we entered a forest of enormous sequoias. This was quite a contrast to the steamy tropical forest. It was cool here, the chill fog hanging high above our heads. As tall and leafy as these trees were, they were spaced far apart. If not for the cloud cover, there would have been little protection from the sun. Nature seemed to work in strange and amazing ways on Boranga.

Ter-ek pointed out several different kinds of birds as we traversed the wood. Except for a few of their calls, it was very quiet. I also spotted a few large rabbits though, as Ter-ek explained, this forest contained very little wildlife.

The long day waned, and dusk was no more than an hour or two away. Ter-ek had been true to his word, however, for Var-Dor was less than three hundred yards away. Ter-ek pointed out the city's location, and through the trees I saw a lofty wall, atop which sat two turrets, undoubtedly manned. As we neared, I saw that the wall ran almost as far as one could see in either direction, with more watch towers popping up intermittently along it. Var-Dor was indeed a large city.

We now stood in front of the main gate. The normally placid Ter-ek was experiencing great joy, for the slightest hint of a smile broke out on his face. He faced north, dropped to his knees, and recited the now familiar *"Noma Kuto Boranga"* three times. When he finished, he signaled to the guards, who observed us from their turrets. They acknowledged his gesture, and the gate began to open slowly. The brave Homaru had come home.

CHAPTER TEN

ADARA

Var-Dor proved a striking contrast to the nearly primitive Mogara. The dwellings were made of wood, quite larger than the Mogar huts. There was more room between each cabin, and some even had small gardens growing on one side. All had at least two windows on the front, these covered from the inside by ornamental cloth drapes, which apparently were rolled up and tied during the day. I could not begin to guess at how many dwellings there were, for I could see only a fraction of them. I was to learn later from Ter-ek that the population of Var-Dor was approximately nine thousand people.

Moments after entering the main gate of Var-Dor, we were on the city's primary thoroughfare, the Street of the Kings. Many people were either moving along it or crossing it at other intersections, and as they saw Ter-ek and myself, they began to move toward us. Some of the guards had fallen in silently behind us and were keeping pace. After walking for perhaps a hundred feet Ter-ek stopped, motioning to me to do the same. We were now surrounded by Homarus. No words of greeting were exchanged, and their faces were impassive.

Ter-ek laid his pouch on the ground, and slowly, ceremoniously, removed the head of the satong and began to peel away the oiled cloth. I had not seen the ghastly thing since the day that he killed it, and the sight brought back the horrors of that morning. With the wraps off, Ter-ek lifted the head high in the air for all to see, walking in circles as he held it. The expressionless faces of the Homarus broke into grins and their voices rang out in praise. They closed in on Ter-ek, pounding him on the back. One of the guards shouted an order to an underling, and within minutes an ornate sedan chair was carried out by four warriors. Ter-ek was lifted bodily by the happily screaming throng and placed in the conveyance. Seemingly unnoticed by all, I followed the procession along the Street of the Kings. People lined the street and waved to Ter-ek, who was still displaying the head proudly.

The procession turned right down another path, the Street of the Warriors. Here I saw something that both surprised and shocked me. About a hundred yards further along was a large, crimson red obelisk, identical to the one in Mogara. A similar door sat next to it, though this one, also with two wide rings, appeared larger. The Homarus, more advanced and civilized than the Mogars, apparently shared the same superstitions and fears. Remembering Ter-ek's

140

actions during the strange ordeal in Mogara, I really should not have found the sight of the tower here in Var-Dor that shocking, but nevertheless I did. A quick glance to the rear revealed an identical obelisk about the same distance in the other direction.

The crowd stopped in front of a cabin about fifty feet short of the obelisk. The sedan was placed on the ground, and Ter-ek stepped off. He looked through the crowd, calling my name, and as I came forward to join him, the people stepped aside to let me through. Ter-ek spoke briefly with the head guardsman, and then placed the head in a receptacle that hung over the door. The people dispersed, still waving and shouting at Ter-ek. One man, however, did not have his attention fixed on the Homaru, but was staring curiously at me. He was an old man and, unlike most of the clean shaven Homarus, had a bushy white beard to go along with his white hair. He was tall, though bent with age. Our eyes met for just a moment in the tumult, and he nodded a greeting at me. I responded in a like manner.

The people now gone, Ter-ek motioned me into the dwelling. It was a clean house, probably cared for by someone in Ter-ek's absence. The ceiling stood nine feet over our heads. There were two rooms, separated by a narrow bamboo screen. The floor was covered with woven straw mats similar to the sleeping mat that Ter-ek had brought with him on his journey. The tools of a warrior were visible everywhere. Finely crafted spears hung on the wall, as did various knives. Brightly-colored feathers also lined the wall, providing the only ornamentation in the otherwise stark house. Truly, this was

141

Ter-ek's home.

"Sometime after dark, the people will return to escort me to Lar-ek," Ter-ek announced, "so that I may present to him the head. You will accompany me, and after the ceremony is concluded I will talk to Lar-ek. Then you shall meet him."

I was tired, and since daylight was almost gone I guessed that we would not have much time before the ceremony commenced. There was fresh water in a receptacle, which I used to cleanse away the layers of dirt. Unrolling one of the straw mats, I curled up in a corner of the house. Within minutes I was asleep.

It was dark without when I awoke, though the house was dimly lit by three small torches. Ter-ek had removed the bamboo screen, and I saw that he had donned fresh clothes, these garments being a bit more colorful than his original outfit. He looked every inch the warrior.

"Soon they will come for us," he said. "The ceremony with Lar-ek will be a short one. Afterwards I will confer with him regarding you, your friend, and our encounter with the Mogars. I will tell him all that is of importance, but will leave out the background of you and the one called Denny. When you speak to him say nothing of where you are from, nor how you came here. Perhaps some day it can be discussed, but for now it would be unwise for any other but myself to know of your origin. You will not be questioned regarding your past. That you are a brave man and a friend is good enough for a Homaru.

"A guest of the Homarus can remain among us for two hundred days. After that, he must return to the

142

outside, or join us, whichever he chooses. Through the years, some of the nomadic peoples of Boranga have joined the Homarus. It is a good life here, but our laws are strict. You would be required to hunt the satong four times, just as any other Homaru. You must serve for a time in the guard. It is not that tedious, and many, such as myself, choose to remain a warrior after the required time is served.''

Ter-ek handed me a poncho made of wool, advising me that the night would be cold. It was a comfortable garment, and I wished that I had possessed one during all the chilled nights of our journey. He rolled up the drape on one of the windows, and I saw the light of many torches out front. The people had come for him. As we stepped outside Ter-ek removed the satong head from its place above the doorway, then resumed his position in the sedan chair, and the crowd, silently this time, moved toward the Street of the Kings. Once again I fell in behind the procession. The curious old man whom I had seen earlier strode a few yards to my left.

At the Street of the Kings, the procession turned right. It marched in silence for about a quarter of a mile past many silent Homarus lining the street with torches. Although there was no cheering, no words spoken, their faces bespoke their pride and respect for Ter-ek. I was able to study these people as we walked along; while their features were similar to those of the Mogars, their faces seemed to reflect a gentle vitality, a self-satisfaction with their lot. They were dressed in simple garments made of wool, which brought to mind the wurra, the animal that Ter-ek had told me was raised by the Homarus, and which I assumed was the source of the fleece.

Children were more visible here than in Mogara. The older ones showed Ter-ek the same kind of respect that their parents did, although the toddlers displayed no interest in the solemnity of the moment, opting to simply have a good time. While they were forced to keep the little ones in check, the parents exhibited no harshness.

At the end of the Street of the Kings was a dwelling only slightly larger than the others in Var-Dor. The majority of the Homarus were already gathered around this cabin, undoubtedly the home of Lar-ek, their king. A small, unpretentious bench stood in front. The sedan chair carrying Ter-ek was brought forward only a few feet from the bench, the bearers then departing. As Ter-ek arose and faced the portal, an elderly retainer appeared from within. After surveying the crowd, he announced: "The King and his family now come!" He stepped aside, revealing a fine figure of a man about forty years old, dressed in garments similar to those of Ter-ek. In his path followed a striking woman and a boy of about ten. The three stood in front of the bench while the assembled Homarus snapped to military attention and inclined their heads a few inches. Observing those around me, I followed suit. This done, the royal family sat down. I felt instant respect for this noble figure who, although a king, saw little need for people to grovel at his feet.

Ter-ek approached the bench, the satong head held high. Standing directly in front of Lar-ek, he again saluted. He repeated the gesture to the queen, and then to their son. Returning to Lar-ek, he knelt down and placed the head at his feet. He then addressed the ruler: "Oh Lar-ek, great king of the Homarus, through you this night I do honor to your mighty and noble ancestor, Dor-ek, who saw to it that we would all be here now to make this offering. Many satongs did he slay, many were the heads that he took during his battles. In that period of seventeen days was the history of the Homarus changed. The satongs were driven off, and from then on did the Homarus prosper. I present this, my second head, to you, his worthy descendent, so that through the chain that binds you to him may he know of my respect. As many have done before me, as many will do in times yet to come, I place this head at your feet, Lar-ek, my king!"

Ter-ek stood at attention, his head inclined. Lar-ek gathered up the head and raised it high. He took it to a blazing fire about fifteen feet away, where he addressed the heavens: "Dor-ek, my ancestor, great warrior, great king, slayer of the satong; I, Lar-ek, blood of your blood, salute you. Ter-ek, a fine warrior of the Homarus, has brought you this head, his second. Twice more in his life will he receive the call, but were it a hundred times, his respect for your deeds would not diminish. Accept the offering of Ter-ek through me, and guide him safely through his next quest."

Lar-ek flung the head down into the inferno, which flared up brightly as new fuel was added to it. The silent crowd now went wild, cheering and shouting. Lar-ek returned to the bench and placed his hand on Ter-ek's shoulder. The two then faced the throng, and Lar-ek raised Ter-ek's right arm high

145

in the air. They were both smiling, as were Lar-ek's wife and son. The queen stood up and entered the cabin, returning seconds later with a lovely young woman. The king pointed Ter-ek in her direction, and, upon seeing one another, they forgot all else and ran to embrace. Ter-ek lifted her high in the air as the cheers of the crowd grew louder. Ter-ek had been reunited with his beloved Aleen.

Ter-ek managed to break away long enough to confer with the king. Aleen stood nearby, watching him with adoring eyes. That she loved him was obvious, yet I wondered how much difference it would have made had he not returned with the head. It seemed doubtful that she would be able to ignore him for three hundred days; but these Homarus took their traditions seriously. I understood now why he risked his life for the wretched prize.

They spoke for about fifteen minutes, Ter-ek occasionally pointing in my direction. Lar-ek listened intently, nodding often. Finally, Ter-ek walked toward me and took me by the arm. We approached Lar-ek, and I saluted him in the manner of the Homarus. I was then presented to Deela, his wife, and their son Val-ek. They were most gracious.

"Ter-ek told me of your exploits, Ro-lan," said Lar-ek in a deep, well-modulated voice. "That you passed through the lair of Tomo Raka alive would indicate your bravery, but to risk the brutalities of the Mogars to save your friend is highly commendable. I grieve with you for what has been done to him, and I hope that he will remain unharmed until the day we reach Mogara. I will discuss Heran's proposal in the morning with the elders, and with my recommendation I am sure they will agree to it. I am honored that you will be accompanying us to Mogara. For now, you are a welcome guest in Var-Dor. The people will know of you, Ro-lan."

Lar-ek faced the populace and raised his hands to silence them. He then related to them the exploits of Ter-ek and myself since the warrior had found me by the river. Somehow, in the retelling of it, the adventures took on mammoth proportions. I knew that I must be blushing, and I felt the desire to hide. The people listened, spellbound. They cheered when Lar-ek announced Heran's proposal. I wondered about spies among them, but I remembered Ter-ek telling me that deceit was practically unknown among the Homarus. Lar-ek knew his people well. When he was finished, the people broke loose in cheers for me. Now I was thoroughly embarrassed as hundreds of them crowded around to shake my hand, slap my back, or just get a glimpse. Many asked me to recount some of our adventures, but no personal questions were asked. I was welcome among them.

Food was brought out, enormous quantities of food. I had forgotten how hungry I was, for we had not eaten since early that afternoon. The C-rations had been used up days before, and we had dined on fruit since. Now platters of steaming hot meat were given to us. The meat, which tasted like veal, was delicious. There were also hot vegetables, unrecognizable to me but palatable nonetheless. There were loaves of dark, tasty bread and a heady, beer-like beverage called *chenna*. It was by far one of the most delectable and welcome repasts I had experienced in my life.

During the feast, Ter-ek brought Aleen to me so that I might meet her. I found her to be as charming and intelligent as she was lovely. She was profuse in her thanks to me for saving Ter-ek's life. Again I felt embarrassed, and I assured her that I owed Ter-ek just as much, if not more. Ter-ek told me that they were to be wed in two days, and that I would be an honored guest. I readily accepted the invitation. The whole population of Var-Dor usually turned out for events like that, and another feast was in store.

Lar-ek was conversing with two men, and they all seemed to be gesticulating at me. I did not recognize one of them, but the other was the old man that had eyed me earlier. Lar-ek finally called me over to where they conversed and addressed me: "This man is Teb-or," he said, pointing to the one that I had not seen before, "and this is Col-in. Teb-or wishes you to stay in an empty house which is his, and Col-in would have his granddaughter care for the house and for you while you are a guest in Var-Dor. Each would consider it a great honor if you accept."

"I would not wish to impose any further on Ter-ek's hospitality than I already have," I announced. "Since he will be wed in two days, the last thing he would wish would be a house guest. Your highness, I accept these gentlemen's kind offers, and I assure you that *I* am the honored one."

The two men smiled at me, and each saluted their king. Teb-or announced that he would show Col-in the location of the house, and Col-in promised me that his granddaughter would have it prepared for me by the time the evening's festivities were over. The two departed happily.

Alone now with Lar-ek, I had an opportunity to get to know him better. He was truly noble in every sense of the word, his hopes, his concerns for his people reflecting his kindly soul. He seemed exceptionally intelligent, and for a moment I almost forgot the deep-rooted fears of the Homarus, which I had witnessed through Ter-ek. His kindly nature almost led me into the trap of asking him some of the questions that troubled me, but I caught myself. I remembered that Ter-ek had mentioned nothing of the Hour to Lar-ek, and he had requested that I say nothing about where I came from. I decided to leave it at that.

Lar-ek was curious as to my encounter with the Guardian, or Tomo Raka, as the Borangans called it. My ax was in my belt, and I showed it to him. He was fascinated with the workmanship, for they had nothing quite like it. I asked him what they used to fell trees, and he described a tool that sounded very much like a long-bladed saw. He called over a fellow, whom he introduced to me as Tor-en, head of the Var-Dor guardsmen. I gave them both a demonstration of ax throwing, sinking it dead center into a target on a tree some fifty feet away. I explained how I had done the same with the Guardian, that the ax had only hurt and infuriated him, allowing me time to escape. They were both impressed, and Tor-en, with Lar-ek's approval, asked if they could use my ax as a prototype for manufacturing others, as it would have many valuable uses to the Homarus. I handed it to Tor-en, who promised its return promptly.

The night wore on, Lar-ek finally gathering up his family and bidding good night to the people. This seemed to signal the end of the festivities, for within a half-hour the streets were nearly deserted. Teb-or returned to guide me to the house that he had provided. Ter-ek learned of this for the first time, and offered his regrets that I would not be staying with him. He was a fine friend, and would not have asked me to leave his home even after he was wed, but I'm sure that he must have felt some relief.

With Teb-or in the lead, Ter-ek and Aleen accompanied me to my new home. Back up the Street of the Kings we walked, past the Street of the Warriors, finally turning left on the Street of the Thinkers. At the seventh house on the left we stopped, and Teb-or made a formal presentation. The three then bade me good night and departed, Ter-ek promising to stop by in the morning with my knapsack and other things.

I parted the curtains on the door of the cabin and entered. Kneeling on the floor, her back toward me, was a girl, rolling out and adjusting a straw sleeping mat. Startled, she turned and stood up as she heard me. Despite the dim light in the cabin, I was able to look at her closely. She was slim, of medium height, with long black hair similar to most of the women I had seen on Boranga. I guessed that, agewise, she was in her early twenties. She was garbed in a simple sarong, this barely concealing her manifold curves and full breasts. But what transfixed my attention was her face: It was impossibly beautiful, the lips red and full, the nose well-proportioned, the cheekbones possibly a fraction too high. No false make-up adorned it and, though her expression was one of surprise, her emerald eyes reflected her good nature, her joy of life.

"Good evening; you must be Ro-lan," she said. Her voice was lilting, her smile enchanting. "I am Adara, and I will be taking care of this house for you while you are a guest here. I am sorry that I have not finished, but I will be done in just a moment."

"Please do not apologize, Adara," I replied. "I am glad that I had this opportunity to meet you."

"There is fresh water in the basin over there," she said, pointing. "In the morning I will bring you your breakfast. I will come late so that you may sleep, for between your journey and this evening's ceremonies, you must be fatigued."

"You are most kind and perceptive," I told her. I was beginning to enjoy her company even more. "My friend Ter-ek will be returning to his duties tomorrow. I would like very much to see Var-Dor, and would greatly enjoy having you as a guide."

She finished unrolling the sleeping mat. "After you have eaten, I would be happy to show you Var-Dor. I will leave you now to rest." She walked to the door and parted the curtains. Her movements were graceful, fluid. Before leaving, she turned and looked at me.

"Ro-lan?" she said.

"Yes?"

"I delayed my tasks on purpose so that I might meet you. I saw you from afar at the ceremonies tonight. I was glad that my grandfather asked that I serve you." The curtains met behind her as she ran out the door. I fell asleep that night with a smile on my face. I believed that I was going to like Var-Dor.

* * *

151

When I awoke the next morning, I found my knapsack lying on the floor just inside the front door. Apparently, Ter-ek had been by earlier and had left it, not wishing to wake me. I had had a fine night's sleep, and felt quite refreshed. Var-Dor was a good place, as were its people. If it was true that I would never be able to return home I supposed that I could be happy here. Only one thing was missing, and that was Denny. If I were able to save him, then perhaps I, or someone here in Var-Dor, would be able to rid him of Oleesha's influence. I looked forward to our return to Mogara, and hoped that the time would pass quickly.

"Ro-lan, are you awake?" I heard a voice outside say.

"Yes, please come in," I replied.

Adara entered, carrying a tray in one hand. She rolled up the drape on each window to allow the morning light into the room. As she turned toward me, a bright smile on her face, I saw that the daylight accentuated her loveliness even more. She placed the tray down next to me. It contained fruit, a small loaf of bread, and a clay pitcher of milk, or at least a similar-looking liquid which was thicker than regular milk, though quite tasty.

While I ate, Adara busied herself by tidying up the cabin, humming softly while she worked. I recalled what she had said before she left the night before, and I found the thought pleasing to me. Her graceful movements were a joy to watch, and I broke into a sheepish grin once when she caught me staring at her. Her smile told me that she did not object.

After breakfast, Adara showed me around Var-Dor, or at least as much of it as could be seen in one day.

Var-Dor was surrounded by the giant trees on all sides, though just a few miles to the west were more mountains. I was sure that the sea was just beyond them. There were small gates on the west and north walls, as well as the main east gate. Outside the north gate were large, cultivated fields, tended by many Homarus, where the bulk of the crops were grown. Irrigation was provided by a number of underground streams that ran below the ground, as was the city's drinking water. Evidently, Var-Dor had not been situated on this particular spot without much forethought.

Also beyond the north gate, about three quarters of a mile to the north, was a small, fertile valley where herd of wurras grazed under the watchful eyes of Homaru shepherds. The wurras were covered with wool and had sheep-like features, but they made grunting noises and were nearly the size of cows. They were a valuable commodity to the Homarus, providing both food and clothing.

Most of the first day was spent exploring the fields north of Var-Dor. Adara was a fountain of information, and her pleasure in walking through the countryside was evident. She was a joy to behold, and I found myself growing more intent on her than on the surrounding beauty. As we sat on the hillside watching the herds of wurras calmly grazing, I felt an inner peace and tranquility such as I had never known. Perhaps the only thing missing was the bright sunshine of a spring day, though never having seen the sun, Adara could not have known of this. We were to return to that spot often in the following weeks.

In the late afternoon we walked back to the city along the perimeter of the fields. Adara slipped her hand into mine, and my head swam until I thought I would pass out. I had known many women in the past, but this daughter of Boranga, in the one day that I had shared with her, had affected me in a way that I could scarce describe. I wanted to spend every minute of my stay in Var-Dor with her. As we walked the short distance from the north gate to my cabin, I found myself absorbed in her. People greeted us, and I nodded absently at them. When we reached the dwelling she told me to wait inside, that she would prepare dinner and bring it to me.

"Bring enough so that we may eat together," I told her.

"Is that a request, Ro-lan?" she inquired, a coy smile on her face. I nodded. "Then I must obey!" she chirped happily, and ran up the street. I watched her lithe figure disappear around a corner and, shaking off the spell, I entered my cabin.

Take hold of yourself, Summers, I thought. You have been flung brutally into a strange and savage world, with little hope of ever seeing home again. Your best friend has become a mindless puppet of two mad women. His life is in danger—that is, if he is still alive. You have much to be concerned with. Yet knowing all this, I felt that nothing mattered but her. I believed that I would lay down my life for this girl who, at this time yesterday, was unknown to me.

In about an hour she returned, bearing food and drink. I had not eaten since breakfast, nor had she, though I daresay I had not thought of food all day. We both did justice to our dinners, after which Adara cleaned up and placed the tray outside the door. We had eaten Japanese-style on a short table, this the only furniture in the room.

We talked all that evening, and I got to learn more about the beauty called Adara. She had just turned twenty-one, and lived with Col-in, her grandfather. Both her parents were dead; her father having died shortly before she was born, her mother soon after giving birth. Her grandfather was an artisan who made tools and weapons for the Homarus. She tended to the housework for them, cared for their small garden, and sometimes served as a shepherd for the wurras, this her greatest joy. She admitted that she had rejected all past suitors, of which, understandably, there were many. Her independence, her strong will, was not in keeping with the male-dominant Homaru society, and she knew that they would only try to change her. She loved the great natural beauty of the surrounding countryside, something that none could understand, for they saw their work in the fields as no more than their duty to Lar-ek. Hesitantly, she confessed that she felt more at peace that day than she ever had before. I beamed inwardly at this revelation.

Ter-ek stopped in briefly to advise me that he would wed Aleen shortly after dark the next evening. It would take place in the same location as the ceremony of the previous night, before the dwelling of Lar-ek. I was to be among those to stand by him. He also invited Adara to accompany me, and she accepted cheerfully.

"Tomorrow, on the drill field, we begin training in earnest for our campaign to Mogara," said Ter-ek.

155

"Perhaps your guide will take you there in the morning, so that you may witness our guardsmen in force."

I looked at Adara, and she nodded her assent. "We will be there, Ter-ek," I told him, "and I look forward to it."

Ter-ek departed, and we were alone once again. It was getting late, and Adara told me that she must go. I asked if I could accompany her home, but she declined, assuring me that it was just a short distance away. She said that she would bring my breakfast early the next morning, so that we could have a longer day. I agreed heartily to this. We stood up together, only inches apart. She raised her face to mine and planted a kiss firmly on my cheek. I lost my control and, grabbing her tightly, crushed her lips to mine. She stiffened for an instant, but then lost herself to her own passions and held me close, the contact seeming to last forever. Finally, we separated.

"Adara, I—"

"Good night, Ro-lan," she sang, and ran out of the cabin, where I heard her fumble with the tray for a moment. After snapping free from my lethargy I went outside, but she was gone. I returned to the cabin and laid down on the mat. Though tired, I found slumber elusive. Was I in love? Impossible! I had just met this girl . . . and yet, it seemed like there had never been another girl in the world; in two worlds, for that matter. After nearly an hour, I fell into a restless sleep.

I was up early the next morning, and realized that all I could think about was when she would arrive.

When she came with my breakfast she was cheerful, though quieter. We spoke little during breakfast, and afterwards she took me to the drill field which was located just outside the east gate, encompassing an area the size of a football field. Four platoons of about thirty men each were practicing spear-casting in unison. One platoon would heave their spears and then step aside, the next one taking their place. Their target was about twenty-five yards away, and their accuracy was uncanny. Ter-ek was one of the lead spears in the first platoon.

Tor-en, head of the Homaru guardsmen, observed the proceedings from the side. He saw us approach and hailed us. In his belt was my hand ax, which he returned to me. "The artisans work quickly, and they have already duplicated it," he informed me. "The other will be used as a guide. We intend to make it a standard part of our weaponry. In five days they will be finished, and I would be honored if you would instruct the men in their use."

"I would be more than happy to, Tor-en," I said. "At least it will make me feel that I am contributing something."

We watched the drills for a while, and then we bade Tor-en good day, for my guide was most anxious to get going. Although the city was large, I realized that there was not much to see. The people all led similar lives and seemed happy. We were greeted cheerfully by those who passed us. The architecture varied little, though there was one large building about the size of an average high school auditorium. This was the Hall of Artisans, and both men and women worked at producing the tools and weapons of Var-Dor. I saw

Col-in hard at work and though he waved at his granddaughter and me, we did not speak.

Next we visited a school. The class we observed consisted of youngsters from eight to twelve years old. Practical things, such as farming, shearing, and crafts, were taught. There was little use for arithmetic, literature, or geography here. What they learned now would help contribute to the Homaru way of life in the future.

As we toured the city, I counted two more of the red obelisks and doors. I thought I would scream until I found out their secret. I saw nothing in Var-Dor that looked like a house of worship, nor did Adara make any reference to religion of any kind.

Toward the middle of the afternoon, we had seen everything of interest in Var-Dor. Adara had once again proven the perfect guide. We had said nothing of what happened the night before.

"Ro-lan, what would you like to do now more than anything?" she inquired.

"I would choose to be sitting on the hillside, watching the herds grazing in the valley," I answered. "Never have I experienced such tranquility."

She stopped and looked at me, her eyes aglow. "I was right! Oh, Ro-lan, I was right. I knew it!"

"Right about what?"

"Last night."

"I'm sorry about last night," I replied, sheepishly. "I—"

"Do not be sorry. I love you, Ro-lan," she stated simply. "Long have I dreamed of one like you. You are different; the Homarus understand only practicality, but your heart is filled with the joy of knowing

158

beauty for beauty's sake alone. You are warm, and you feel as I feel. I know nothing of your background, and I dare not ask. You are a guest among the Homarus. Some day you must choose whether to stay here as a Homaru, or leave. I should not say this, Rolan, but I must: whatever your choice, I wish to be with you."

For one of the few times in my life, I found myself speechless. I held her gently in my arms, her head on my shoulder. She was sobbing quietly, joyfully. People passed by us, but I did not notice them. The most incredible girl in two worlds had just proclaimed her love for me, Roland Summers. I held her at arm's length and wiped her tears.

"I have never met anyone like you in my life," I told her. "I love you, Adara, and I too wish to be with you. I do intend to stay with the Homarus when the time comes, but to know that you would leave if I chose to do so is more than one could ask. Let us go now to our spot."

We walked silently toward the north gate, each lost in thought. Now, more than ever, I wished to have Denny here with me. Were he safe and well, I would feel like a king. I hoped that he would be as fortunate in finding a girl like this.

We spent the rest of the afternoon in that lovely spot, lost in each other, watching the thick, overhanging clouds, the protectors of Boranga. As it started to grow dark, we remembered the wedding. We would be late for the ceremony! Laughing and tripping, we ran all the way back to the north gate. She left me at the door, advising me that she would be back as soon as she freshened up. I told her that the time would be far too long.

After cleaning up, I put on some fresh clothes, which Ter-ek had provided for me. I was ready in minutes, and I waited outside for Adara, who was not long in returning. She had changed into a bright blue sheath and dainty sandals, while in her hair was a large white flower. Her beauty was incomparable.

Nearly all the citizenry attended the brief ceremony, which consisted of a simple mingling of the blood from the small fingers of Aleen and Ter-ek, a blessing of sorts from Lar-ek, and the entire populace facing north and intoning *"Noma Kuto Boranga."* Amidst congratulations I presented Ter-ek with the finely crafted Mogar spear, which he appreciated, having lost his own in the deep crevice atop the outcropping days earlier. Adara presented to Aleen, who was a dear friend, a bolt of brightly colored material. Then the wedding feast, which was a repetition of the other, began. Food was plentiful, and the chenna flowed like water. I was careful not to overdo it with this potent drink because even the slightest amount was too much.

The party continued, with everyone enjoying themselves. Adara and I sampled every kind of food that we could get our hands on. Adara offered me one tidbit which looked like nothing I had ever seen before.

"Try this, my love. But be careful, for it will fight back," she warned, laughingly.

Emboldened by the chenna, I put the whole thing in my mouth. It was like biting into a jalepeno pepper that had been dipped in hot sauce. I enjoyed Mexican food, but this was too much.

"Blast it! That son-of-a-gun is hot!" I yelped.

As I spat the fiery morsel out, I quickly realized my mistake. I had uttered the words in my long unused native tongue! Fortunately, no one had heard me except Adara. She stared at me, dumbfounded. I started to speak, but she motioned me to silence. She told me to wait where I was, and ventured through the crowd. Soon she was conferring with her grandfather who listened intently, then walked away. Adara watched him for a moment, then returned to where I awaited her.

"Please, Ro-lan, come with me," she said.

"What's this all about?" I queried.

"Do not ask me now. You will know shortly. Now come." She was insistent.

We walked through the deserted streets in silence. Past my cabin we went, where we turned down a smaller street. We stopped in front of a particular house.

"This is my home, Ro-lan," she announced. "Please go in."

I entered the house, which was well lit within. Col-in was standing in the middle of the room. He smiled at me and extended his hand. Then he spoke: "Welcome, Yank, my name is Peter Collins. How's everything in the States?"

I had had many surprises since I reached Boranga, but very few approached this one. Adara's grandfather had spoken to me—*in English!*

CHAPTER ELEVEN

PETER TELLS HIS STORY

Adara and her grandfather were looking at each other, and both were smiling. I stood frozen in the middle of the room, stunned. Finally, Col-in spoke again: "When I first saw you, and some of the garments you wore when you arrived, I had a hunch. When I saw the workmanship on the ax, which was brought to me for duplication, I was almost positive. Still I hesitated, hoping that in Adara's presence you would slip. Now we know for sure. What is your name, and where are you from?"

"I am Roland Summers, and of late I have lived in Hawaii," I told him, finding my tongue. "Why didn't you just ask me if you were not sure?"

"Forgive me, but I should have. Years of living on Boranga, amidst the superstitions of these people, has made me cautious. But come; sit down, and you shall hear my story, after which I would like to hear yours."

Adara took my arm, and together we settled upon a straw mat. Col-in sat down cross-legged opposite us and began his story.

"As I told you before, my name is, or at least was, Peter Collins. I lived in Melbourne, Australia, where I was a banker. I was reasonably successful, and in middle age I was already semi-retired. My greatest love being sailing, I owned a small but durable schooner, the *Sea Star*. Nearly twenty-two years ago, I embarked on a cruise of the Pacific. Accompanying me were my wife, my daughter, and her husband, all experienced and capable sailors. We sailed first to South America, then up along the west coast of North America as far as Vancouver. All of us were having a smashing time.

"It was in Canada that I learned my daughter was pregnant. Her time was months away, and we felt sure that we would reach home long before that. We pointed the *Sea Star* southwest toward home, planning a short stopover in the Hawaiian Islands along the way. The weather was perfect, as it had been for most of the trip, and we encountered no difficulties.

"We were no more than a few days from the islands when it happened. I had just made my log entry for the morning. Our coordinates: 28° Longitude, 152° Latitude, almost to the mile. That was where we were when it started. First, the water turned a ghastly white, and then we began moving due west. There was a good breeze that morning, yet the *Sea Star* seemed to have a mind of its own. The sails would not respond no matter what skills we employed.

"We traveled for what seemed hours, although this was hard to tell, for our timepieces had ceased functioning. A fog began to creep in all about us, even though the morning had started out dazzlingly sunny. My family remained calm on the outside, but inwardly I was sure that they all were as frightened as I was. I especially worried about Patricia, my daughter, and her unborn child.

"Patricia's husband, Laurence Walker, had been keeping watch off the bow. He hailed me, and I joined him. What had caught his attention was a dazzling light up ahead that glowed through the heavy fog. The strange path of white water was also bright, and it was difficult to look at. We began to slow down, and I returned to the women to inform them of what we had seen.

"Now we were in the midst of the strange glow. The *Sea Star* began to spin, slowly at first, then faster. Caroline, my wife, grabbed my arm, and together we held tightly to a mast. We called to Laurence to leave the bow, but he hesitated. Patricia went to join him, but the wildly moving vessel forced her to the deck. Laurence saw her go down; he rushed to help her, but the motion of the ship was too much, and he stumbled forward head first. Patricia screamed, and Caroline dug her nails into my arm. We had both been forced to the deck. It was as if we were pinned. The speed at which the *Sea Star* was spinning was unbelievable. The last earthly sounds I heard before blacking out were my daughter's cries.

"I was the first to awaken, and I felt strangely euphoric, but this feeling was quickly replaced by a terrible thirst. We were well provisioned, and I promptly satisfied this. I then realized something else: I was burning up. The huge sun was incredibly hot. According to its location, it was about mid-morning. I moved both Caroline and Patricia to a cabin, out of the sun's rays. Patricia was breathing regularly, but my wife's inhalations were quite strained.

"I went back on deck to retrieve Laurence, but found him dead. His skull had been shattered by the fall, and it was not a pretty sight. As I covered his body, I grieved for him. He was a fine young man, and I was proud to have him as a son-in-law. I dreaded having to face Patricia with the news.

"For most of the afternoon, I kept a vigil over the rest of my family. Patricia came to first, and I immediately gave her water. I found it difficult to look her in the eyes, but the absence of her husband had already told her what I dared not. She laid back resignedly and stared at the ceiling. She had always been a strong-willed girl, and her fortitude under this adversity was reassuring to me.

"Caroline was still unconscious, and her breathing was labored. I applied wet cloths to her face and tried to get her to take some water. Patricia, seeing that her mother was ill, offered her help. I told her to remain in bed and recoup her strength, but she insisted that she was all right. Together we worked on Caroline until nightfall, but she did not regain consciousness that day.

"After dark, we went up on deck. It was cooler now, and bearable. Patricia said her goodbyes to Laurence, and we gave him an improvised, but dignified, burial at sea. When it was over she stood at the railing and stared out into the black night. I went to comfort her, but she shook her head. Realizing that she wished to be alone, I returned to Caroline's side.

"That first night, after the two moons rose, I realized that we were no longer on our own world. I seemed to accept this calmly, though it was possible that I had still not recovered from the shock of the whole experience. Strange phenomena had always interested me, and I believed myself more open-minded than most in those days. I first ruled out a space warp, for I did not believe that anyone could survive the journey; or, even if they did, what were the odds against landing on a world capable of sustaining human life?

"After much thought, I narrowed my choices down to a time warp and a dimensional warp. If it were a time warp, then I believed that we had been cast millions of years in the future. But what of the fact that the sun was hotter, when it was expected to cool in the future? And what about the dual moons? I tended to lean toward the dimensional warp, and my experiences on Boranga strengthened this theory. Now, your appearance here cements it. If it were a time warp, then the chances of your being flung to exactly this period would be infinitessimal.

"We learned to avoid the sun's rays, though one of us stayed on deck at all times to keep watch, while the other cared for Caroline. I took the bulk of the vigil, fearing for Patricia and the baby. I hoisted all the sails, but the breeze was minimal. We moved slowly in an easterly direction, assuming that the sun rose and set as it should. Caroline, in the meantime, regained consciousness for brief intervals, during which she raved incoherently, struggling with whomever was sitting by her. She acted as one caught in the grip of fever, although she did not feel like she was burning up. She had always been a vital, athletic woman, and it broke my heart to see her like this.

"On the afternoon of the third day, Caroline died. We buried her at sea also. Patricia held tightly to my arm after she was gone, and together we mourned our losses in silence. Finally, the enormity of the situation was too great for her; she put her head on my chest and sobbed quietly. In a few seconds I had joined her.

"The next morning Patricia was standing watch, and she called to me excitedly. I came on deck, and together we gazed upon an island directly in our path. For hours we watched as it loomed larger and larger, until finally we could make out the cliffs that appeared to surround most of it. With my glass I sought out a place where we might land, eventually spotting a strip of beach toward the northern tip of the island. We were not headed for it, but through some tricky tacking manuevers we managed to work the *Sea Star* closer to it. Soon we were anchored less than one hundred feet from the shore. Despite our anxiety to land, we decided to wait until an hour or so before sunset, for we knew that to challenge the sun during the afternoon would be suicide.

"We spent the day making preparations for the exploration, Patricia gathering the most essential food and supplies, I putting together some make-shift torches. One of the two moons was full the night before, the other half full, and I hoped that this, plus the torches, would enable us to see our way.

"The time came, and we rowed to shore in one of our small lifeboats. We dragged the boat far up on the beach and started inland. In only minutes we were traipsing through a swamp, the muck emitting a terrible odor and grasping at our feet, this making the footing treacherous. I feared traveling this swamp after dark, and suggested to Patricia that we return to the *Sea Star* and circle the island in an attempt to find a less hazardous inland route. She agreed with me, and we were about to turn back when, far in the distance, we heard what sounded like a human voice. We looked at each other, deciding to push on so that we might investigate the source of the sound.

"We continued our trek inland. The mud, besides being sticky, was quite hot. Only our leather boots prevented our feet from burning. We were now able to find stretches of semi-solid land to walk on, while all around us the mud pits boiled. I guessed that it was quicksand, and knew that we must be cautious. We heard the sound again, still distant, and were determined to solve the puzzle.

"Darkness had fallen, the light of the two moons casting eerie shadows through the swamp. I lit the torches, and we felt our way along gingerly. But one misstep to my right deposited me waist deep in the mire. There was no doubt now that it was quicksand, for I began sinking slowly. Although the night air had begun to cool the mud on the surface, below it was still exceptionally hot. I knew that I could not survive for long.

"Patricia, reacting quickly, planted her torch into

the ground and got down on her knees, grabbing my hands. My downward movement was now checked, but she could gain no leverage to haul me out. Slowly, painstakingly she pulled, exerting every ounce of energy. I was helpless, and could offer no aid. But inch by inch I emerged, until finally I was able to grab on to the ground. In a few minutes I was free.

"We sat on the ground together, fatigued. I cleaned the mud off my body as best I could, and soon we were walking again. Moving cautiously, shoulder to shoulder, we tested every inch of ground in front of us before setting foot on it. We progressed slowly, but steadily. The voice sounded closer now. It was unmistakably a woman's voice, and it was calling for help in a language that I immediately recognized as one of the Polynesian dialects that I had picked up in my many travels. I was amazed at the revelation.

"Suddenly, Patricia dropped her torch and fell forward, clutching her stomach. I grabbed her and tried to help her to the ground, but she waved me off, protesting that she was fine, just a slight pain. The baby was still some months off, but I feared the ordeal she was undergoing was creating some problems. I cursed myself for not leaving her on the *Sea Star*, and begged her to let me take her back.

"A scream pierced the air, and this time it sounded only meters away. Patricia hastened her steps, and I followed, pleading with her to slow down. Minutes later, we came across a grim scene. A man was in one of the quicksand pits, neck deep, his fingertips grasping feebly at those of a woman, who was attempting to save him. She was small and frail, and had apparently been holding on to his hand for some time. He had not been sinking, nor was he able to climb out. Now, her strength all but gone, his hand had slipped from hers, and she was helpless to prevent it.

"Patricia and I threw off our gear and rushed to her side. She was shocked to see us appear so suddenly, but she stepped aside quickly. Only moments later, the man reposed safely on the ground at our feet, nearly unconscious. We worked on him for a while, and soon he was breathing regularly. The woman thanked us profusely and asked if we could help her get him back to their dwelling, to which we agreed. I turned to retrieve our gear, but found, much to my chagrin, that it was gone. By tossing off the sacks in haste, we had consigned them to the quicksand pits. We had made another foolish mistake, and I knew that I would have to return to the *Sea Star* for things we needed, though to try that night would be folly.

"The woman's name was Azena, her husband Vor-an. Although unconscious, Vor-an was not heavy, and with Patricia's help he was easy to carry. Azena guided us deftly through the swamp, and in about an hour we came to a heavily wooded area. The ground was solid, the quicksand pits gone. I breathed a sigh of relief for all our sakes.

"We continued on for another hour to the south, stopping once to rest. In the moonlight I saw that we were approaching some hills. It was into these hills that Azena led us to their dwelling, a small but well constructed hut of wood and straw. It was well hidden amidst large rocks and trees, offering them safety as well as shelter. We deposited Vor-an on a straw mat within. Azena thanked us, and offered us the use of the hut. We refused, assuring her we would be most comfortable outside. She gave us two mats and one wool blanket, and then retired. I prepared the mats, covering Patricia with the blanket after she had reclined. She fell asleep almost instantly, her breathing heavy and irregular. I laid there for a time and worried about her, until weariness finally overcame me.

"The next morning I awoke to a cloud-filled, sunless sky. I have seen the sun only a few times since in the more than twenty-one years I have been on Boranga. Patricia was still asleep, but her breathing had become a bit easier. Vor-an emerged from his dwelling, looking none the worse for wear considering his ordeal of the night before. He offered his personal thanks for our assistance and told me that Azena would be out shortly with food for us. I was famished, and the prospect was pleasing.

"As the four of us breakfasted that morning, I learned of my hosts. Vor-an and Azena were Homarus, and both had been shepherds. Vor-an had also been a Thinker, one of a small group who, among themselves, discussed questions which had no apparent relevance in the Homaru way of life. The Homarus led a simple life, governed by the ways of their ancestors and dedicated to service to the Master. The Homarus were farmers, shepherds, artisans, miners and warriors when they had to be. To question useless things was wasteful, to question holy things forbidden. Science was the prime interest of the Thinkers, and for a while they were tolerated.

"As a young man, Vor-an saw some of his friends

banished, some even executed, for failing to kill the satong. Vor-an was not a violent man, and he feared the time when he would be called. When that time came, he refused to go. He argued that it was a waste of human life to attempt to honor a tradition steeped in antiquity. Although some might have agreed with him, none would stand by his side except for Azena, whom he had recently taken as his wife. Together they were banished from Var-Dor, never to return. Family and friends turned their backs on them. The meetings of the Thinkers were banned, though to this day some of the original Thinkers and their descendents still wish to question, still desire to know. I have spoken with some of them, but I have never told anyone my true background.

"Vor-an and Azena had lived alone in the hills for ten years when we met them. At times they traveled across Boranga, seeking to answer questions of which the Homarus have little interest. They had scaled some of Boranga's mountains to ascertain the reason for the clouds; they sought to understand why the river flowed as it did, although they had never been to the source. They puzzled over the Sands of Fire, not willing to accept the Homaru belief that it was a place to be left alone. Once, Vor-an confided, they even journeyed north to seek the answer to the biggest mystery of all, but found that they could not go all the way. Some fears were just too deeply inbred in the Homarus. I did not ask him at that time what he meant.

"When they were done, we told them our story. They listened silently, intently, and when we were finished they stared at each other, nodding their heads. They had never believed that Boranga was all, that other life must exist beyond the sea. Now they had learned of another world, and as intelligent people strove hard to understand. In the weeks we were to live with them we spoke much of our world, and we learned about Boranga. The only difficulties seemed to arise when I questioned them about the . . . Master, and the secret of the north. They assured me that they would answer my questions in time.

"During our first week with them, Patricia seemed to be doing well, but in the second week she fell ill. I had no reason until then to return to the *Sea Star*, but now I wished to retrieve those things that I thought might help her, so I asked Vor-an to guide me there. We set out late in the afternoon, reaching the swamp shortly after sunset. Vor-an told me that he had been through the Sands of Fire many times, that what had occurred weeks before was the result of carelessness on his part. He seemed to know the trail well, and after an uneventful trek we reached the coast. We were a little south of our original landing site, but it took only a few minutes to find the life boat.

"It was a little darker than usual that night as we walked down to the shoreline. One moon was in its new phase, the other darting in and out from behind some high clouds. I stared out into the black sea, straining to locate the *Sea Star*. Finally the moon popped out from behind the clouds, its light shining on the still sea. A still sea, yes, but an empty sea also, for the *Sea Star* was gone!

"How could it have happened? I had secured the anchor myself. It could not have broken loose, but apparently it had. Why had it not come aground on the shore? There was medicine aboard, food, clothing, tools. Now there was—nothing. Why? Had the ship been taken? Vor-an assured me that navigation was unknown on Boranga.

"Dejected, I followed Vor-an back into the swamp. A million thoughts raced through my head as we trudged through the mire. Patricia was all I had left, and now I feared losing her. The *Sea Star* was gone, relegating us to a life on Boranga. I cared not for myself, but for Patricia and the child. What kind of a life could it be for them? With the *Sea Star*, I might have sought after the warp in a year or two. Now it would be impossible.

"We reached the dwelling some time later. Azena had prepared a place for Patricia in the hut, and kept watch over her constantly. I knelt down and spoke with her, telling her what had happened. She smiled at me and took my hand, assuring me that everything would be all right. She then fell asleep, and Azena shooed me out of the hut.

"Patricia never rose from her mat again, although we took her out into the air a number of times. Her condition worsened, and she grew weaker. Vor-an prepared medicine from herbs he had gathered, and I believe that she would have died sooner without them. In our fifth week there, she gave birth to a tiny daughter. With her dying breath she told me that the child was to be called Adara. She had wished to name her Azena, to show her love for the fine woman who had never left her side for a moment; but Azena, embarrassed, pleaded with Patricia to name the child Adara, after her own mother. I told Patricia that it was a beautiful name and, with a smile on her face, she died.

"Azena cared for the child as if it were her own. Vor-an left that night and was gone for days, finally returning with a wurra to provide milk for the child. Only much later, when I discovered that none but the Homarus kept wurras, did I realize that he had risked his life to obtain it. The child thrived on the milk, and grew considerably after the first month.

"One evening, I sat in front of the hut with Azena, who was holding the infant in her arms, playing with it. Vor-an was late in returning from a hunt for food. Suddenly, Azena placed the baby on the ground. She stood up, as if in a trance, and began walking toward the north. I picked up the infant and yelled at her to come back, but she did not hear me. I ran after her, but my legs were as leaden weights, and the gap between us widened. I could not understand how this was happening. In minutes, she was gone from my sight. I never saw her again.

"Vor-an returned shortly thereafter, and I told him what had happened. I was aware of his great love for his wife, and expected him to charge into the forest after her. To my surprise he made no motion to leave, but stood there silently. Finally he dropped to his knees and faced north, mumbling something unintelligible to me. When this was done, he sat down cross-legged in front of the hut and stared blankly into space.

"For three days, Vor-an was like a caged animal. He paced back and forth, fighting a violent battle deep within himself. I pleaded with him to go after Azena, telling him that if it were not for the child I would go myself. He ignored my pleas and continued his inner torment.

"Finally he made up his mind; he would go after his wife. He had overcome the final barrier of Borangan superstition. His life was nothing without Azena, and he felt that he must try and find her, or die in the attempt. Since he assumed that his life was already forfeit, he believed that it would not matter any more if I knew the truth. Before he left, he told me of the Master. I almost wish that he hadn't, for I have lived with the nightmare ever since. I understood then why he felt doomed.

"He gave me instructions as to the location of Var-Dor. I then bade farewell to this fine fellow, silently praying that he would once more be reunited with his Azena, whether in this life or another. Then he was gone. I took little Adara to Var-Dor, where we were accepted by the people. No one sought to know of my background. I became a metal worker, and raised Adara with the help of the local women. She has been the only joy left to me."

I sat quietly for a moment, touched deeply by the old man's story. Adara looked at me and smiled, clutching my hand tightly. Col-in, or Peter, as I now thought of him, held his head down. He was tired, and his eyes were moist. The memories must surely be painful for him.

"I have seen what affect the Master has on the people of Boranga," I told him. "I am not superstitious, but I must admit that the experience was unnerving. I wish to know more about the Master, to perhaps understand. Will you tell me?"

Peter did not answer me. He was nodding, and his eyes were closed. I realized that he was asleep. Adara went to his side and helped him down to his mat. She kissed him on the head and returned to me.

"My grandfather is old, and tires easily. He will answer your questions tomorrow night. He also wishes to know of the occurrences on his own world since last he saw it. I am glad that you are what you are, Ro-lan, for his sake. It pleases him greatly to speak to someone in his own tongue again. For me it does not matter, for I would love you either way."

She kissed me good night, and told me that she would be by in the morning. I walked the short distance to the cabin in somewhat of a daze. I treasured each day that I could spend with Adara, but I knew that it would seem an eternity until Peter related to me the story that he had heard from Vor-an some twenty-one years ago. I slept poorly that night, my head filled with thoughts of the torment of Peter Collins. That he was still alive was a testimonial to the love he felt for his granddaughter, his only link with the life he knew.

I shared the next morning with Adara on the hill overlooking the herds. We spoke of nature, we spoke of love. We did not talk about her grandfather. The afternoon I spent on the drill field with Ter-ek, where plans were going ahead in earnest for the bloodless siege of Mogara. I took the opportunity to keep myself physically fit. That night I had dinner with Adara and Peter, and afterwards I heard the story of the Master. As Ter-ek had warned me, it would prove to be deadly knowledge.

CHAPTER TWELVE

RAS-EK VARANO

"The story of the Master," Peter began, "is very old, by my guess probably about a hundred and fifty years. Madness was inherent in many of the Homarus, and because they could not be helped, they were driven away. They journeyed north, beyond a broad valley, until they could travel no more, for the mountains barred their way. Here they settled, their common affliction the only unifying force. At the time there were perhaps fifty of them. They hunted, for game was plentiful on Boranga then, and they tried to plant fields, but they were as likely to destroy the crops in their madness as they were to tend them when coherent. They lacked leadership, and some died. Wild beasts killed them; they killed each other, or committed suicide.

"Working amidst the crops one day was a young man named Ras-ek. Among the Homarus he had been a shepherd, and tended to his chores well. One day, for no apparent reason, he murdered an old woman, mutilating and dismembering her. Many witnessed the act, though they were too late to stop him. He wandered off, and the guard was notified. They found him watching over a herd. He was whistling happily, and did not understand why they had come for him. He was to be beheaded, but he escaped and traveled north, joining the mad ones at the place which is still called the Other Side, north of the valley. No one among them cared about his action, for all were as capable of committing similar atrocities, and some were even as guilty of one as he was.

"Who can guess at what thoughts went through his diseased brain as he toiled? All that is known is that, while turning the earth, he discovered something. He looked around furtively to see if anyone had noticed what he had found, but none were within twenty yards. He dug dirt up from around the object, until he was able to loosen it. Then he covered it with a garment and began running north, toward the lower hills. It is said that those who saw him run that day noted that the object he carried was very heavy, and he ran awkwardly, his eyes ablaze. No one attempted to stop him, for on the Other Side such actions were commonplace.

"Ras-ek was not seen again for many days thereafter, though few were concerned by his absence. Then one day, the people of the Other Side were summoned. No one knows how, but as one, they stopped whatever they were doing and began walking north. Even those in the throes of madness

179

went, for the force that drew them was stronger even than their maladies. Into the hills they climbed, until they stood before a dwelling the like of which none of them had ever witnessed. From the description given to me by Vor-an, I pictured an antebellum mansion from the days of your old South. It was crimson red, and pulsated with life before their eyes. Rising to a height of about fifteen meters, it covered more than three acres of the mesa upon which it sat.

"The people stared at the house without emotion, as if they had seen it often before. Suddenly, the large metal door opened, and there stood Ras-ek. He wore a silver cloak that shimmered blindingly, and a silver turban sat atop his head. His eyes blazed fiercely as he looked over the people, a malevolent, twisted grin on his face. In a loud, hollow voice he addressed them: 'My people, I am Ras-ek Varano,' he told them, adopting the name of the once beloved deity of Boranga, 'and this is Sekkator, my home. You, and only you, have been chosen to be my kuta. We have been sent to the Other Side for a purpose, and now I have learned of it. I am to be the Master of Boranga; you are to be my servants, the rest my slaves. They will learn to live for me, to die for me. They will teach their descendents to fear me. I will rule them forever, for I cannot die! Your own descendents will be my kuta. You are honored, you are blessed. Return to the outside and tell them. Teach them, my kuta! They will laugh at you, the fools! They may even try to injure you, but they will learn. Oh yes, they will learn! They will fall to their knees and pray to me. *Noma Kuto Boranga!* Beloved is the Holiest of Boranga, this is what you will teach them. Go, my kuta, go, for Ras-ek Varano has spoken to you!'

"The people fell to their knees and faced Ras-ek Varano, screaming *Noma Kuto Boranga* over and over. The Master raised his arms in benediction and then disappeared inside, the door closing by itself after him. It is said that he did not walk, but instead floated within, as if carried gently by the wind. The others, still on their knees, lost control; they began to scratch and tear at everything within reach, including each other. In their ecstatic madness three were killed, their bodies left by the door. These 'Holy Ones,' as proclaimed by Ras-ek Varano, composed themselves, and the trek downward began as though nothing had happened.

"Messengers were chosen from among the Holy Ones and sent across Boranga to spread the word to the people. In Var-Dor they were taken prisoner, for were they not ordered to stay away from the land of the Homarus? They shouted their warnings, but the people scoffed. 'Build monuments to the Master,' they screamed, 'great crimson monuments of stone! You may not gaze upon him when he visits you, so dig chambers deep into the ground, where you can tremble and pray when he comes among you. He will take what he wishes, when he wishes it, and you will not stop him. He is Ras-ek Varano, the Master of Boranga, your Master!'

"The Homarus were incensed by these blasphemies. The mad ones were sentenced to die, but none did. Instead, they disappeared. It was shortly after that the Master visited Var-Dor for the first time. What happened remains unspoken to this day, but within weeks the crimson obelisks rose, and the chambers were dug. The fear of the Master had been instilled in nearly all the Homarus.

"Some were still unconvinced by all that had occurred, and these brave souls were determined to eradicate the problem. They ventured north, until they reached the land overlooking the valley. It was the middle of the afternoon, but as they gazed down into the once fertile vale they could see nothing, for it was dark. Some were frightened, and chose not to go on. Eleven brave ones opted to continue, and their companions vowed to wait for them there.

"The fearless eleven descended into the valley, disappearing in moments. Hours later, the ones who stayed behind heard a hideous shriek, and they jumped to their feet. From out of the abysmal blackness of the wretched vale emerged Zol-ek, the leader of the group, one of the bravest of all Homarus. His eyes blazed with fire, while his skin was pasty white. He shrieked and gibbered like a monkey, and the men could make no sense from what he uttered. They did all they could to calm him down, and finally got him to sit on the ground. Foam flecked the corners of his mouth as he panted heavily. They relaxed their vigilance for just a second, allowing Zol-ek to snatch a knife from one of the men. With an insane cackle rising from his throat he plunged the blade deep into his heart.

"The men were overwhelmed by this action. They waited silently for more to return, but none did. As it grew darker their terror overcame them, and they ran as far away from the Vale of Fear as they could. To my knowledge, Zol-ek is the only man to have emerged alive from the Vale of Fear. Until Vor-an left to find his Azena, I doubt if any have even risked the Vale of Fear. The Master apparently summoned Azena twenty-one years ago, as he has summoned women for all of his decades. What he does with them is unknown. Some come back, many do not. Those that return are not the same as before they left. All eventually destroy themselves.

"That, Ro-lan, is the story of Ras-ek Varano. Although telling it to you could cost me my life, I care not. I am old, and would die soon anyway. I care only for my granddaughter, and long have I prayed for someone like you to come to her. I fear that some day the Master will send for her. The very thought infuriates me, but I am helpless. I gave much thought to venturing north in an attempt to destroy him, but discarded this as folly. You must get her away from here, Roland Summers. After you have rescued your friend from the Mogars you must leave, for as an outsider you too are in danger. How I avoided it for so long I do not know. Perhaps it is because I am old. No matter. I have a plan, one that I have worked on for fifteen years. No one knows of it, not even Adara.

"Five years after joining the Homarus, I went for the third time to hunt the satong. Yes, even a middle-aged man is not exempt. The hunting was poor, and my search took me all the way to the hills in which they roam. I finally found and killed one. As I removed its head, I happened to spot an opening in the rocks. Entering, I discovered that it was a cave. I decided to explore it, though I feared that it might be the home of a satong. At no point, however, was the ceiling more than two meters high. Most of the way I was forced to bend over, and this fact allayed my fears, since the huge satongs would find such a dwelling most uncomfortable.

"The cave continued on for a few miles, at some points so narrow that I was forced to squeeze through. Finally, the floor sloped downward, and I saw light pouring in. As I neared the opening, I could hear the sound of waves lapping gently against the rocks. I now stood in an enormous cavern, the walls seven meters away from me on either side, the ceiling half as high. The sun stood overhead and offered little danger as I gazed out at the sea, which I had once loved so dearly. But no, this was not the same sea, but an alien one.

"The water had been rising as I stood there, and soon it covered the floor of the cavern. I was forced back into the tunnel, but found myself hesitant to leave. I knew that I must, for it was getting late, and to camp near the hills would be suicide. As it was, the time that I had spent there had negated any chance of exiting the forest before dusk. I was fortunate that the night passed without incident.

"An idea had been born in my mind that night, and I dwelled on it during the return to Var-Dor. I had spent much time around the shipyards of Melbourne, and had some small knowledge of boat construction. I decided to build a vessel of some kind, deep within the tunnel. If the time ever came to use it, it could be easily floated out of the cavern at high tide. The risks would be great, for I would have to contend with the Mogars, the satongs, and the chance of discovery by my own people. Also, implanted in my brain by this time, was the risk of incensing the Master.

"After my return to Var-Dor, I started my project in earnest. The process was slow, for all work had to be done in secret. I spent many late hours in the Hall of Artisans, constructing each piece to my specifications. During the day I was able to get these pieces out of Var-Dor unnoticed, where I hid them in the forest to the east. After a full year I had progressed very little.

"When the fourth call came to me, I was glad. I was now sixty years old and though still in fine physical condition, I knew that age would soon make a satong hunt for me akin to suicide. If I was to finish this boat I must stay alive, for I knew that it would take a long time.

"I left Var-Dor that morning, stopping after three kilometers to gather up the finished pieces. Carrying them across Boranga was difficult, but I finally made it to the forest. Luck was with me that day, for I came across a feeding satong and killed it. With that done, I could now concentrate on the boat. I took the pieces to the cave and left them there, making sure they were high and dry. I then returned to Var-Dor and continued my work.

"One of the prerogatives of age is that it provides for a limited work schedule. Once a year I left Var-Dor, and usually did not return for a month. Each time, I took the pieces that I had completed to the cave and fit them together. As each year passed, the journey became harder. I built a wheelbarrow-like contrivance to haul the pieces with, for I was having trouble carrying them. I had withstood a number of attacks by the satongs, but in the ninth year I was almost killed by one. I was weak, and only by cunning did I dispatch it.

"The following year the job was done, but I'm afraid that I was also. I was nearly seventy, and the physical as well as the clandestine aspects of my project had nearly killed me. Returning to Var-Dor, I suffered great pains in my chest, and was unable to travel for days. When I was able to walk, I could accomplish no more than a few kilometers a day. It took me weeks to reach Var-Dor, and when I finally did I knew that I could not make the journey again. My vessel was complete, but the effort seemed to be for naught. To the best of my knowledge it lies there still, ready for use. When you have returned from Mogara, I want you to take Adara and leave. She is a lovely young woman now, and I fear that her time will soon come."

I looked at Adara, and saw her crying softly as she thought of the ordeals that her grandfather had suffered these many years. She had not previously known of his illness.

"Oh, Grandfather!" she sobbed. "Why did you not confide in me? I could have helped you. I would have done anything for you!"

"It is because you are so dear to me that I could not have you risk the dangers that were involved," he told her. "I was a vain man, expecting the vitality of my younger days to last forever. Now Ro-lan has come. You both love each other, and I am glad. Boranga is not for you, for you will only know suffering here. You must leave the island, together."

"No, Grandfather!" she cried. "I will not leave you. I cannot leave you!"

"I am old, my dear," he told her, as he cradled her head on his chest, "and I am also sick. I have little time left. To know that you at least attempted flight from Boranga with Ro-lan would make what time I have left more bearable. Please believe me, for it is what I desire most."

Adara kissed her grandfather on the head, and then wiped her eyes. As I watched the two of them, I was deeply moved by their devotion to each other. How did I deserve to have the love of one such as Adara? Surely there must have been some purpose, far beyond my ken, for why I was brought to this world.

"I'm sure that there would be some way to take you with us, Peter," I said.

He shook his head. "I would only slow you down," he replied, "and in the long run I would not make it anyway. Come, let us stop all this talk! I wish to hear of my own world, of Australia, of America. Please, fill me in on all that has occurred since last I saw her."

"One more question please, Peter," I said. "How sure are you that Adara will be taken by the Master? You indicated to me that not all the women of the Homarus are called."

"Not all the women are called, Ro-lan," he answered, "only the most beautiful of them. Does that justify my cause for alarm?"

I nodded my agreement, and the matter was left at that. For the next two hours I spoke of my world, of all that had been accomplished over the past two decades. Adara was especially fascinated by my description of television. Peter was also interested, for he had witnessed some of the earliest prototypes while still there. I told him of the war, and his brow wrinkled thoughtfully as he absorbed some of the black side of his world. He wished to hear as much as possible, but once again he wearied, and Adara laid him gently down on his sleeping mat. We visited for a short while, and then I left.

My next couple of weeks in Var-Dor became somewhat routine. Adara brought me my morning meal, and then stayed to care for the cabin while I joined Ter-ek on the way to the drill field. A quantity of the hand axes had been duplicated quite expertly by the artisans, and I delighted in teaching the Homarus how to utilize them. The metal that the craftsmen used was similar to steel and just as strong, but its color was a deep, rich brown. I made a mental note to inquire as to the source of the metal.

After four or five hours with the guardsmen, Adara would stop by, and we would spend the rest of the afternoon together. I loved this part of the day best, for in those two weeks that followed we grew to know and understand the deep, innermost feelings of the other. She spoke much of her mother, whom she had never known. Her grandfather had told her that they were much alike. I wished that I had known Patricia Walker, for I was sure that she had been a fine woman. I also spoke of my parents, and I told her that they would have loved her as I do. She felt the same regarding them.

I dined with Adara and Peter every evening, for Peter was unable to hear enough of his own world. As I loved his granddaughter, so I grew to respect and admire this brave old man. Over twenty-one years ago he had lost nearly everything, and now he was willing to sacrifice what was left to assure Adara's safety.

Soon I began my third week among the Homarus. In less than two weeks I would join the warriors in their march to Mogara, to seal the rift that had separated them for so long. It seemed foolish to think that war could exist between two peoples on an island where all of them were, in effect, slaves; at least, that is what their superstitions and fears had made them. Perhaps this self-proclaimed Master reveled in the follies of these people, letting them live their own lives for his amusement, knowing that he could take it all away from them if he so desired.

One afternoon, while watching the wurras, I asked Adara to be my wife. She was overjoyed and, wrapping her arms around my neck, she covered my face with kisses. We ran all the way back to the city so that we might tell the news to Peter. He beamed proudly at his granddaughter.

"You forget one thing, Adara," he reminded her. "Ro-lan has not lived among us for two hundred days. Lar-ek will not perform such a ceremony until he has become a Homaru."

Adara buried her face in her hands and began to sob. I too was dejected until I looked at Peter's face and saw, even through his bushy beard, that he was smiling. He winked at me, a gleam in his eye.

"All of us are what we are, my granddaughter," he said brightly. "None of us were born Homaru, and therefore should not be totally bound by their laws. Somewhere in my own world I am still listed as the captain of a sea-going vessel, and world-wide authority recognizes my right to carry out a marriage

189

ceremony. I have performed a few in the past, but none will give me greater pleasure than the one I will conduct tonight."

Adara hugged and kissed her grandfather, unable to contain her great joy. I left them together, returning shortly after dark. That night, in the presence of God, here in this world as in all worlds, Captain Peter Collins joined together Miss Adara Walker, Boranga, and Mr. Roland Summers, U.S.A. My school ring now graced her finger. I was sorry for only one thing—that my best man, my *best friend*, was not with us.

Peter laughingly shooed the two of us out of his house, assuring the concerned Adara that he was capable of caring for himself. We ran, ecstatic, to my cabin, *our* cabin, where we consummated our unbounded love through the surprisingly brief hours of darkness. As I think of that night now, our sole night of joy, I wonder just how much of it was real.

The next morning I was again on the drill field, where most of my pupils could now outdo me in their accuracy with the hand ax. This fighting force was now honed to perfection, and I was sure that if any unforeseen circumstances arose in Mogara, they would be more than capable of handling themselves.

I spent the afternoon with my bride, and for the first time in weeks we discussed her grandfather's plan. She insisted that she would not leave him, and I vowed to her that if I had to physically carry Peter across the entire width of Boranga, he would accompany us. She was much relieved, though she knew that I would have it no other way.

That night, the two of us once again dined with

Peter, who talked about the boat that he had built in the distant cave. The vessel was a large skiff, about the size of a whale boat. He had built two oars, and had fashioned metal oarlocks. There was a portable mast that could be affixed to a hole in the center of the boat once it was at sea. He had rigged a special set of sails, designed to function as an umbrella as well as to catch the wind. There was plenty of storage space for food and water. It sounded simple, yet it had taken him ten heartbreaking years to complete.

Suddenly, Peter stopped talking and cocked his head, as if hearing something. We both listened, but discerned nothing. I started to speak, but Peter motioned me to silence. We waited, and then I too was aware of its presence. It was—a low humming noise, the same that I had heard in Mogara!

"It is the Hour!" Peter announced, and he sighed deeply, as if everything had suddenly been taken from him. Adara grabbed my arm and held it tightly.

"It is over, Ro-lan," she said, resignedly. "Please remember me always, and know that I loved you dearly."

"Adara, please, don't talk like that!" I pleaded. "Nothing will happen to you. I will see to that. Peter, please tell her!"

"Come, we must go," said Peter, trance-like. "It is the Hour."

They exited the house, and I had no choice but to follow. Outside, people were hurrying toward one of the four obelisks, but their movements were more controlled than those of the Mogars. As we neared the closest obelisk I saw Ter-ek and Aleen, but they seemed not to know me. The hum grew louder every second. The red door was open, and the Homarus filed down the stairs in an orderly fashion. I held on to Adara and Peter, so that we would not become separated.

The stairway plunged into the earth for some distance before reaching the underground chamber, which was huge. Countless people were already on their knees, lined against the wall. We stopped about twenty feet from the foot of the stairs. The two of them knelt down, and I followed suit. Ter-ek and Aleen were close by. As the large door creaked shut above us, I knew that the last Homaru had entered this chamber.

I gazed at my beloved and her grandfather, realizing that it would be futile to attempt communications with them. Despite all their apparent strength and intelligence, they were still affected by this strange power. I wondered why I was not. As I dwelled on this the humming noise, by this time ear-shattering, stopped. All around me the peoples' eyes widened as they knelt in the midst of the silence. It remained that way for long minutes, until a series of new sounds pierced the air. There were screams, moans, pathetic wails, and—a mocking laugh. The asylums of past days, meant to hide the sick rather than help them, surely must have sounded like the chamber of horror far below Var-Dor did that night.

For nearly ten minutes the blood-chilling noises continued, and after a while they did begin to affect me. It was not hard to understand why these people, conditioned as they were since childhood, could fall under the spell of this madness. I was holding Adara's hand but, unaware of me as she was, her own was limp. My nerves were shaken, and I was starting to feel very much alone amidst the multitude.

Suddenly, high above, the door flew open, admitting the throbbing red light of the obelisk, which glowed with an eerie luminescence. A strong wind seemed to escape from the chamber through the portal, whistling as it made its continuous exit. As one, the Homarus bent their heads down until they touched the ground. The terrible sounds had increased in intensity, but the loudest of all was that horrid, mocking laugh. I felt on the verge of snapping, but somehow I rose to my feet and glanced around, trying to understand, trying to comprehend this nightmare.

From the far end of the chamber a young woman arose, and slowly, silently, she began to move toward the stairs. As she passed me I saw the blank, witless expression on her face. I noticed something else too: though she was moving, her legs were not. It was as though—as though she glided above the floor! She reached the foot of the stairs and rose upward, much in the same manner. In seconds she had disappeared through the opening, while the insane laughter continued.

A second young woman met a similar fate, quitting the chamber in the same manner. None of the Homarus had even seen them, their heads buried as they were. I should have done something, but I was frozen where I stood. It was only when the third woman rose up that I felt compelled to take action, for that woman was Aleen! She floated past me, and I went to grab her, but I was now physically unable to move, for my legs were paralyzed. Frantically I shouted at Ter-ek, hoping that the departure of his wife would force him to act, but he did not move, nor did he even look up. As Aleen disappeared above, I grieved inwardly for both her and Ter-ek. The cackle seemed to mock me even more.

Shortly after Aleen had gone, the laughing stopped. The other sounds abated, though they were still audible. Although I could see nothing, hear nothing, I sensed a presence in the chamber. I knew it was there, but I could not begin to understand how I knew. It permeated the chamber, studying all who were gathered there. As it reached me, I could feel my skin prickle. It was all around me, and it seemed to linger there. I felt myself losing control; for the slightest part of a second I was on the ground near the obelisk, and I was looking down into the opening at the scene on the floor of the chamber. It was then that I understood what was happening: The presence was trying to enter my brain! It wished to learn my thoughts. Desperately, through sheer power of will, I fought to ward it off. I knew that, at all cost, *I must keep it out!*

Moments later I had regained control of my thoughts, though the effort had weakened me considerably. I doubted whether I would be able to withstand another assault, but fortunately I did not have to, for I felt the presence moving away. That it was still nearby I was sure, for suddenly I saw Ter-ek's head jerked off the ground, as if he had received a severe shock. His eyes bulged, his fists clenched and unclenched as he fought a losing battle with the presence. For nearly a minute he jerked spasmodically from side to side. Two times he fell forward, his head smashing against the hard ground. At no time did he leave his knees.

When it was over, Ter-ek slumped to the ground in a heap. I wanted to assist him, but I was still unable to move. The presence was floating again, and it seemed to gravitate to the opening above. Soon, I knew that it was gone from the chamber. Slowly the Homarus began to raise their heads. Dreamlike, they focused their eyes on the opening. The weird sounds, which had quieted, were once again louder, and the mocking laugh resumed.

"Roland Summers!" a voice called, and I knew that it came from no one in the chamber. It was a hollow, monotonic voice, and it emanated from above. It mingled with the shrieks and moans behind it, and it made my skin crawl.

"Roland Summers!" it repeated. "You are not of Boranga. I am so pleased that you are here. We will have much to talk about when next we meet. You are strong of will. It was only through your friend that I learned of you."

"Who are you?" I shouted. "Why can I not see you? Do you wish not to be seen?"

"Who am I?" the voice shrieked. "Have you not been here a sufficient time to know? I am Ras-ek Varano! I am the Master of Boranga! An entire world cringes in the dirt from the thought of me. They fear to whisper my name, for they may be struck down where they stand. They would unhesitatingly kill another who mentions it. You ask who I am, fool? Then see me, and know me!"

The wind blew sharply through the chamber while the red glow from the obelisk intensified. Gelid

195

fingers entered my flesh. From above, a head appeared. At first it seemed normal in size, although it was detached from the body that it belonged to. It moved through the air in a slow, circular motion. As I watched it the head grew, and the aura that surrounded it brightened. The Homarus once again placed their heads on the ground, and their bodies trembled.

This strange, light-enshrouded countenance now filled the entire chamber. Its glow made gazing at it difficult, but I studied the face as best I could. I read malevolence in its piercing eyes, both of which burned like red-hot coals. It was an ageless face, neither young or old, with a small, pointy nose and thick lips, these curled back as it grinned wickedly. On its head sat a silver turban. The ears were partially hidden by the headdress, but signs of deformity were evident.

"Do you see me, Roland Summers?" Ras-ek Varano screamed. "Do you not fear what you see?"

I admit now that I was terrified, but at the time I gave no thought to it. I was just as curious to know what was going on, and I defiantly questioned the thing.

"Why do you keep me paralyzed?" I asked. "Surely you do not fear me."

"Had you interfered with the women you would have died," he shrieked. "I wished to learn of you, and so chose to preserve you. You may move."

I was free, and my first thought was for Ter-ek. As I moved toward him, I heard the Master scream. "You fool! Never do you ignore the Master when he speaks to you! Your friend is unharmed. I merely borrowed his brain for a short while." His tone quieted down. "Now, I will invite you formally to visit me at Sekkator. I wish to know much, as I'm sure you do. You will be a welcome guest, and will find the hospitality on the Other Side most refreshing. Come, Roland Summers, and join me."

"I am not ready to leave Var-Dor at this time," I told him, rebelliously.

The face twisted into a mask of rage as he absorbed my reply, and the flaming eyes bore through me. The dirge-like noises in the background rose, while the aura burned brighter. Soon I was unable to look directly at him, and I covered my eyes.

"I shall release the demons of the underworld into your soul!" he shrieked. "I will see Ama burn the flesh slowly from your body! I . . . !" His tone altered once more, and the brightness abated. "No, I must expect this from one like you. Your kind must be fascinating. Yes, you *will* join me, Roland Summers. Soon your only thought will be to reach Sekkator, though you will find it far more difficult than had you simply accepted my invitation. You need a cause, a purpose, and you shall have one. Yes, you *shall* have one."

He cackled demonically, a blood-freezing sound. The accompanying noises rose again, all blending in a chorus of insanity. The head grew smaller and smaller, until it was merely a speck of light that contrasted with the blackness of the Borangan night, visible through the opening above. Then it was gone, but its laughter remained. For a moment all was as it had been before; then, once again, it spoke: "The Hour grows short, Roland Summers, and I must take leave of my beloved Homarus. I await you on the Other Side, and I almost wish that you could make it there, though of course you will not. Pity. Farewell, Roland Summers. I daresay that you shall remember this night."

His mad laugh resounded through the chamber once more, and now I began to understand what he had meant: Adara, my dear one, had risen to her feet and began to glide slowly toward the stairs! Once more my arms and legs were paralyzed, and although I struggled mightily, my efforts were futile.

"Save her, Roland Summers," a voice from above cackled. "Go ahead, try and stop her!"

I started after her, but my legs moved as though bound by leaden weights. Always did she remain just out of reach. The insane laughter taunted me, tortured me as I grabbed helplessly for her. Although the stairs were only twenty feet away, it seemed like minutes before I could reach them. When I did, Adara was once more out of reach, inches above my head. I started up the stairs, but with each step I took the preceding stair dropped into the ground. I was unable to climb them, and my beloved was drifting further away.

"Adara!" I screamed. "Don't let him take you! Fight it, please! You can do it! Break the spell with your mind!"

As I watched her, I saw her head turn slowly. She looked down at the floor of the chamber and saw me. The zombie-like expression on her face altered into a look of stark terror as she realized what was happening.

"*Ro-lan!* Oh Ro-lan, please help me!" she screamed

pitifully, her cries nearly wrenching my heart out. "Don't let him take me, Ro-lan! Grandfather, please help me! Grandfather! Ro-lan, *please!*"

Her hands were held out to me pleadingly, but I stood there, helpless. Adara was three quarters of the way up, and though cognizant of her dilemma, was unable to stop herself. As I stood watching her, a figure raced by me and began acscending the stairs. It was Peter! The pleas of his granddaughter had broken the spell, and he was attempting to save her. The Master had not foreseen any resistance from the docile Homarus, and was not prepared for it.

"Adara, I'm coming!" Peter screamed, climbing the stairs. The laughter ceased as the Master absorbed the scene. Peter was more than half-way up when he suddenly clutched his chest. Gasping for breath he fell down the stairs, landing at my feet. Adara saw him and screamed. It was the last thing she witnessed before she disappeared through the opening. Seconds later, the door slammed shut. The mad cacophony had stopped, and the Homarus were getting to their feet. I saw that Ter-ek was rising with them. Hastily I bent over to examine Peter, but he was dead. I grieved deeply for this wonderful old man who had given his life trying to save Adara. That she witnessed his fall before she disappeared would be torture for her, for she could not guess his fate.

Knowing that Peter was beyond my help I started up the stairs, but was restrained by a strong hand on my arm. It was Tor-en, the captain of the guard. I grabbed his wrist and tore his arm away from me."

"For God's sake, man," I shouted, "I've got to get up there! They've taken Adara! And you, Ter-ek.

They've taken Aleen! Don't you care at all? Don't you want her back?"

"There is nothing we can do, Ro-lan," he replied, his eyes averted to the floor. "It is the Master's will. You must not interfere."

"He already has interfered," Tor-en yelled, "and for that he must be punished, lest the Master be angry with us for harboring him. Take him!"

I leaped up the stairs, but Tor-en grabbed my ankle and pulled me to the ground, where four Homarus, including Ter-ek jumped on me. I kicked and punched frantically at them, injuring two, but more took their place.

"Fools!" I screamed. "Ignorant, superstitious fools! Can you stand by and watch your women taken like that? You are intelligent people. You can fight that thing, or at least die honorably in the attempt. I am not afraid to challenge the Master. I will journey to the Other Side, and attempt to save the one I love. Who will join me? What about you, Ter-ek? Your Aleen has been taken. Would you not sacrifice your life for her? How could you let this happen? Col-in was a sick old man, yet he died attempting to rescue his granddaughter. Learn a lesson from one such as him, you brave Homarus!"

Ter-ek's grip loosened, for he was beginning to waver. But Tor-en shouted: "Silence him! Silence him now, before he can speak more words such as these! Lar-ek will decide what to do with him later, but for now he must be silenced!"

A Homaru withdrew an ax from his belt. I struggled wildly, managing to kick him in the face. Once again all hell broke loose as my violent rage gave me a strength heretofore unknown. I grabbed the ax from the felled one's hand and leaped to my feet, swinging aimlessly. I was able to cleave the skull of one, and the rest backed off. I moved slowly toward the stairs, watching them closely.

"Cowards! All of you are fools and cowards! Never have I seen—!"

My words were silenced as I stumbled backwards over the body of Peter. My head struck the stairs, dazing me. The Homarus swarmed over me, and with a blow from the blunt end of an ax, I remembered no more.

CHAPTER THIRTEEN

THE VALE OF FEAR

What a difference a day can make! The previous morning, I was an honored guest of the Homarus. My new bride had been in my arms when I awoke, and the busy day that I had spent, both with Adara and the warriors, had been enjoyable. The evening with Peter Collins had been, as usual, a pleasure. Yes, that was all yesterday. This morning I woke up, or rather, came to, a prisoner of the Homarus. My beloved had been taken by the apparition known as Ras-ek Varano, and Peter Collins—lay dead.

At first, I thought that I was still in the same underground chamber of the previous night, but a cursory scan showed me to be in error. Although similar, this room did not have a stairway. A rope ladder hung down from the opening, but it was far out of my reach. A man was peering down from above, and as I stared upward I was sure that the opening was much further from the ground than the other had been. I guessed that this chamber served solely as a place of incarceration.

The daylight that filtered in from above afforded me the opportunity to explore the chamber. It was warm and dank here, suggesting the presence of water nearby, but I was unable to discover any. The chamber was about seventy-five feet long, its width varying from fifteen to twenty feet. The stone walls were bare with the exception of a number of unlit torches which hung on them. The dirt floor was covered in various places by torn, not-too-clean straw mats. There seemed to be no other egress other than the hole far above. Indeed, this was a prison!

My explorations proving fruitless, I sat down dejectedly on one of the filthy mats. My head ached terribly from the blow of the previous night, and I was weak. I did not plan on staying here long, and I knew that I must rest in order to build up enough strength for an escape. I had no idea what Adara's fate might be, but if she had been taken to the Other Side, then my goal was clear. Somehow I would get out of Var-Dor, though the chances of that seemed poor at the moment.

I laid on the floor of the prison chamber for what must have been hours, alternating between sleeping and staring at the opening. I must have dozed off for a moment when the Homaru began descending the rop ladder, for he was more than halfway down before I noticed him. He released the lower portion of the ladder, which fell to the floor. Motioning for me to stay where I was, he negotiated the rest of the ladder. No words were spoken as he removed a leather pouch from his back and laid it on the floor, all the time eyeing me carefully. Far above, another guard observed the proceedings.

The Homaru, a stranger to me, had completed his assignment, and now scampered quickly up the ladder, hauling up the lower part behind him. Again he refastened it, and then continued his ascent, until he disappeared through the hole. The other guard watched me for a few more seconds, and then his head also vanished. I scooped up the parcel, pleased to discover that it contained food and water, and for the next hour I ate and drank very slowly. More and more I could feel my strength returning, and for this I was glad.

Shortly after I finished the repast, I noticed that it was getting dark. I had been unconscious longer than I thought, and must have come to in the middle of the afternoon. Soon I was unable to see anything, the light from the fires of Var-Dor unable to penetrate these depths. I sat in the dark and mulled over my predicament. The two people most dear to me were both in terrible danger. I knew that I must seek Adara, but what of Denny? Even if the Council kept him alive until the Homarus came, what would his fate be here in Var-Dor? Ter-ek knew of his background, as did Heran and Dovan. Would they not find it simple to kill him rather than cure him, so that any further incidents could be avoided? Should I try and rescue my friend first, and then go after Adara? True, it would upset the plans of the Council, but what did I care now for the problems of these people? My only thoughts were for Adara and Denny.

In considering my plight, I realized that the

journey to the Other Side would take many days. Each day would increase the fears in my already tortured mind as I tried to visualize Adara's plight. I would lose more time if I journeyed to Mogara, and the chances were great that I would lose my life attempting the rescue. It was likely that my fate would be no different if I headed north, but I knew that it was there I must go, for my life would be worthless without her. I hoped that somehow, some way, Denny would understand.

Hours later, I paced restlessly back and forth in the stygian darkness, unable to sleep. The night had brought out the other inhabitants of the chamber, large, cricket-like beetles that chirruped loudly, the sound echoing off the chamber walls until I thought that it would drive me mad. I must have crushed hundreds of them beneath my feet, but still they came, from where I could not perceive. They were fearless devils, and I was kept busy brushing them off my legs. One of them managed to escape my scrutiny longer than the others, and I yelped as it bit me on my right calf. It was apparent that there would be no rest for me that night. My only hope was to sleep during the next day, and attempt escape during the dark hours. I was still at a loss for ideas as to how I might undertake this.

A torch appeared above, and I could see some one descending. I stood directly below the hole, and the rope ladder dropped only inches from me. Desperation now guided my actions as I grabbed hold of the rope and shook it vigorously. The torch clattered to the floor as my unknown visitor tried to keep from losing his hold. I hoped that whatever noise was made would be inaudible to anyone without. I continued shaking the precarious ladder, until I heard a voice.

"Ro-lan, it is I, Ter-ek! Please stop this! I must talk to you!"

I released the ladder, though why I did I could not say. Was this man not my enemy? Did he not choose to assist in my capture the night before, when he might have helped me? No, I owed him nothing. Yet I recalled the friendship that had grown since he first saved my life along the Otongo. I could not destroy him. He reached the floor of the chamber and retrieved his torch, while I turned my back on him.

"You choose not to talk to me, and I understand," he said quietly, "so I will ask you to listen to what I must say. Last night, I felt shame for the first time in my life, and I have been tormented by it ever since. You faced the Master last night and you defied him, even though it would have meant your death. Since childhood I have cringed before him, as have all the Homarus. Never do we challenge or question, but simply bear our yokes of slavery. Our women are taken, and we accept it. To question is to die, and as many die at the hands of my own people as by those of the Master. Lar-ek has decreed your own death, and for the first time I realize the unjustness of it. You are to die because you are a brave man who only wishes to recover that which he loves most. My own Aleen is taken from me, and I do nothing. You asked me last night if a man should not sacrifice himself for his beloved, and I tell you now, Ro-lan, that the answer is yes!

"I most probably will die for what I do tonight, if

206

not for what I say. It matters not, for I owe you this much, and more. I will help you to escape from Var-Dor tonight, so that you might seek your Adara. If I am not discovered, I will journey to Mogara and make sure that no harm befalls your friend. I swear this with my life. Please believe me, Ro-lan."

I turned and faced Ter-ek, noting the sincerity in his demeanor. I placed my arm on his shoulder, and he responded in a like manner. He then motioned me toward the farthest part of the chamber, and I followed. At the wall he dropped to his knees, where he appeared to be measuring something from the ground up. Satisfied that he had found what he sought, he made an indentation on the wall and stood up.

"After I depart, begin digging as quietly as possible where I have left a mark," he instructed, handing me a small knife. "Do not worry, the wall is not solid. Once through, you will see an underground stream below you, and you will follow its flow. You will be able to keep your head above water most of the way, but at one point the stream disappears under some rocks. It will be necessary to swim underwater for a short time, but I believe that you can make it. Shortly after you have surfaced, you will see your knapsack on a small bank to your left. It is well provisioned. Near it, you will find easy access to the forest. The direction in which you face as you leave the tunnel is the one that you will travel in to reach the Other Side. It will take six days to reach the Vale of Fear. If all goes well, I will follow in your path after my return from Mogara. I too have lost something that I wish to recover. I must go now, or they will question my tardiness."

"Ter-ek—"

"Do not speak, Ro-lan. It is imperative that I return. I know not if we shall ever see one another again. You have shown me what it is to really be a man, and I am proud to call you my friend. Good luck, Ro-lan. If you reach the Other Side, tell Aleen that I come for her. Tell her this for me. Convince her to fight the will of the Master, as you convinced Adara and Col-in. Goodbye, my friend." With these words, Ter-ek ascended the ladder in haste. Moments later, he was gone.

The opportunity that I had hoped for was now at hand, and I felt much relieved. I returned to the far wall and began digging cautiously with the knife. The wall started falling away in large pieces. Fearing investigation due to the noise, I slowed my efforts, pulling each chunk away by hand. In about fifteen minutes I had torn through nearly three feet of wall, and I was rewarded with the sound of rushing water. I now concentrated on widening the hole, until I was sure that I could pass my body through. In the excitement I had forgotten about the beetles, but a few stinging bites from them served to alert me.

I crawled through the small tunnel until my head protruded from the other side, and I looked down. The rushing stream was only a few feet below me. I pulled myself through and lowered my body into the icy water. Although narrow, the stream was very deep, and I was unable to touch bottom. I kept my head above water and let the current carry me for a while, trying to preserve my strength for when I needed it. I found passage easy for the first ten minutes or so.

The rocks that Ter-ek had spoken of now loomed directly in front of me, the water disappearing beneath them. The force that pulled the water below was great, and I knew that I must prepare for the quick submergence. I breathed deeply a number of times, filling my lungs with air. Only yards away, I took one more long, deep breath; then the water sucked me under.

I swam as close as I dared to the rocks, being especially careful not to crack my head on them. My eyes were open, though the water was quite murky. The current remained steady, but I did not rely on it alone, for I had no idea how long I would have to be submerged. I swam as quickly as the situation would allow, but after about two minutes I felt my lungs beginning to strain. I felt overhead quickly, but the rocks were still there. The exertions were making my lungs scream for air. Perhaps this was the death sentence placed on me by the Homarus, although it was inconceivable that Ter-ek could be guilty of deceit.

I now began to release the air that I had stored in my lungs. Only seconds remained before I would drown. During my last frantic movements I raised my hand up, and this time it met no resistance. I paddled upward at a slight angle, feeling above me. Nothing was there to impede my progress, and at the last possible instant my head surfaced. Gratefully I sucked in the clear, beautiful air. My heart pounded rapidly, as if it wished to escape from my chest. Whether this was from my exertions or my fright I could not say.

The current was gentler on this side, and I floated leisurely down the stream. A narrow bank appeared on my left, and soon I spotted my knapsack lying on it, about a hundred feet from where I had broken the surface. Ter-ek was as good as his word, and I felt ashamed that I had doubted him. I pulled myself from the stream and reclined next to the knapsack, exhausted. While resting I examined the contents, which consisted primarily of food, water, and weapons. Two hand axes were included, one of them being my own, the other a fine duplication.

I drank my fill of water from the stream, leaving the canteen in my knapsack full. Cool air was entering the tunnel from a small opening over my head, and I knew that this was the way out. I donned the knapsack and pulled myself through the hole, this depositing me in a small cave. I followed it for a few moments, and after turning a corner I was breathing the crisp night air of the Borangan forest. I was still close to Var-Dor, so without hesitation I set off straight ahead, as Ter-ek had instructed. My destination being the Other Side, I could only assume that I journeyed north.

For the rest of that night I traipsed past the giant trees of the still forest, the silence broken only occasionally by the shrill cry of a bird. Visibility was limited by the clouds hiding the two moons, but the sparsity of the flora made the going fairly easy. I felt strong, my purpose, perhaps, giving me additional strength, and I was determined not to rest until the next night. Ter-ek had said that it would take six days to reach the Vale of Fear, but I desired to get there in less time than that.

Daybreak found the landscape changed but little. I continued on all day, stopping briefly just twice for food and water. Not until many hours after dark did I sleep, and I resumed my journey at the first hint of light. A second long, uneventful day brought me to the base of an enormous sequoia, where I paused for a few hours' rest.

Some time during the next two days the trees disappeared, and once again I found myself traveling over a barren tundra, pocked with broken rocks and dry shrubs. As I rested on the fourth night near a small pond, I felt fortunate that I had encountered no difficulties. I was sure that the Vale of Fear was not far, that I might reach it the next day. That I relished the thought seemed ludicrous, since nobody had ever survived the unspeakable place; yet I did not fear it.

I was asleep, but deep within my subconscious I heard the low, humming sound, and I immediately knew what it was. This time, it rose quickly to its ear-shattering pitch, for it did not have to wait for the exodus of hundreds, thousands of subservient beings to reach their chambers. It was meant for me, for me alone.

"Roland Summers!"

I woke with a start and leaped to my feet, clutching my hand ax. The still night air was charged with electricity, and as I jerked my head from side to side to locate the source of the voice, I discerned the unbearable chorus that had permeated the underground chambers of Var-Dor. Then the laughter began, and the malevolent countenance of Ras-ek Varano appeared, growing larger in the sky above me.

"I applaud your tenacity," the hollow, mocking voice spoke. "You have come a long way, and still you do not hesitate, you do not turn back."

"I have no intention of turning back," I announced, "not until I have recovered that which was taken from me. You may kill me, but I still do not fear you."

"Kill you? Oh, no, I would not think of it," said Ras-ek, his tone sugary. "You are much too interesting for that. If you die before you reach me, it will be of your own doing. I am only sorry that you have not truly undergone the rigors of a difficult journey. By late morning tomorrow you will reach the Vale of Fear. However, as much as I wish to witness your passage through the valley, I feel that I must lengthen your trek. Yes, that is what I'll do! Oh, but I wish to get this over with! What should I do?"

As Ras-ek argued with himself, I found myself growing dizzy. My head was spinning, and everything around me, including his evil face, became a blur. I did not stagger around, but instead found myself riveted to one spot. How long this went on I could not tell, but finally my head cleared. The insane chorus was gone, and so was Ras-ek Varano. There was, however, another sound, that of rushing water. I looked around quickly, and the answer, while impossible, stared me in the face. I stood, inexplicably, on the bank of the Otongo, close to the spot where Ter-ek had first found me, countless miles from where I had just been! I should have been terrified, but the only emotion that surfaced was rage, for I had been so near my goal, only to end up here. I screamed loudly, shaking my fist in the air.

"Ras-ek Varano, you cowardly devil! I wish to be back where I was! Surely you do not fear me, a mortal man! I will get you some day, you bastard! I am not afraid of you, or your menagerie! Take me back, you—!"

Once again the dizziness overcame me, and all was blurred. Moments later, I stood alongside the small pond, far to the north. Ras-ek's detached head still floated in the sky above me, but it was smaller than before. His invisible entourage wailed and, amidst cackles, he spoke to me.

"I have decided to let you continue, Roland Summers, for I drool with anticipation to see you attempt the Vale of Fear. You have not been alone on your journey, as I'm sure you now realize. Farewell, Roland Summers. Perhaps we shall meet again on the Other Side. Hee hee hee. Yes, *perhaps!* Hee hee hee!"

The apparition faded amidst maniacal laughter. Soon the deathly silence of the Borangan plain had returned, as if nothing had occurred to break that silence. I slumped to the ground, drained both mentally and physically by the encounter. My sleep was restless and disturbing, filled with the night-marish creations of a depraved mind. Were they my own, or were they Ras-ek's? I did not know.

I slept far past daybreak, and this disturbed me for I had wanted to depart as early as possible. After a quick meal I got under way, and as I walked briskly I dwelled on the occurrences of the night past. Had I really been visited by Ras-ek, or had I dreamed it? Could he have transported me to a place many miles from here? Impossible! Yet—I had been there. I know I had! To what bounds did the powers of this monster extend? Was I the biggest fool in two worlds, to be making this attempt at rescuing Adara? Perhaps—but whatever her fate, I wished to share it with her.

Hours later, I knew that I was nearing my objective. It seemed to be growing darker all about me, even though the searing orb burned brightly, high above the fleecy nimbi. A sinister tenseness permeated the atmosphere, causing me to shudder. As I studied the clouds, I suddenly stumbled over something. I examined the obstacle, finding it to be a thin slab of stone lying flat on the ground. There was writing on it, and, while time had worn the stone considerably, I was able to make out what it said. I had discovered the grave of the long dead Zol-ek, the only man known to have emerged from the Vale of Fear alive.

I stood on the south rim of the valley, likely in the same spot where the eleven brave Homarus first descended. While I should have been able to gaze into the valley, as well as across it to the north edge, I could not. Darkness filled the entire vale, and also hovered atop it; not clouds, not fog, just—darkness! It was as if night had fallen in only a single spot. For the first time since escaping Var-Dor I hesitated, but only for a moment. Somewhere beyond that valley, yes, on the Other Side, was Adara. I could not stop now. I stepped over the rim and began my descent along the slight incline, into the valley below.

Darkness encircled me completely before five steps had been taken. There would be no thought of turning back now, for I had made my commitment.

The first thing I noticed was that, as hazy as it was, I had no difficulty in seeing for some distance ahead. I observed many trees, both small and large, and they were all dead, their rotted, black branches twisted grotesquely. Grass had grown here once in abundance, but the hard, brittle ground offered little evidence of that. All through the air there was an odor, a vile effluvium, the smell of death.

I had descended the south slope about a hundred yards when I saw something ahead that brought me to a halt. It was moving toward me at a brisk pace and from the choking, coughing roar that emanated from its throat, I knew what it was: The Guardian, Tomo Raka, or at least a duplicate of the horror, was approaching. This time, however, it was not limited by the confines of an underground lake. It traveled quickly, albeit awkwardly, on four large, flipper-like feet, each one attached to a short, stubby appendage.

Its size and speed precluding any possibility I might have had to outrun the thing, I decided to stand here and fight it out. Tomo Raka slowed as it neared, and as the wicked eyes studied its potential morsel, it roared and sputtered hideously. I drew both my axes and backed away slowly, my eyes affixed to it. The head swiveled wildly as the beast closed the distance between us. Soon it was only yards away, and its jaws crashed together as it twisted down toward me. I could smell its fetid breath as it neared, and the odor, melded with the rancid smell of the valley, made my stomach turn. I heaved one of the axes at its snout, and in the same motion I leaped to one side, landing on my stomach. The blow winded me for a couple of seconds, but I managed to roll over and jump to my feet, the other ax raised high. To my amazement, the Guardian was gone! Not a trace was left to show that it had even been there.

I moved briskly down the slope, stopping only to retrieve my ax, which had landed harmlessly some twenty yards further down. I dared not even ponder the incident, for already I was beginning to learn what the Vale of Fear was all about, and I still had far to go. The blackened trees were more numerous now, a foreboding forest of death. I maintained a close watch for anything else that might appear, though I questioned whether weapons or skills would be of any use in battling whatever I might encounter in this hellish valley. As I dwelled on the thought, I realized that the ground was now level. I had reached the floor of the Vale of Fear.

The stifling silence was suddenly broken by the pathetic sobs of a woman which seemed to emanate from everywhere. I was unable to discover the source; I called out aloud, but received no answer. For many minutes the sobbing continued, a bitter, heart-rending sound that unnerved me considerably. Finally, when I thought that I could take no more, I espied its author. Twenty-five feet ahead of me, a girl sat on the ground, her face buried in her hands. I called to her and she raised her head. It was . . . *Adara!* She stood up as she saw me, a smile on her face, her arms outstretched. I ran toward her, but I could not shorten the distance. She continued to hold her arms out to me, frustrating me beyond belief.

A figure appeared just behind her, to the right. I strained to catch a glimpse of the face, and saw that it was—Denny! They were both here! He waved at me, a broad grin on his face. I must reach them, I must! But the harder I ran, the further away they seemed. Now there were hundreds of figures across the floor of the valley, all bearing the face and form of either Adara or Denny. Every one beckoned to me, each spoke my name. I stopped for a moment, bewildered. They surrounded me on all sides. I called their names, but no individuals among them responded. I continued on toward the original ones, though I was scarcely able to tell them from the rest.

Suddenly they were gone, all of them! Once more I stood alone amidst the gloom of the vale. Like a wild man I waved an ax in the air, issuing challenges at no one in particular. I charged the nearest tree and hacked at it until nothing remained but a blackened pile of wood chips which I then crushed beneath my feet.

Take hold of yourself, Summers, take hold! What you see here are figments, shadows from your own mind. Perhaps because this is his own ground, Ras-ek has been able to penetrate your thoughts; or, maybe your will was stronger in Var-Dor. You're weakening, and this is not the time for that! Ignore what you see, and continue onward!

Yes, the arguments were clear, but how could I discount what occurred? I *had* seen Adara and Denny; I *was* attacked by the Guardian. How could I deny this. But . . . what was I hearing now? It sounded like—an automobile engine! It was distant at first, but then it grew louder, louder. There it was, a sleek, black '47 Buick with a long running board and a fancy, rearing horse on the hood. *It was my parents' car!* Mom was on the passenger's side, and I could clearly see her ever-present blue hat. She smiled as she waved to me, but I was unable to move. Dad, ever the careful driver, had his eyes glued to the road ahead, but he did manage a quick glance in my direction, and I knew that he was grinning.

I heard something else, a loud roar that all but drowned out the sound of the Buick's engine. From the other direction came a broken-down truck, a farm vehicle. The back of it was loaded with bales of straw. It weaved from side to side as it rolled along at high speed, the driver undoubtedly drunk. Head on toward the Buick it sped, while Mom continued to wave at me. I tried to cry out, but the sound stuck in my throat. Closer, closer the two vehicles came, until the air was shattered by the crash of tons of steel involuntarily merging, and the futile, final screech of brakes. I faced the heavens, and now the screams came. For minutes I shrieked wildly, until reason took hold once again, if only temporarily.

The vehicles were gone from the spot of the collision. In their place were two gravestones and a hospital bed. I could read the inscriptions on the stones: *Mary Summers, 1904-1948; Richard Summers, 1902-1948*. In the bed lay Virgil Willis, the drunken farmer, the survivor of the crash. Through the swath of bandages that covered most of his body I could see the grin on his face. His left arm, only slightly injured, was raised feebly, and he waved at me. I lifted an ax and heaved it at him; it lodged deeply in his chest. He clutched at it, screaming. The bandages were now gone, and I saw that it was not Virgil Willis who grasped the haft but—*Peter Collins!* His eyes looked at me questioningly, as if trying to understand why I was killing him.

I began to run; I did not know which direction I raced in, nor did I care. Again, the laughter began, the insane cackling, and the moaning chorus. My audience was undoubtedly enjoying the show. On and on I went, blindly. I stumbled over rotted logs, but these proved only a temporary hindrance as I continued my mad rush.

Suddenly I no longer ran, but instead was falling. I had stepped into a satong trap, one dug to capture the beasts alive. Far below me I could see two of them at the bottom, exhorting me with their shrieks and roars to arrive quickly so that they might tear me apart. The wind whistled past me as I fell, but I seemed to make little progress in my descent. I fell for long minutes, until finally I was only inches above their heads. The veins on their bloated skulls flared brilliantly as they anticipated the carnage. Hands clutched at me; I kicked and flailed wildly with my feet. My descent was then checked, and once more I lay on the floor of the valley, listening to the ungodly sounds of my gleeful hosts.

I started forward again, this time slowly, for I had become numb to all that was happening to me. Had my mind truly snapped? If not, then why was I laughing? I was walking uphill now, my trek through the valley nearly over, but I did not care. My body shook as I roared with laughter, and I finally had to sit down on the incline to compose myself. I raised my left hand to wipe the tears from my eyes, when I noticed something crawling on my wrist. It was a white grub, a hideous little devil. I brushed it off, only to see two more of them on my right hand. I rose quickly, the laughter now forgotten. Hundreds, thousands of the vermin covered my body up to my waist. Frantically I brushed them off, but it seemed to make no difference. They covered my chest, my arms, until finally they were on my face. I closed my eyes to protect them, and ran blindly up the hill.

Through the verminous cloak, I became aware of standing ankle-high in water. Deeper, deeper in I went, until the water was over my head. I shook my body vigorously to free it from the insects and, after surfacing, found that they had disappeared. The body of water was a small pond, and the cool liquid was refreshing. I started to trudge the ten feet back to shore when the pond began to churn. Soon I was knee-deep in bubbling quicksand, unable to move. I struggled futilely, and began to sink. Adara stood at the edge of the pit, throwing kisses to me. At her feet was a coil of rope. I screamed at her to throw it, and she complied. The end fell just inches from my right hand but, as I grabbed for it, the rope reared and snapped at my fingers. I was looking into the fangs of a huge snake! Quickly I withdrew my hand, disgusted. I heard Adara laugh, but when I looked for her she was gone.

The reptile slithered away and disappeared, leaving me alone in the quicksand which soon swallowed me completely. I felt strangely euphoric as I sank downward, as if the warm ooze that engulfed my body was comforting me. For minutes I descended the shaft of mud, until finally I was dropped from it, and I struck the ground with a violent jolt. I was on the hillside once more.

What would be left of me by the time I exited this

vale of horror was open to conjecture, but I continued up the hill nonetheless. Even the appearance of Ras-ek Varano could not slow me down. He leered at me, but did not speak. Behind him, his entourage made their first appearance. There were men, women, and even children, all floating ethereally behind the Master. Their twisted faces were alternately masks of pain, pleasure, horror, insane joy, and the grotesque sounds emanating from their throats reflected each emotion. Some were cowled, though most were not. All were staring at me, but I averted my own eyes. They fell in behind me and followed me up the hill.

Ahead of me, slightly to my left, stood a sacrificial altar. Adara lay on this slab, her hands tied, while Oleesha stood over her with a long dagger. The princess grinned wickedly at me as I passed, while Adara screamed my name. The wails of the ghostly entourage rose as Oleesha plunged the dagger three times into Adara's heart. I kept my eyes straight ahead, and did not look back.

My mother held my father's head in her lap as he lay on the hillside, unconscious. Blood was trickling down the side of his face. Mom cried uncontrollably and held her hand out to me, begging my assistance. Ophira suddenly appeared behind them, a squat Mogar accompanying her. The queen barked out orders to the underling; he raised his barbed spear and brought it down with great force toward my mother's back. I continued to fight the torment, and my pace quickened.

Closer! I must be getting closer! Somehow I could sense the end of the valley nearby. I must hold out; I cannot break! Only a little further now. No, not Adara again! She appeared to the right of me, and was running from something, or some one. There, behind her! It was Ter-ek! There was a malicious grin on his face. In a few strides he caught up to her, and he grabbed her. She screamed, and tried to break away, but her clothes were torn from her body. Ter-ek snatched at her arm and flung her to the ground. He then leaped atop the tortured beauty and began to ravage her! She screamed pitifully . . .

I climbed over the rim of the north slope. The spectral chorus was gone, as was the darkness. I had emerged from the Vale of Fear. In front of me stood two elders, a man and a woman. They smiled benignly at me, but I stared at them blankly. The woman spoke: "Welcome, Ro-lan," she said, in a delightful voice. "We have been expecting you, haven't we, Vor-an?"

"Indeed we have," the man chirped. "Azena and I have been looking forward to your arrival for some time."

"Azena?" I replied, absently.

"Yes," said the old woman. "I am Azena, she who cared for your dear wife when she was first born. We—"

"*No!*" I shrieked, my control now gone. *Nooooo-oo! You're not real, you're figments of my mind! I'm mad; you're mad! Get away from me, or I'll tear you to pieces. I'll tear you to pieces! Noooo-oo!*"

I leaped to the ground at their feet and began pounding my head into the hard earth. Vor-an grabbed my shoulders and tried to stop me. Evidently he was real. I continued to strike myself, the two elders no match for the strength of a madman. The last speck of rational thought left in my mind before blackness engulfed me was this: the Vale of Fear had once again claimed another victim.

CHAPTER FOURTEEN

THE OUTPOST OF THE AGED

The woman's back was turned toward me, and I could not see the expression on her face, but I heard the noises clearly. Throaty mewling sounds were coming, I could only assume, from her lips. Although sounds of contentment, they changed occasionally to squeals of surprise and anger. She rocked on her heels, both hands held high above her head. In each there was a flat rock, and these were smashed together at regular intervals.

Behind her, the old man lay prostrate on the floor, silent. The woman leaned over and smashed the rocks together near his head. He rose to all fours with a start, and growled at her. She retreated a bit, and he commenced shaking his entire body, like an animal throwing off the last vestiges of sleep. With his final stretch he eyed me, and he emitted a low, husky roar. He moved toward me slowly, stealthily, as if stalking his prey. He was only yards from me when his motion was halted by something thrown in his path, apparently by the woman. The object was a rodent of some kind, and it was quite dead. The man pawed it questioningly, turning it over and over. Then, holding it down with his hands, he began to tear small bits of it away with his teeth, chewing each piece slowly.

"Ro-lan, wake up," the sweet voice sang. "You must come out of it now. Everything is going to be fine, I assure you."

"Look, my dear, his eyelids flutter," another voice spoke. "I believe he is going to join us."

"I am so relieved, Vor-an. It has been nearly two days, and he has hardly moved. Oh, how wonderful."

I opened my eyes and saw her bending over me, the expression of motherly concern evident on her face. She smiled at me, and I managed to return it. Behind her, the old man was grinning broadly, his hands clasped together in front of him. I made a feeble attempt to get up, but a thousand rocks crashed mightily upon my head, and I laid back down. The old woman placed her hands on my chest as if to dissuade me from another try, but I needed no further convincing.

"You gave yourself quite a beating when first we saw you," she explained. "You were fortunate that you did not kill yourself. I advise you to lay still, as it will take you a while to recover."

"Wh-where am I?" I asked, feebly.

"Do you not remember?" said the old man. "You passed through the Vale of Fear, and you are now on the Other Side. You are a welcome guest in the home of Azena and Vor-an. We will care for you until the time when you are well enough to resume your travels. You must rest now, to regain your strength."

"N-no, I cannot rest," I gasped. "I must keep going. I must . . ."

My head throbbed mercilessly, and as I put my hands up, I could feel the numerous bandages that encased it. Vor-an held me down while Azena dabbed my lips with a cold, wet cloth. In only moments I was unconscious again.

The sleeping mat was tucked away in the far corner of the spacious room, affording me an overall view. Two figures were rolling around on the floor, engaged in some sort of battle. They hissed and shrieked violently at each other, never resting for a moment. The woman finally gained an advantage, and with a sputtering sound she ran her fingernails down the man's left cheek. He squealed and leaped backwards, feeling with his hand at the blood that trickled from the gash. Angered, he jumped on top of her and began to pummel her with his open palms, growling loudly. The woman shrieked pathetically, trying futilely to divert his blows.

For two more days, I straddled the thin line between life and death. The two old people cared for me constantly until, five days later, I awoke feeling much better. The pain in my head had subsided considerably, and I was able to sit upright for short periods of time. In another day I left the interior of the hut and took short walks, always accompanied by one or the other. My hosts treated me well, and I began to feel like a human being again, though my purpose here was still foremost in my mind. I tried to forget the experiences of recent days but the memories haunted me, both during my waking and sleeping hours.

During my stay, I told Azena and Vor-an my story. They had known of my coming to the Other Side, but knew little else of me, and they found the story fascinating. They were especially saddened to learn of the death of their friend, Peter Collins. I then asked them to tell me all that had happened to them since they last saw Peter. It was Vor-an who spoke.

"There is so little to tell, Ro-lan," he began. "I followed Azena north until I reached the rim of the Vale of Fear. At the grave of Zol-ek I hesitated, but finally I journeyed through the valley. I emerged alive, much as you did, and found my beloved waiting for me. We have settled here, and have been happy ever since. The Master provides for us. We have little wants, little needs. You'll see, Ro-lan. You and Adara will be happy here, I promise you."

No, Vor-an, I thought to myself, I could never be happy in this evil place, nor could Adara. I knew that I must leave here as soon as possible. The two of them were smiling blankly at me, and in a way I was glad that Peter could not know the fate of his once noble friends. As I looked at them the grin vanished from Vor-an's face, and he sat frozen, his eyes glazed. Azena, still smiling, rose to her feet and escorted me outside. It was late afternoon, still quite light. We were about fifteen feet from the house when I began to hear noises emanating from it. The sounds were those of an animal. I wanted to go back and investigate, but Azena held my arm tightly.

Suddenly, she froze. She released my arm and stared upward at the sky, her eyes widened in an expression of stark terror. She moved her head slowly, painfully, until her eyes met mine. Her lips parted, and I heard a voice, but it came from deep within her, and was faint.

"Ro-lan, listen to me, and do not speak," she whispered. "Sometimes, only for seconds, I am what I once was. You must leave today, right now! Find your Adara, and save her. If you cannot, then destroy her, and yourself also, for death would be preferable to this. The madness has come every night that you have been here. Vor-an has tried to destroy you, but I have been able to stop him. I fear, however, that I will not be able to any more. Do not blame him, for it is not of his doing."

Her voice was getting weaker, and I strained to hear her words. The expression on her face grew more pained. She raised her arm and pointed a shaking finger at a clump of dead trees.

"Behind those trees are your weapons and other things," she gasped. "I hid them so that he would not find them. Take them and go, Ro-lan, for time grows short. Listen!" The shrieks and roars from the house were louder now.

"Beware the Holy Ones, Ro-lan!" The voice was nearly inaudible. "Heed this warning! *Beware the Holy Ones! Beware, beware . . . !*"

I held my ear closer to her lips, straining to hear each word. Suddenly I felt a sharp pain, and I realized that she had scratched my face. I jumped back and looked at her. The torment had been replaced by a cunning, malicious grin, and she hissed as she held her hand poised to strike again. I backed up slowly, cautiously, but she did not follow. With a loud squeal she turned quickly and ran to the hut. At the doorway, she turned and stared at me. Although I was now some distance away, I could see that her face again reflected terror and pain. She held her hands out to me pleadingly, and I was able to hear the final words from the Azena within.

"Ro-lan, please kill me!" she cried pitifully. *"Kill us both, pleee-ase!"*

Once more she was like an animal, and she disappeared into the dwelling. Sickened by all that had occurred, I nonetheless wondered if I should go back and help them. Instead, I decided to heed the words of Azena and depart. They had survived here like this for twenty-one years, and I doubted if there was anything that I could do for them now. To kill them was unthinkable to me, and yet I could feel her anguish. Perhaps some day I might be able to help them; perhaps, though I was beginning to doubt it more and more. I dove into the clump of trees and withdrew my gear; then I turned to the northeast and trotted slowly away.

I ran for a few miles, stopping shortly after dark. The night was spent alongside a huge boulder, in the middle of an open meadow. Not the slightest noise disturbed the silence, no animals, no birds, nothing. I used the opportunity to take stock of myself, and was not too pleased with what I found. That the Master had gotten to me was evident, for had I not tried to kill myself after journeying through the Vale of Fear? The lumps protruded prominently from my head, and to this day I still suffer from excruciating headaches. My hands, once steady as rocks, now shook uncontrollably. I continually glanced around me, fearful of every shadow. My sleep was disturbed by constant nightmares. Perhaps death was the only escape from this place. Maybe I would have to destroy myself, and Adara. Maybe . . .

Now I knew that I must be going mad, to think such thoughts! I had come this far, and I still maintained some degree of sanity. I *would* find Adara, and I *would* get her away from here. If there was some way I could rid Boranga of this evil menace, I would do that also. That was the way to think, the *only* way for me to think. I finally succumbed to another night of broken, restless sleep.

Mid-morning found me many miles from the previous night's campsite. My head had ceased pounding, making the journey more comfortable. If not for the abundance of dead trees that surrounded me as I walked, the Other Side would have seemed no different than any other place on Boranga. I had heard nothing further from the Master, though I had been here a week or so. That he knew of my movements I had no doubt. One time, I was certain that he was trying to probe my mind while I walked, but I strengthened my will and fought against him. However, it was impossible to avert this while asleep, and I did not doubt that this had much to do with the constant nightmares that haunted me.

A range of mountains loomed far to the north, and it was toward them that I traveled. They had been visible ever since I reached the Other Side, but it seemed difficult to shorten the distance. I could not be certain that I journeyed in the right direction, but somehow I sensed that I was.

It was early afternoon, and I had stopped for a short rest when I heard a sound, that of a child crying. Remembering all that had occurred in the Vale of Fear I rose slowly, almost disinterestedly, and strolled toward the source of the sound. Fifty feet ahead, amidst a dense clump of dead trees, was a small girl of about eight. She had apparently stumbled, and her foot had become wedged in the gnarled branches of a nearby log. She saw me approach, and held out her hands.

"Please help me," she sobbed. "Oh, please help me!"

"Are you real?" I asked, cautiously.

"Please help me," she cried again, "my foot is caught, and it's bleeding."

Her pathetic pleas made it impossible for me to ignore her. I ran to her side and bent over, noting that her foot was wedged tightly between two thick branches. The bleeding was from a slight, superficial cut. She appeared more afraid than injured, and I was sure that the foot was not broken. I carefully extracted the member from its trap, breaking one of the branches in the process, and then cleaned the small cut which had already stopped bleeding. In a minute she was on her feet, none the worse for wear. She was a pretty child with long, black hair, but there was a dullness about her eyes that was startling.

"You saved me," she chirped, in a delightful voice. "I think I like you."

"Well, thank you," I replied. "I think I like

you too."

"What is your name?" she asked.

"Ro-lan. And yours?"

"Mara," she answered. "Ro-lan is a nice name. I would like to give you a kiss for helping me. Bend over, and I will give you a big kiss."

I did as she asked, and was rewarded with the heel of her foot driven hard into my nose. The blood began to pour from my nostrils as I leaped back, stunned. Mara looked at me as though nothing had happened, and without further word she turned on her heel and strode away. I yelled for the little brat to stop, but she ignored me. Irate, I took off in pursuit of her, doing my best to stanch the flow of blood. Her foot was surely unharmed, for with deceptive speed she was able to maintain a comfortable lead on me. I swore that if I ever caught up with her, I would paddle her backside until she was unable to sit down.

Mara led the chase for nearly a mile, finally slowing down. I slowed also, and examined my nose. The bleeding had stopped, and I did not think it was broken. I wondered why such an incident should surprise me, since the unexpected seemed the rule on Boranga, especially here. Perhaps it was the fact that a small child had performed such an act of cruelty that was disturbing.

The girl was about thirty yards ahead of me, when she disappeared beyond a hillock. Determined to keep her in sight, I quickened my pace. Without pause I raced down the knoll, where I found myself amidst a group of people! There were about eight of them, although others might have occupied the dozen or so small huts that were scattered haphazardly throughout this tiny village. Mara stood ten yards away, clasping the hand of a man who looked to be in his late thirties. They were both smiling at me, as were all the people in the village. I eyed them carefully as they gathered around me, mechanically drawing my ax.

"This is Ro-lan, Father," said Mara cheerfully, pointing at me. "He saved my life in the forest, where I would have died a terrible death. I gave him a big kiss to thank him. Did I do well, Father?"

"You certainly did, Mara," he replied, patting her on the head. "It is well to thank people for such fine favors."

I stared reproachfully at the lying little imp, but her face showed not the slightest bit of deceit. She smiled sweetly at me, but I resolved myself to keep a safe distance away. Her father, meanwhile, let go of her hand and approached me. He looked like a fine fellow, although he exhibited the same dullness in his eyes as his daughter. His hand was raised in greeting.

"Welcome, Ro-lan, welcome to our humble village. I, Zan-ak, wish to thank you for saving my daughter. You have done a fine thing, and we will honor you tonight."

"I didn't save her," I protested. "She was only—"

"You will stay among us for as long as you wish," he continued, seeming not to hear a word I said. "A hut will be prepared for you, so that your privacy will be assured. Falla! Come meet the one who saved your daughter's life."

Falla emerged from a hut. She looked much like Mara would in twenty years or so. Her long hair was disheveled, and her dirty garments were scanty, as were those of all the people here. She ran to Mara until she stood directly in back of her. Inexplicably, she drove her knee into the girl's back, knocking her face down into the ground, all the time grinning broadly. I believed Mara to be injured severely, but she rose to her feet as if nothing had happened, smiling affectionately at her mother.

"There is Ro-lan, Mother," she announced. "He saved my life. Is he not wonderful?"

Falla looked at me and smiled. As she neared, I braced myself for anything. She stopped alongside Zan-ak and dropped to her knees. With her head on my feet, she spoke: "As mother of the beloved daughter that you have saved, it is my privilege to initiate the honors which you so richly deserve. A feast will be prepared, and you will be the guest of honor. Thank you, Ro-lan, for saving my daughter."

With her last words, she sank her teeth into my right ankle. I yelped in pain and kicked her away, but the others were upon me immediately. They praised and welcomed me, all the while biting, kicking, and punching me. Cries arose, shouts of "Feast of Honor!" and "Ro-lan, our welcome guest!" sounding amidst the bedlam. By sheer numbers they overwhelmed me and brought me to the ground. I was sure that they would kill me, but instead I was dragged to a nearby tree and bound to it. I ached badly in many places, and I bled profusely from a nasty gash on my cheek.

After tying me they backed off, and I was able to have my first good look at these people. Aside from Zan-ak, Falla, and Mara, all the others, fifteen in all, were incredibly old. Two of them, a man and a woman, were already rolling on the ground, gibbering incoherently and foaming at the mouth. The others, including Mara and her mother, were all experiencing lesser degrees of madness, though it was apparent that they would soon join the others on the ground. Zan-ak stood quietly and watched his people, smiling happily. I tried to reason with him, but it was no use. He seemed not to hear anything I said.

"Oh, Master, you have chosen to honor our Outpost of the Aged with such a guest as Ro-lan," said Zan-ak dreamily, as he faced the mountains. "I, the Keeper, thank you, as do all your kuta here. *Noma Kuto Boranga, Noma Kuto Boranga!*"

In ecstasy, Zan-ak ran to the nearest person, a writhing old woman, and with a mighty kick he caved in the crone's skull. Joined by five or six others he leaped on the body, and together they tore it to shreds. Though sickened by this orgy of insanity before me, I was also fascinated, and I kept my eyes glued. All the people were on the ground now, some moaning quietly, some striking their heads on the earth, some fighting with others, all quite mad. The most pitiful sight of all, however, was that of Mara, the girl, sharing the stage with the other maniacs. She had pounced on the dismembered arm of the crone, and was beating it violently into the ground, her mouth foaming like a rabid dog.

After what seemed like hours, the sickness abated. Seven of the old people were dead and dismembered, the rest lie panting like dying animals. Mara slept next to her mother and father, clutching a bloody arm much as another child would hold a doll. I had puked a dozen times since this began and, although I had nothing left, I continued to retch uncontrollably. What I had seen in the Vale of Fear was illusion, but this was real, this was very real! Never, for as long as I live, could I forget the sight of that little girl lying so calmly with a dismembered arm. I prayed that death would quickly release me from this scene.

One of the old men nearest me began to stir. He started crawling feebly toward me, chattering incoherently. When he reached me, he sat up; then, may God help me, he started gnawing on my leg! I screamed at him, but I was helpless to do anything. As he gnawed absently, I realized that he was toothless and incapable of doing much damage. However, the sucking, slobbering noises that he made were disgusting, and I began to choke again.

Zan-ak arose suddenly, as if shaken from a deep sleep. He took four steps and dropped to his knees, his head lowered, facing north. After a couple of minutes he chanted *"Noma Kuto Boranga"* three times, and rose. At the spot where the fiends had first felled me, he gathered up my ax and my knapsack. He approached the tree, stopping in front of me, and with the ax he clove the skull of the madman who was gnawing on my leg. The old ghoul fell silently at his feet. He then looked at me, and once more raised the ax. I assumed that it was all over, and closed my eyes; but after the ax had fallen harmlessly a couple of times, I realized that he was cutting my bonds. Once I was free, Zan-ak dropped my things on the ground and returned to Falla and Mara, collapsing in a heap next to them.

The circulation in my arms and legs was poor, but I managed to grab my ax and stagger away from this place of horror. I left my knapsack, an excess burden now, withdrawing only Ter-ek's knife from it. Why Zan-ak would wish to free me I could not say, but I had the feeling that there was something more involved than his benevolence. I reflected on this as I shambled painfully, my only thought to put some distance between myself and the Outpost of the Aged.

Pain wracked my entire body, and my head throbbed mercilessly. I had traveled for a few miles, though it had taken hours of slow, agonizing effort to cover the distance. Now dusk approached and I knew that I could go no further. I stopped alongside a small pond, the first body of water that I had seen on the Other Side. The water was refreshing, and after drinking deeply I bathed my wounds. Save for the gash on my cheek, many of them were superficial, most of the damage done being in the form of bruises and welts.

Food was the furthest thing from my mind that night. Even the water that I drank was unable to stay down as I thought of the Outpost of the Aged. Why was I doing this? Surely I could not succeed. I would be killed eventually, just as soon as Ras-ek tired of this sport. What Azena had told me in her moment of sanity now became even more clear. Death would truly be a preferable choice to life in this Hell. Should I reach Adara, I would have to convince her that it would be the only way. She would understand; yes, of course she would. I fell asleep thinking these shameful thoughts, and the nocturnal visions that came were by far the worst of all.

CHAPTER FIFTEEN

THE HOLY ONES

"Roland Summers?" the voice spoke, calmly.

"Yes?" I answered.

"You are near, Roland Summers, very near. I look forward with great anticipation to your arrival. I have observed most of your journey, and I must say that you have come a long way. Yes, I must know more of you and your people. Truly, they must be a formidable race. Hurry, Roland, and perhaps we shall meet tonight."

"Tonight?"

"Yes, tonight. The Holy Ones will welcome you as you pass. Do not fear them, for they will not harm you. Tonight is the Night of the Touching Moons, the night of the Great Sacrifice. You will be fortunate to witness the Holy Ones as they observe this. Consider the Great Sacrifice to be in your honor also, Roland Summers, for I have so willed it. Come,

Roland, for Adara awaits you."

"Adara?"

"Yes," said the voice. "Your beloved is here."

I leaped to my feet, darting glances from side to side, but I saw nothing. Had I been dreaming, or had he spoken to me? Was I really as close as he had said? There was only one way to find out. It was still dark, but the first hints of dawn were beginning to appear. To attempt further sleep would be futile, so I decided to resume the journey. I ached terribly, but it did not matter.

With the day's march undisturbed, I was afforded the opportunity to do much thinking. The events of the previous day continued to haunt me, although I struggled to push them from my mind. I thought of Denny, and of Ter-ek. I had lost track of the days, but I knew that the Homarus were at least on their way to Mogara, if not already there, to enforce the peace between the two. I prayed that Ter-ek would be able to save Denny; that is, if he were not already dead. But foremost among my thoughts was Adara, my beloved, the woman I had wed. I wanted so badly to see her again, but for real, not some perverted illusion. Would I really be with her tonight, or was that just more additional torture? What would she be like when I found her? She had a strong will; perhaps she continued to fight the Master and had not succumbed to his evil. Was she aware of my approach? I prayed that somehow she knew.

As the day wore on, the terrain began to alter appreciably. Harsh, barren plains became fertile fields and abundant orchards. Fruits and vegetables of every description grew there, as well as various grains. There seemed to be little skill involved for the furrows in the fields ran unevenly, and the trees were scattered haphazardly. The earth was rich and dark, however, the finest I had seen outside of Var-Dor, and this made the growing easier.

People began to appear, men, women, and children, all tending the crops. I held tightly to my ax, prepared for anything, but none showed any hostile intentions. Indeed, many smiled and waved happily at me as I passed. Keeping in mind what these people were, and remembering my welcome at the Outpost of the Aged, I felt little desire to have any contact with them.

The fields stretched for many miles, and the people became more numerous. A glance to the rear revealed that the people had been falling in behind me, albeit at a cautious distance. The knowledge of this served to increase my awareness, and for the next half hour or so I kept a close eye on them. At no time, however, did they narrow the gap.

A small group of people suddenly appeared in front of me. I stopped short, my fingers squeezing the handle of the ax tightly. Behind me, the few hundred also halted. One man in the group began walking toward me, a broad grin on his face. He looked to be in his forties, and was well muscled. His left ear, however, was practically non-existent, while his cranium seemed slightly larger than one should be. He spoke in a loud voice as he approached me: "Welcome, Roland Summers," he boomed, cheerfully. "I am Gaz-ek, foremost among the Holy Ones."

"Stop right where you are, Gaz-ek," I ordered, "and don't come any closer."

"You may refer to me as Kuta," he said, continuing toward me. "It is a title of respect."

"I'll refer to you as *dead* if you don't stop!" I responded.

"The Master told me to expect this from you," Gas-ek replied, stopping in his tracks. "No matter, for you are still a welcome guest. See, it grows dark. We will show you the way with torchlight to the field of the Great Sacrifice. Come, for it is late, and soon the moons will touch."

"I will follow you, Gaz-ek," I told him, cautiously, "but you will keep your distance. The first one to come near me will die. Do you understand?"

"It will be as you wish, Roland Summers," he shrugged. "Now come!"

Gaz-ek backed up slowly and rejoined the group. The Borangan night had arrived somewhat unexpectedly, and the flickering shadows produced by the hundreds of torches being lit by the Holy Ones were eerie. They began to walk, and I followed, the larger contingent bringing up the rear. For the next hour, this strange procession snaked its way through fields and orchards. It was amidst the trees that I was most alert, for it was nearly impossible to keep all of them in sight. But my fears proved to be unfounded, for I was not approached.

The two moons, both full, were now visible. Zil, the larger of the two, was already high in the sky, while Dal had just risen in the northeast. I had noticed the last couple of nights that the arcs of the two moons were getting closer as they hurtled through the sky in nearly opposite directions, this affording me a reasonable idea of what the Night of the Touching Moons was all about. It was the Great Sacrifice that concerned me, for I did not know what, or who, was to be offered. Animals were practically non-existent on the Other Side, with only an occasional rodent to be seen. Maybe *I* was to be the sacrifice. I had been welcomed heartily before, and nearly died from the honor. Such was the way of the Holy Ones. I was determined that they would not get another chance.

The foothills, which had been visible during the latter part of the day, now loomed less than a hundred yards ahead on the far side of a vast, open meadow, which was brightly lit by scores of huge bonfires. Two identical stone slabs, spaced ten yards apart, stood near the base of the hills. Each was about twenty feet long and five feet wide, their tops rising three feet above the ground. In the light of the many fires, the two slabs glowed a vivid red.

Many people covered the field, these clearing a path for Gaz-ek and his party. All were smiling at me, and I could feel the tenseness increasing. The faces of the people were varied; some of them appeared normal, but many showed signs of deformity, either in the shape of the skull or the visible organs. I noticed a man with only one eye, located slightly left of center on his face, creating a grotesque, cyclopean effect. He smiled obscenely as he realized that I was staring at him, and I quickly looked the other way.

Gaz-ek's group reached the slabs, where they halted. The leader turned and faced me, while the rest, eight in all, divided in two, each half striding solemnly to a slab. They stood along one side of their respective slab, spaced evenly apart, and were perfectly still, their heads bowed. Gaz-ek, still smiling, raised his hands high over his head, silencing the murmurs of the multitude. Satisfied, he turned around completely and dropped to his knees. The people followed suit, and all chanted the three words that I had come to loathe: *"Noma Kuto Boranga!"* Over and over they repeated it, while I stood my ground, disgusted. Gaz-ek finally rose, as did the others.

"Holy Ones, listen!" Gaz-ek shouted. "We are doubly honored that on this, the most sacred of nights, we have a personal guest of our Master, Ras-ek Varano. We welcome Roland Summers to the Other Side, and commence the Great Sacrifice in his honor!"

A loud cheer went up from the people, and many began to shout my name ecstatically, all the while crowding in closer. I drew Ter-ek's knife from my belt, and with the two weapons waving menacingly I circled about, daring anyone to come within range. One wide-eyed devil broke from the crowd chattering like a monkey and tried to grab me, but I promptly spilled his brains and kicked him aside. Two more came at me, a man and a woman. I drove my knife into the man's heart, but I could not bring myself to kill the female, so I rendered her unconscious with a blow to the jaw and laid her none-too-gently on the ground.

Seconds later I was surrounded, and I knew that it would not be long before I succumbed to the overwhelming numbers. I swung my weapons wildly, this time caring little whether I destroyed man, woman, or child. They were all devils, mindless, bloodthirsty devils, deserving nothing less than death. Twenty, thirty were dispatched, until finally I was brought to the ground. So much for the Master's pledge of safe passage! I thought. My arms were pinned, but I kicked and bit anyone I could reach.

"It is time!" shrieked a voice that I recognized as Gaz-ek's. "Look, kuta, Zil and Dal draw closer! Commence the Great Sacrifice! It is time!"

The Holy Ones stopped what they were doing and jumped to their feet. Moments later, aside from the dozens of bloodied corpses that surrounded me, I found myself alone, my weapons lying on the ground near me. I knew that I should have run as far away from this place as I could, but I was unable to move. The crowd was facing in the direction of the stone slabs, their backs to me, straining to get a better view. I could not see the slabs, nor could I see Gaz-ek, but I did hear him shouting.

"Make way, make way, fools!" he screamed. "Let our honored guest through! Let Roland Summers pass!"

The Holy Ones parted, and I was afforded a path nearly ten feet wide to walk through. My weapons were raised, and I was alert, but the people ignored my passage in deference to the pending spectacle. Gaz-ek motioned me to his side, but I made sure there was at least ten feet between us. In the sky above, the two moons neared. In only minutes their paths would cross, and they would appear to touch.

Torches appeared in the foothills, and people

became visible, these wending their way down the slopes. As they reached the meadow, I could see them more clearly. Six men wielded the torches, and they were leading eight women, all naked except for a large, glittering necklace. The latter glided along, trance-like, and I was stunned as I realized that I knew one; she was—Ter-ek's beloved Aleen!

The party split in two, Aleen in the group to my left. The women were helped onto the altars, as I now realized them to be, where they laid down on their backs. The purpose of the Great Sacrifice was becoming clearer each moment, and now there could be no doubt, for each of the eight Holy Ones stooped over and gathered up a long, shining dagger, gripping the haft with two hands and holding it high in the air.

"Look, Holy Ones, Zil and Dal touch!" Gaz-ek shrieked, pointing to the sky. "Begin the Great Sacrifice, my brothers; *begin!*"

A quick glance skyward revealed Gaz-ek's proclamation to be true. Dal, the further and smaller of the two, appeared to be sitting directly on top of Zil, and together they resembled a child's snowman. With little time left, I raced between the two altars, but I was too late. The four madmen on my right had plunged their daggers deep into the hearts of their victims simultaneously, and the crowd moaned in ecstasy. Without a second's hesitation I leaped atop the other altar and drove my ax deep into the skull of Aleen's would-be executioner. With my knife, I slashed the throat of the next closest one. I had saved two of the women, at least temporarily, but the others on this slab were less fortunate. As they drove their knives deep into the poor women, the two remaining Holy Ones screamed defiantly at me and then made a hasty retreat.

"Fool!" Gaz-ek shrieked, as he and five others raced toward me. "How dare you interrupt the Great Sacrifice? The Master proclaimed this in your honor. Is this how you show your gratitude?"

"*Honor?* Is this what you call honor?" I screamed. "I call it *murder!* Do you understand me, you devil? *This is cold-blooded murder!*"

The other girl came out of her stupor and, after quickly absorbing the scene around her, ran screaming into the crowd. Aleen proved to be more difficult, and as I frantically tried to snap her out of it, the Holy Ones, those left on their feet, surrounded the altar. The rest, frenzied by the blood-letting, were ignoring my blasphemies as they rolled around on the ground in various stages of insanity. I saw that the four bodies on the other altar had been dragged off, and I shuddered as I thought of their fate.

The number of Holy Ones intent on my destruction decreased every second, as one by one the madness overtook them. Those who chose to persist were cautious, for they knew what I was capable of, and they feared their own demise. Gaz-ek screamed obscenities at me, all the while shaking his fist. I judged that he too was on the brink, and would not last long.

Suddenly Aleen's eyes opened wide, and as she stared at me I could read the terror on her face. She darted quick glances all around, her eyes finally coming to rest on Gaz-ek. Before I could speak to her, she leaped from the altar and began to run. I shouted her name, and that of Ter-ek. For a brief instant she stopped and looked at me, the least hint of recognition in her eyes. Seconds later she was crossing the field, running between the maze of writhing bodies. I took off in pursuit, but the bravest of Gaz-ek's madmen blocked my path, and once again I was forced into combat with these travesties of humanity.

"Kill him, kill him!" Gaz-ek shrieked. "Zil and Dal no longer touch. He has ruined the sacred ceremony! Kill him! The Master will understand!"

I dispatched two of them quickly, but there were six or seven left, and some were armed with the long daggers used during the sacrifice. What worsened matters was the fact that there were Holy Ones crawling all over the ground, making the footing precarious at best. That my assailants were having similar difficulty was little consolation, for the gibbering maniacs were clutching at my feet and legs. One woman even sank her teeth into my ankle. I fought my way back to the altar and jumped on it, displacing a woman who had prostrated herself on it, and was banging her head down on the heavy stone. My attention turned quickly to the attackers, and I was gratified to see that their number had been reduced by madness to two, one of them weaponless. I cleaved the latter's skull instantly, but the other put up a formidable defense, and I was hard-pressed to destroy him. When he finally lay dead across the stone slab, I continued to drive my knife into his chest. Seven, eight times I struck, until I finally realized what I was doing and stopped, horrified by my actions.

After quitting the altar I began to search for Aleen,

but I soon realized the futility of my efforts. The field was a churning sea of depravity, with hundreds, thousands of wriggling, squirming, clutching maniacs. They performed unthinkable, unmentionable deeds on themselves and on others. Their moans and laughter filled the air like a ghastly, spectral symphony. Many piled on top of each other and formed writhing hills. I stopped to examine a naked, partially dismembered body, and discovered that it was one of the girls who had been murdered on the altar. She was a lovely young woman, and I grieved deeply for her.

The sight of that young girl, added to the unspeakable horrors that surrounded me, was more than I could take. I began to scream, and soon I was destroying anything within reach. Totally losing control of myself, I hacked, stabbed and kicked my way through this ocean of insanity. I had no idea how many of them I felled, nor did I care. The only one I was able to recognize in my frenzy was Gaz-ek, who somehow sensed my actions and scampered away on all fours, like a terrified rodent.

Low clouds began to gather, dark, ominous puffs. Soon the two moons were obliterated, and it began to rain. The pelting liquid brought me temporarily to my senses, and I began to wipe off my hands, which were covered with blood. But as hard as I tried, I could not remove the crimson stains. I cupped my hands to try and gather some of the rain, and only then did I understand what was happening: *it was raining blood!* The Holy Ones seemed to be aware of it also, for they shrieked and wailed ecstatically, the noise reaching ear-splitting proportions.

Sickened, I flung the blood that I had gathered away from me. The laughter began, the insane, demonic cackle; *his* laugh! It was clearly audible, even over the sounds made by the Holy Ones. With my ears covered I raced toward the foothills, my head shaking from side to side. I ran as fast as I could, until the steepness of the incline forced me to slow. My hands were necessary to help me climb, and once again I had to listen to his laugh, although the shrieks of the Holy Ones were now distant. I dared not look back, for I could not bring myself to set eyes on the scene that I had just quitted. He said that I would see him tonight, and I knew that I must get there. I *would* get there!

The rain stopped, leaving me drenched in blood. As the clouds dissipated, the hills became bathed in the light from the two moons. A well-defined, albeit steep and treacherous path lay ahead of me now. I climbed for hours, never giving thought to resting, although I was all but spent. One thought, only one, dominated my entire being: I would find the Master, and I would destroy him! I would slash his throat, tear out his heart. I would . . .

No, it cannot be! I'm thinking like them, acting like them! Back there, did I really do what I think I did? It could not have happened, yet—yet I did not imagine it! I killed all those people! Regardless of what they are, of what they were doing, I killed them. *Oh, my God!*

Years ago, Uncle Jack stopped by the house. It was late, and I was surprised to see him, but pleased nonetheless. He seemed nervous, and was stammering. I made him sit down, and, amidst sobs, he told me what had happened. I stared at the wall, not wishing to believe what I had just heard. Then it struck me: they were dead! *Oh, my God!* I dropped to the floor and sobbed uncontrollably. Uncle Jack tried to comfort me, but I wept on and on. I cried no more after that, not even at the funeral.

That night, in the hills, I fell to my knees and cried again. I wept for Adara, for Denny, and for Aleen. I cried for Peter Collins, and for his long-dead family. I wept at the thought of what I had become, at the atrocities I had performed. His laughter grew even louder, until it echoed through the hills. I hated him for what he had done to those I cared for, and for what he had made me.

After regaining some control of myself, I resumed the ascent. The hills gave up distance grudgingly, as each yard became an effort. The blood that had fallen from above had dried, but already I could see my own appear from numerous injuries. I continued to push myself, for I feared that if I fell asleep, I might never awaken again.

The insane laughter stopped suddenly, and I glanced around, startled. A short distance above me, beyond a ridge, I discerned a red, throbbing light. I hastened atop the rim, and found myself standing on a broad mesa: There, less than a hundred yards before me, stood Sekkator!

My pains were forgotten for the moment as I approached it. I was able to distinguish every feature clearly. Peter Collins had visualized Sekkator as resembling an old, antebellum mansion, and at first glance this description seemed correct. The columns, like the rest of the house, glowed crimson. Their ornamentation, as well as that on the facade of the building, was ghostly gray, the figures they represented grotesque, shapeless horrors. Oversized double doors on the front were made of silver, and a similar metal constituted the floor of the portico. Upon closer scrutiny, I realized that the main columns were not uniform. Some were only a couple of feet apart, others separated by many yards. The whole house reflected the dementia of its builder. No, this was by no means what Peter had thought, for the traditional old dwellings of the South were far more lovely than this monstrosity.

Sekkator was enormous, covering nearly three acres of land. The mesa on which it sat encompassed about four times this. Beyond the edifice, both to the left and straight ahead, sheer cliffs rose to heights of many thousands of feet. To the right, the mountains inclined more gradually. Although steep, they appeared scalable. There was no flora on the mesa, nothing but thin, dead trees. Their shadows, cast by the pulsating red light of Sekkator, gave the appearance of a vast, spectral army.

I approached to within fifty feet of the main portal, when my legs began to buckle, and I was forced to grab hold of a dead tree to keep from falling. The wood cracked, becoming splinters, and I fell forward on the crusty earth, breaking the fall with my hands. Now unable to walk, I began crawling to the doors. I had drawn to within a few feet of the portico when the huge doors were flung open. There, resplendent in silver robe and turban, stood Ras-ek Varano! I was sure that I was witnessing him in the flesh this time, and not seeing a disembodied image.

"You're late, Roland," he sneered. "Surely you encountered no difficulty in finding Sekkator. Whatever could have happened to delay you? Hee hee hee!"

"Where is—Adara?" I gasped, ignoring his laughter.

"Oh, forgive me, Roland," he mocked. "You have come all this way to be my guest, and I must seem inhospitable to you. I will have the one you seek care for your wounds, for as soon as you are well, we must visit. See, she comes!"

Ras-ek stepped aside, and for the first time in weeks I saw her. As she came toward me she glanced fearfully at Ras-ek, but he did not interfere. She was as beautiful as ever, though her face was a mask of great sorrow, and I shuddered to think of what she must have been through. I rose weakly to my feet and awaited her.

"Adara?" I asked, praying that she was not an illusion.

"Ro-lan, my beloved!" she cried, now running.

I took one step and crumpled, falling at Adara's feet just as she reached me. She held my head in her soft hands and buried her face on my chest, sobbing softly. The last sound I remembered was the obscene chuckle of Ras-ek; then I heard no more.

CHAPTER SIXTEEN

THE ARENA OF JOY

A first baseman's glove! Gee, thanks, Dad. I'm a cinch to make the team now. None of the other kids . . . The starter's gun is in the air. I know I can swim faster than these other guys. I hope I don't . . . Why does he have to go, Mom? He didn't start the dumb war. Will he be on a destroyer, or maybe a carrier? Boy, when I'm older . . . It's him Mom, I know it's him! Look, he's waving at us from the gangplank. Here he comes . . . Yes, I'm positive! As soon as I graduate, I'm going to enlist. I love the sea, and . . . Yes, Chief, I'll get on it right away. Oh, Chief? I'll need some more paint . . . How much beer did I drink? Too much, probably. Denny, get off the lifeguard's stand! I'm going to tip it . . . What's happening? We've lost control of the Queen! *Where the devil is this thing taking us? Oh, God! What's that up ahead . . .*

"Ro-lan?" the voice whispered, softly.

"Ummmphhh," I groaned, my eyes still closed.

"Ro-lan, can you hear me? It's Adara. Oh, Ro-lan, please wake up!"

I opened my eyes slowly, for the light hurt them. At first everything was blurred, but as my vision cleared, I found myself staring into the face of my beloved. I smiled at her, and she returned it. The straw mat that I was lying upon sat on the floor of a strange room; Adara was next to me on her knees, holding my hand. The cubicle was a nightmare of colors. Three of the walls were dirty brown, flecked with olive green, the fourth solid black. The ceiling, some fifteen feet above, was gray and yellow. There was little need to ask where I was.

Upon examining my body I noted that I was clean and wore fresh clothes. My wounds had been tended to and were beginning to heal. My head ached, albeit only slightly. I rose to my feet slowly, testing my arms and legs. They felt much better than before, though I knew that I was still weak. Adara made me lie down again, scolding me as she helped.

"How long have I been out?" I asked her.

"It has been three nights since you arrived here," she told me. "This is the first time I have seen you conscious. Twice the Master has come for you and taken you from this room, but I know not what he has done to you. Do you have any memory of it?"

"I recall having many strange dreams," I replied, raising my hand to my head. "They were all about my past. My mind feels drained, empty. That's all I seem to remember."

"Ro-lan, why did you come here?"

I stared deeply into her eyes for a few moments before replying: "Need you ask that?"

She threw her arms around my neck and covered my face with kisses. I held her tightly and pressed her lips to mine, and for a couple of minutes I forgot where I was. All that mattered was Adara, all that would ever matter would be her. I loved her dearly, and I swore that I would never let her be taken from me again.

"Oh, Ro-lan, I have grieved for you so!" she cried. "He informed me of your progress in coming here, and I was certain that you would be killed. Had he told me of your death, then most surely would I have killed myself, for death would be preferable to life here."

"Has he harmed you in any way?" I queried.

"He has not hurt me physically, but he has shown me things that—that—no! I cannot even think about them!" She shuddered, and buried her head in her hands.

Thinking back to my own experiences, I understood what she meant. I held her head on my shoulder and stroked her hair, trying both to soothe her and to keep my own memories from creeping back into my head.

"Ro-lan, my grandfather is dead, isn't he?" she asked suddenly.

My silence provided her with the answer, though I was sure that she had guessed it long ago. She turned and stared at one of the walls for a minute. I had thought little of Peter Collins since that night in Var-Dor, but now I stood by Adara's side, and together we mourned the loss of that wonderful old man.

There was a tiny, barred window near the ceiling and through it I could see Zil overhead, more than three quarters full. It was quiet all around us, and I found it hard to believe that this was the core of the evil that dominated Boranga.

"How much freedom do you have here?" I asked Adara.

"Much of Sekkator is free to us, except for a few areas. You must not enter a room with a red door. There is but one portal leading to the outside, and only the Master can open it. Otherwise, there is very little to see, aside from more cubicles like this one. There is a room where food and water are stored, and it always seems to be full. Many people walk through the lengthy corridors, even some I know from Var-Dor, but their minds are blank, and they do not recognize me."

"What does he do with these people?"

"One day they are here, the next they are not. Some eventually reappear, but others are never seen again. Only once did he send for me, and—" She began to cry again.

"Try not to think about it," I implored her, holding her tightly. "Think only of this: I'm going to get us out of here, as far away from the Other Side as we can flee!"

"Oh, Ro-lan!" she cried, wiping her eyes. "If only we could! But I'm afraid it is impossible. You have seen the Master's powers. What could be done to stop him?"

"I know it won't be easy," I shrugged. "Somehow, I wish that I could discover the source of his power.

Ras-ek was once an ordinary mortal, just as you and me. Whatever he found that day in the fields so many years ago must have been responsible for the transformation. Perhaps if I could locate this source and destroy it, I could destroy Ras-ek also."

"Ro-lan, you must not speak of this!" she exclaimed, looking furtively around her. "He will hear you! He—!"

"Nonsense!" I retorted. "The Master has some perverted reason for wishing me alive, or he would not have allowed me to come this far. If he has probed my mind, then he is well aware of the fact that I would like nothing better than to tear his heart out. Come, let us explore the corridors together."

Adara regained her composure and took my hand. We stepped out into the corridor, which was at least fifteen feet wide, and ran as far as one could see in either direction. Its walls were built of a granitoid stone, quite indestructible. The outer wall was smooth, unbroken throughout, save for a few randomly-spaced sconces, while the inner wall was dotted sporadically with the doorways of other small rooms. Through the open doors I was able to look into the cubicles, all similar to the one Adara and I had been in. Many were empty, but some contained either one or two occupants. Most were women, though I did see a few men. All sat listlessly on the floor, their backs against a wall, and stared blankly at the ceiling. Not one of them acknowledged our passing in any way.

We continued traversing the bleak corridor, stopping only at the sound of footsteps to our rear. My ax and knife were still in my belt, for which I was thankful. I drew the blade and wheeled around, making certain that Adara was behind me. A man and a woman were ten yards away, and walking toward us. They appeared harmless enough, but I kept my weapon ready, for appearance had proven deceiving more than once on the Other Side. My caution, however, was unjustified, for the couple strode past us without even the slightest hint of awareness. Like all the others I had seen their faces were blank, their glazed eyes affixed straight ahead.

The long hallway turned sharply to the left, and we followed it. We passed by many other Borangans now, but in their trance-like stupor they were unaware of us. As I stared at their blank faces, I found myself becoming both enraged and frustrated, and I decided to attempt communication with one. I grabbed a passing fellow by the shoulders and began to shake him, but he did not respond. Four, five times I slapped him across his face, gently at first, then harder as my frustration grew. Adara laid her hand on my shoulder and shook her head admonishingly. I released the poor soul, and he continued on his way, unruffled.

The first red door loomed just ahead of us, and I noticed that Adara's eyes were averted to the floor. As we reached the door her pace quickened, but I held her hand tightly and slowed her, for I was curious. She tried to hurry me along, but I stopped in front of the door and stared at it.

"Ro-lan, you must come quickly!" she pleaded, tugging anxiously at my arm. "It is a red door!"

"Perhaps this is the answer we seek," I told her. "I must find out."

"Ro-lan, no!" she screamed. "You mustn't!"

I smiled at her and placed her at a safe distance from the door, imploring her with a curt gesture to stay put. Slowly, hesitantly I approached, for I had no idea what to expect. The crimson portal appeared larger than it actually was, and I guessed that fear could create such an illusion. Inexplicably, it contained no knob or other device that would allow it to be opened. I pushed on the door, but it did not give even an inch. It was built of thick, solid wood. I felt around the portal with the tips of my fingers, searching for some way to slide it open, but I discovered nothing. With a shrug I rejoined Adara, whose face had whitened from observing my efforts, and we continued along the depressing corridor of Sekkator.

The next room we came to was the food storage chamber. This room was twice the size of any other that I had seen, and contained vast quantities of fruit, nuts, and water in pottery jugs. As we entered the room, we discovered three women already occupying it. They sat on the floor and munched absently at various victuals. Ignoring them, I gathered up a large helping for myself, for I was famished. Adara commandeered a smaller portion and followed me out into the corridor, where we ate as we walked.

Once again the hallway turned, and two more red doors were revealed, but I chose to ignore them both, much to Adara's relief. There was little variance in what we saw, so we quickened our pace in an effort to cover some distance. In this part of the corridor we ran into very few people, and most of the small rooms were empty.

We had covered about half of this particular corridor, when the first variance in the blank wall appeared. Here were the main portals of Sekkator, the steel guardians of this Hell. On the inside, naturally, these doors were painted red, and they dared anyone to come and touch them. For a moment I stared longingly at them, dreaming of the freedom that beckoned on the far side, but Adara's tightened grip on my hand brought me quickly back to reality. I glanced wistfully over my shoulder a couple of times after we passed the doors, and I prayed silently that soon we would emerge from Sekkator into the eternally overcast Borangan day.

Further down the corridor, not far from the main portals, we discovered two staircases, one spiraling upward and disappearing into the blackness above, the other angling sharply down and ending at a closed door. Both stairways, as well as the door at the foot of the latter, glowed a bright crimson, and the meaning was clear. Sensing that the answer I sought was close by, I decided to return Adara to our room to insure her safety and explore this place alone; but before I had a chance to inform her of my plan, she spoke:

"I know that you wish to learn the secrets of this place, and I fear for you, my darling. But my fear is even greater when we are apart. While we are in Sekkator, I will never leave your side. Now that you are with me, I am no longer afraid. What you seek is not below, for I know all too well what is. Let us ascend the other staircase together, and see what there is to be seen."

I could not contain my pride as I gazed upon this

brave woman, *my* woman. If we were indeed doomed, then it would be better to die together. I held her closely for a few moments, and kissed her on the head. She took my hand, and we ascended the spiraling crimson staircase, each step deliberate and silent.

The deathly stillness that had prevailed through the corridors of Sekkator was suddenly shattered by the sound of a thousand mad demons being released from a long-sealed Hell. We had climbed only about a dozen steps when the cacophony of horror reached our ears. At first it emanated from above our heads, but soon it surrounded us. Adara grabbed my arm tightly, but made no sound; her face, however, displayed the terror that she felt. We were halted by a potent force, unable to advance any further. Frantically, we tried to steady ourselves as we descended, but we were unable to maintain our balance, and fell the last five or six steps to the floor.

I was unable to help Adara to her feet, for the two of us were forced to clamp our hands over our ears in a futile effort to block out the depraved chorus whose shrieks and wails had reached an intensity far above any that I had heretofore encountered. This fact alone convinced me that we had reached the core of evil, and what we next witnessed confirmed it. Directly above us floated the authors of this death knell, appearing amidst a ghostly cloud. The nimbus contained heads, thousands of tiny, grotesque heads, the mouths of all agape, as if in pain.

The cloud drifted closer, and the shrieks rose. It now swirled all around, seeming to pass through us, though we could feel nothing. The faces were more distinct now, and I could clearly make out the pained, twisted expressions, the degenerate faces of both males and females. Adara had uncovered her ears, and was swatting at them as though they were insects, but her hands merely passed through the ethereal haze. I screamed at her, trying to advise her of the uselessness of her efforts, but my shouts were lost amidst the ear-splitting din.

Far above our heads a light appeared, increasing in intensity as each second passed. The cloud gravitated upward toward the light, though the noise abated little. Three-quarters of the way down, the glow began to take shape. The turban-like headpiece was visible first, as were the bottom portions of the malformed ears. Soon the whole evil face could be seen leering wickedly above, the piercing eyes burning more brightly than I had ever seen them. His thick lips were curled back, revealing the most perverse of grins. The rest of the body took shape, the shimmering, silver cape reflecting the light blindingly. Ras-ek Varano, the Master of Boranga, had appeared once more, the energy he was emitting seemingly unbounded.

Ras-ek floated down the stairs, his feet inches above them. The cloud of heads, his obscene entourage, surrounded him, and he seemed to revel in their maniacal wailings. Adara had buried her head in her hands, and appeared to be near breaking. I put my arm around her in an attempt to comfort her, though I feared that I was little better off. Ras-ek's descent had brought him to within a few feet of us, where he stopped. He raised his hands high above him and, in response to his command, the terrible nimbus drifted hastily up the stairs, disappearing into the darkness. An ominous silence prevailed for long seconds, while Ras-ek absorbed the scene.

"How kind of you to come, Roland," he sneered, the hollow voice emanating from every corner of the corridor. "I was just on my way to fetch you, but it appears that you have saved me the trip. I'm glad to see that you are well, and that you have brought your woman with you. She has already been my guest in the Arena of Joy, but I know that she will enjoy another visit, just as you will enjoy your first."

Adara looked up at Ras-ek suddenly, her face contorted in horror, and she would have fled, but I held on to her tightly. She swung her fists wildly, even striking me a couple of times. Then she began to scream.

"No, Ro-lan, no! *Oh, no!* Don't let him take us there! Oh, Ro-lan, please! *Please!*"

I struggled to control Adara, all the while glaring at Ras-ek's twisted face. He began to laugh, the hideous, insane cackle that made the hairs prickle on the nape of my neck. He floated to the head of the second staircase and gestured downward with his right hand. The red door at the foot of the stairs slid open, though this revealed very little.

"The Arena of Joy awaits us," Ras-ek hissed. "I know that you will enjoy it, Roland."

"My wife is terrified!" I screamed. "I can't take her down there. I won't take her, Ras-ek!"

"Dear Roland," he mocked. "There is nothing to fear. It is a pleasurable experience. Must I be forced to take other means to convince you again? How tedious. Perhaps this time I will do it in a way that is more to your understanding. Yes, yes; that's what I'll do. Hee hee hee! Yo, Willo!''

He had shouted the latter words toward the open door. I had no idea what they meant, but Adara evidently did. She screamed loudly and renewed her struggles, finally fainting in my arms. I placed her gently on the floor and knelt beside her, keeping a watchful eye on the portal below.

Seconds later, a figure appeared at the doorway, nearly obliterating the dim light from within. It ascended the stairs slowly while Ras-ek laughed, and as it drew nearer I had my first look at Willo. It, or he, I imagine, stood well over seven feet tall, larger than a satong, though he was definitely not one of the Borangan man-beasts. He was naked but for a filthy loin-cloth, which hung loosely around his middle. One of his feet was clubbed, the other normal. There was coarse, black hair on his legs, chest, and arms, but it was not overly plentiful. His left arm was longer than the right, and there was an extra stubby appendage on his left hand. A scrawny neck led to an obscene, chinless face. Two pig-like eyes peered lazily from under thick, half-closed lids. The nose was naught by two tiny pin pricks in the middle of a smooth face, while the small, round mouth exhibited two pointy, protruding cuspids. His two enormous ears were the final travesty, sticking out as they did from under the coarse, unkempt hair. Gurgling noises came from deep within his throat, but whatever he might have been saying was unintelligible.

I understood now why the mere mention of Willo's name would have caused the reaction that it did from

Adara. The anticipation of his approach triggered me to action, and I drew the knife as I leaped to my feet. Out of the corner of my eye I saw Ras-ek gesture with one finger, and as I raised the blade behind my ear to throw it, I felt it being jerked from my hand. I turned around quickly, just in time to hear the knife clatter as it struck high on the stone wall, where it hung suspended. The ax met a similar fate, leaving me unarmed and defenseless, just as Willo reached the top of the stairs.

Whirling about, I placed myself between the sub-human and Adara, determined to protect her as best I could. Willo was only yards away when I lunged at him, attempting to land a fist in his stomach. His torpid appearance belied his agility, and he easily dodged my projected blow. With nothing more than a slight flick of the wrist he knocked me backward, where I landed with great force next to Adara's slumped body. The fall had hurt me, but nothing seemed broken, so I struggled to my feet once again. Willo, obeying a gesture from Ras-ek, stood his ground.

"Willo will only hurt you severely if I so instruct him to," Ras-ek announced in an oily tone. "You're an intelligent fellow, Roland, and I know you would wish no harm on yourself or your woman. Come with us; Willo will guide you."

"Let me take Adara back to the room first," I pleaded. "She's in no condition for—"

"Oh, I wouldn't dream of it," he crowed. "The woman will love the spectacle in the Arena of Joy, just as she did the first time. Now come! I tire of this talk. My strength is full, and I crave the Arena!"

Realizing the futility of further arguments, I scooped up Adara in my arms and strode silently to the top of the stairs, ignoring Willo as I passed directly in front of him. The Master was already gliding effortlessly down the stairs, his silver robe flowing behind him. I followed him down, Willo a few yards to my rear. One thought raced continually through my mind as we descended, and it was not the fear of whatever unknown horror might await us below. The Master had said something that made little sense, yet I felt that it was of significance: 'My strength is full.' What the devil could he have meant by that? Could I write it off as the ravings of his deranged mind, or was it important?

We reached the foot of the stairs, and the time for dwelling on the mystery had passed, at least for now. Ras-ek had already passed through the open doorway, and was temporarily out of my sight. With Adara still unconscious in my arms I entered, and I had my first look at the Arena of Joy, a place that I pray I might never set eyes upon again. Immediately upon entering I stood on the floor of the arena, which was covered with sand. The two walls on either side were bare, save for a single door. In front of me, about forty feet, tiers of benches angled upward, much in the style of an amphitheater. There were ten rows of them, the highest reaching almost to the ceiling of the arena, thirty feet overhead. The Master occupied a huge, padded chair that was located before the first row of benches. To either side of him, about five feet away, were pairs of strange looking stone seats. Two other unusual looking structures sat on the floor in the center of the arena, but I was unable to get a good look at them initially.

Ras-ek, smiling wickedly, gestured to the stone chairs on his right, and I carried Adara, who was now beginning to stir, to them. Willo strode to the Master's side, assuming a position at his left. Adara opened her eyes as I placed her down gently, and I smiled at her. She looked around quickly and, realizing where she was, heaved a deep sigh and slumped down in her chair. I took my place in the other one and resignedly awaited developments.

I now had a chance to examine the two strange pieces of apparatus and, as I looked at them from this side, I realized just how familiar they were. As a child I had loved the circus, and I never passed up the opportunity to see one when it came to town. One of my favorite performers was the knife thrower, who would strap his beautiful assistant to a large wooden wheel and hurl knives at her. The highlight came when he would spin the wheel and toss the blades while she was in motion. He would invariably form an outline of her body, after which she would jump, smiling and unharmed, from the wheel. The two structures that I now looked at in the Arena of Joy, a world away from my past, were nearly identical to those circus props, the only difference being their bases, these blocks of stone, denoting the fact that they were stationary. What their presence portended was a fact known only to the madmen on my left.

Ras-ek raised both hands high in the air, and the door that we had entered through slammed shut, while the others flew open. A man emerged from one portal, a woman from the second. They walked slowly, expressionlessly, to the center of the arena, the doors closing behind them, and it was obvious that they were mindless slaves of the Master. Each one stopped as they reached their respective wheel, and waited. Willo strode to the center of the Arena, going first to the woman. He fumbled with the apparatus for a moment, until he was able to tilt the wheel back. It was now parallel to the ground, resembling a large table-top. He lifted the woman up and placed her on top of it, tying her wrists and ankles securely with leather straps, though his thick fingers made this a tedious process. A fifth strap was bound around her waist, and when this was done he once again tilted the wheel upward so that the young woman, completely nude, faced Ras-ek. Willo repeated the procedure with the male, while Ras-ek wrung his hands together, impatient with the clumsiness of his sub-human servant. With his work finally finished, Willo returned to the Master's side.

The Arena of Joy was illuminated by a multitude of small torches, which now began to flicker and fade. Soon it was nearly dark, the dim light from the few remaining lit torches casting eerie shadows throughout the chamber. I had been glancing all around the arena, but a strange whirring noise now brought my attention back to the center, where the two wheels had begun to rotate. They moved very slowly at first, and, as I watched, I saw that the two unfortunates were struggling, now aware of their predicament. Ras-ek apparently wished them awake, so that he might fully enjoy whatever fiendish tortures he had devised for them.

Faster, faster they spun, until the two faces were nothing but blurs. My instinct told me to try and help them but, as I went to rise, I found that I was frozen in my chair, all but my head and neck paralyzed. Now helpless, I could do nothing but observe the spectacle. Adara, who also could not move, had averted her eyes, and was biting her lip. The other spectators in the arena, however, were enjoying the scene thoroughly. Ras-ek grinned broadly as he pounded his fists down on the arms of his chair, while Willo gurgled disgustingly, spittle dribbling from his mouth.

Minutes later, the wheels began to slow down, and soon they had stopped completely. The man's head hung loosely, for he was unconscious, while the woman shook hers slowly from side to side, moaning softly. Willo picked up a receptacle from alongside the Master's chair and walked over to them. He cupped a few handfuls of water from the pitcher and splashed them in the woman's face, pouring the remainder over the man. The poor fellow sputtered and coughed, while Willo held his head up by the hair for the Master to see. Ras-ek, apparently satisfied, ordered his ghastly servant back to his side.

Silence reigned in the Arena of Joy for long moments. The woman, more alert than her partner, gazed fearfully around at the surroundings, her eyes finally coming to rest on Adara and myself. There was a question on her lips, and I was sure that she was about to speak, when the rest of the torches flickered out, and the arena was engulfed by blackness. For a moment the only audible sound was that of Willo's gurgling, but even that was drowned out as the wailing began. I knew immediately what was to come, and a quick glance upward confirmed my fears. Near the ceiling a cloud was visible, small and milky. It dropped slowly to the floor of the arena, encircling the victims, and the woman screamed loudly as the first of the horrid heads appeared.

The nimbus grew larger than it had been before, while the size of the heads increased also. By the illumination emitted from the cloud, I saw the Master standing on his chair and clenching his fists, his face contorted in ecstasy. Willo was on all fours, digging his nails into the ground like an animal. They too were encircled by the cloud, as were Adara and I, but they seemed to revel in it. The wailing was louder than ever, and with our hands paralyzed we were unable to shield ourselves from them. I watched Adara as she struggled frantically to move, and I doubted if either of us could take much more.

The cloud now filled the Arena of Joy, and a feeling of unbounded energy permeated the air. The man and woman screamed insanely as the densest part of the nimbus encircled them. I began to pull against the paralysis that held me, and for just an instant I was able to move my arms. I glanced cautiously at Ras-ek and Willo, but they were totally enraptured by the scene in front of them. All my conscious thought was channeled into one extreme effort, and in a few seconds I had freed my arms. I quickly leaned over and clamped my hands over the suffering Adara's ears to block out the deathly sounds. She looked at me, and in the midst of this unspeakable Hell we each managed a meager smile.

For long minutes the scene varied little, the increasing dementia of Ras-ek being the only possible change. Finally, the cloud began to dissipate, and the noise abated. Smaller and smaller it shrank, higher and higher it floated, disappearing in a final puff. Not wishing my secret to be discovered, I promptly returned my arms to their previous position, just as the lights in the arena flared up again. Ras-ek had slumped down in his chair while the frothing Willo was once again standing. The man and the woman were both conscious, but their eyes were glazed and they babbled mindlessly. The energy in the arena, strongest during the time the nimbus had appeared, was still evident, but it was not nearly as forceful.

Ras-ek reclined in his chair, seemingly exhausted, for a minute or two, after which he rose slowly to his feet and raised his arms high in the air. Once again the insane, malevolent leer dominated his wicked face, and I shuddered as I realized that he would inflict more punishment on the two helpless creatures before him. Willo swung his arms like an ape as he watched the Master, eagerly awaiting what was to come.

A clanking noise, very much out of context in this hellish place, became evident. It reminded me of the sound made by the chain as we drew the anchor aboard the *Maui Queen*. The stone bases that supported the two wheels began to rotate, obviously not stationary, as I had supposed. They turned slowly, until the man and woman faced each other, and then stopped. The two showed no signs of recognition, for their reason was all but gone.

Ras-ek gestured with bent fingers, and the wheels once again began to spin. The man revolved counter-clockwise, the woman clockwise. Once again the clanking was heard, and the wheels started moving toward each other. Four feet separated them, then three, when I suddenly realized what was happening. I looked at Adara, who had already guessed what was to come and, quite mercifully, had passed out. Ras-ek had quitted his chair, and now sat atop the back of Willo, who had resumed his animal-like stance. The Master pounded his servant as he stared, glassy-eyed, and the two of them foamed heavily at the mouth, like mad dogs.

Two feet apart, then one foot, until finally the two unfortunates met. Bones splintered and cracked while geysers of blood shot out in all directions. I started to gag, sickened by the sight before me. The stench of death filled the arena as the two wheels moved closer together. Ras-ek shrieked loudly as he rolled fitfully on the ground, while Willo moaned and crammed dirt into his mouth. The wheels now touched, and what was left of the two victims oozed sickeningly from the small cracks.

I screamed and gagged alternately, and with an effort only attributable to madness I pulled myself free of the chair that held me. My legs were unsteady, but I slowly made my way to the two prone monsters, determined to tear them apart in a modest act of retribution for the atrocities they had committed. The Master, though in the midst of a seizure, somehow became aware of my approach.

"You were an honored guest here!" he shrieked. *"How dare you interfere with the spectacle in the Arena of Joy? You shall pay severely for your affrontery. Willo, stop him!"*

The frothing sub-human leaped quickly to his feet

and came at me with surprising speed. Ras-ek seemed helpless where he lay, but I knew that I would be unable to reach him. I tried vainly to dodge Willo's rush, but my legs would not respond to the wishes of my brain. Slowly, helplessly I swung at him as he reached me, but he lifted me high over his head, tossing me toward the center of the arena. I landed hard near the wheels, in a sickening pool of ooze. Willo charged at me again but, as I rose slowly to my feet in a feeble effort to defend myself, I slipped. My head hit the ground only inches from the stone base of one of the structures, which surely would have killed me. Darkness overwhelmed me, and the last sight I recalled was that of Willo's grotesque face bending over me, his hands extended toward my neck.

CHAPTER SEVENTEEN

THE MASTER'S CHAMBER

Adara sat on the floor in one corner of the room, whimpering softly. At first she was unaware of my consciousness, but the noise that I made as I tried to prop myself up on one elbow caught her ear. She turned and stared blankly, never once making any attempt to come to me. I spoke her name quietly, but she turned and buried her head in her hands. I wanted to go to her, to comfort her, but the pain in my head was severe, even worse than it had been before. Helplessly I lay on my back in agony.

I must have blacked out again, for when I came to I found Adara kneeling at my side. Some assorted fruits were on the floor nearby, as was a jug of water. My head was not throbbing as severely as before, but I remained still nonetheless. Adara placed her hand gently under the back of my head and tilted it slightly forward, lifting the water to my lips. The liquid was refreshing, for my throat was parched. After easing me back down, she offered me one of the fruits. I had no appetite, and with a feeble wave I indicated this to her.

"How—how did we get back here?" I stammered.

"Who knows?" she answered, blankly. "Who knows anything of what transpires in Sekkator? Willo brought us back here, I imagine." She folded her arms and shuddered at the mention of his name.

"I wonder why he did not kill me."

"I came to just in time to see him standing over your body," she informed me. "He was in a rage and beginning to choke you when the Master ordered him to stop. For a moment it appeared that he would disobey, but the Master continued to scream, and he released you."

"Did you see Ras-ek get up?"

"No. He remained on the floor throughout. Willo lifted him up and placed him gently in the chair."

"What happened then?" I snapped, suddenly very interested.

"Willo returned to your body and scooped it up with one arm. He then carried you over to where I sat."

"Then what?"

"The thought of you being dead, and the sight of his horrid face, were too much for me to bear. I fell faint at Willo's feet."

"Are you sure you fell to the floor?"

"Yes. It was the last thing that I remember. Why?"

"The paralyzing effect of the chair did not hinder you at all?"

"No. Ro-lan, what do you mean by all these questions?"

"I don't know, my love," I replied, scratching my head. "I have a handful of small pieces, but I'm having trouble putting the puzzle together. I need time for my head to clear, so that I might concentrate."

"Your words are strange to me, darling," she stated, "but I hope that I will be able to help you. Ro-lan, when you awoke before and I did not come to you—"

"No explanation is necessary," I interrupted, putting my fingers to her lips. "Now, I think that I might need some more sleep. Perhaps a kiss would be helpful to achieve this."

"What is that you taught me? 'Your wish is my command, sire!' Yes, that's the one," she chirped, and happily complied with my request.

It might have been a few minutes, or perhaps hours, when next I opened my eyes. Adara lay sleeping next to me, the expression on her face indicating the troubled nature of her dreams. I sat up slowly, discovering that the pain in my head was nearly gone. The various bumps and bruises that covered my body ached, but I tried to ignore them. My recent sleep had been a refreshing experience in more ways than one, for this time I did not dream of the Vale of Fear, or of the Holy Ones. I was not troubled by the atrocities I had witnessed in the Arena of Joy or the Outpost of the Aged. Instead, the various bits of the puzzle had flashed through my mind, and for the first time they appeared to be falling into place.

Adara sat up suddenly, her eyes wide open. It was likely that something in her dreams had startled her. A glance in my direction assured her that everything was fine for the moment, and with a sigh of relief she rested her head on my lap. I stroked her hair gently as I looked at her, this wonderful woman that I loved. After all she had been through, all she had seen, I wondered if time could somehow erase those memories in the future. I doubted if either of us could withstand much more of the Other Side. My own reason had been slipping, of this I was sure. A move had to be made soon, for once Ras-ek learned what he wanted from me, I would be as good as dead.

"Ro-lan, remember that American saying you taught me as we gazed at the herds?" Adara asked, softly. "I believe it was 'A penny for your thoughts.'"

"You learned it well, my love," I replied, laughingly. "Earlier, I told you that many unexplained bits and pieces regarding all that has happened were troubling me. I have used these to develop some theories. They may be correct, or dead wrong, but I feel that we must apply them in an attempt to escape from this terrible place."

"Even death would be preferable to Sekkator," said Adara, shuddering. "I will do anything you say. Please, tell me of your ideas."

"The first time I encountered Ras-ek," I began, "was that night in Var-Dor, during the Hour. The name alone has a hidden significance: the *Hour*. Has he never terrorized the city for two hours, ten hours, a day? No, only for the better part of an hour. If he is all-powerful, then why limit his time? Does the long-distance effort weaken him?

"On the night that I arrived at the portal of Sekkator, Ras-ek walked out to greet me. He did not float out, but he *walked* out. If he means to frighten people with his powers, then why not be consistent?

"Do you notice the great periods of time that pass here while nothing happens? What does the Master do during this period? A diseased brain like that does not willingly stay idle for so long. There must be some need that has to be satisfied before he can resume his activities.

"I know that you would rather not be reminded of this, but it is important. On the night we explored the halls of Sekkator and encountered Ras-ek, do you recall the incredible energy that surrounded him? In the confines of that horrid arena I could feel this force even more. However, after he had expended a great deal of his powers on the earlier tortures, the energy subsided, and I was able to free my hands. With the final atrocity his power was spent, and I was able to free myself from the chair, just as you were able to when Willo approached, and you passed out on the floor. Ras-ek needed Willo's help to get to his chair, and I'm just as sure that Willo must have carried him to wherever his quarters might be afterward."

"What does it all mean, Ro-lan?"

"On that night, Ras-ek said something that, until now, made little sense: 'My strength is full.' I thought that perhaps he was raving, but now I'm sure the key lies in that statement. Ras-ek was once an ordinary, albeit mad, human. His immortality and his power began after he discovered something buried in the ground. I have no idea what this thing is, but I believe that the power it gives him is of short duration, and must be replenished often. Why else would he need a bodyguard like Willo? When we first saw him that night, he was descending from some unknown room above. I believe that the answer is up there."

"What will we do?" she asked.

"We must wait until we are sure that he has expended all his energy. He is less than mortal at that time. I will seek him out and destroy him. If I fail in this, then we must escape from Sekkator, and our knowledge must be used as a weapon against him in the future."

"But how will we escape from Sekkator? The doors are closed tightly. We are trapped in here."

"If my theory is correct, that will be the least of our worries. I'll show you later."

"If you cannot destroy him, then what will happen when he regains his strength and discovers us gone? He will find us and bring us back—or kill us."

"I do not believe that he can locate anyone at will. When I followed you to the Other Side he was with me most of the way, but that is because he knew the route I would be taking. If we do get away from here, I think he will be hard-pressed to find us. There is a gamble involved, but I feel it's one well worth taking. If I'm fortunate enough to kill him, however, all of our fears will be academic."

"When do you wish to start, Ro-lan?"

"The sooner we start, the better," I told her. "Do you feel up to it?"

"Certainly. But what about you? Your injuries—"

"I am fine, my love," I assured her. "I will worry about them when we are away from here. Let's go!"

We entered the corridor and began walking purposefully toward our objective, not even aware of the dozens of poor, mindless souls that wandered aimlessly by. Again we came to the first red door, which I approached without fear, and this time my brave Adara remained at my side. I placed both palms on the door and tried to slide it open. To establish proper leverage was difficult, but after a few seconds' exertion I had opened it a few inches. I wedged my foot in the opening and grabbed the side of the door with my hands. Now I was able to slide it open about one-third of the way, but the great pressure was too much, and I was forced to let it shut again. I did not see what was on the other side, nor did I care, for my theory had proven correct.

"When I first tried the door, I could not budge it," I explained to Adara. "At that time, the Master had just replenished his strength. I am sure that it is only his will that keeps these doors locked. When he is weakest, these doors are not secured. You and the others here were conditioned to stay away from the red doors, therefore you would never have attempted to open one. The fact that this door opened slightly cannot tell me if he is renewing his strength or using it right now. We must find this out for ourselves."

We entered the third corridor, moving more cautiously. No other people were visible, and the silence in the bleak hall was ominous. We passed the main portals of Sekkator, but did not stop. The two staircases appeared next on our left, and we hurried past them, stopping just for a moment to scoop up the knife and ax, both of which lay unattended on the floor. In the instant that we paused I became aware of distant noises, but I could not be sure where they emanated from. Another twenty-five yards further on we entered a small, deserted room. It seemed a bit far away for effective surveillance, but I was concerned for Adara's safety. I looked back down the corridor, assuring myself that I would be able to see clearly. While waiting, we took the opportunity to rest, but my impatience got the best of me, and I found myself continually popping my head out into the hall.

I have no idea how long we had occupied that room when we heard the first sound, but we became instantly alert. The noise, though distant, was unmistakably that of a door opening, and it was followed by slow, heavy footsteps. These continued interminably, until finally the huge form of Willo filled the corridor. He had just ascended the stairs from the Arena of Joy, and in his arms he carried the lifeless form of Ras-ek Varano, the Master of Boranga. For a second he hesitated, then climbed the other staircase only after being certain that nothing was amiss. Soon he had disappeared from sight, only the dull sound of his receding footfalls indicating the continuation of his mission.

It seemed like forever until he returned, but eventually he did. Again he hesitated in the corridor for a moment before returning to his hellish pit below. Certain that all was clear, I motioned Adara to follow me closely, and we re-entered the hallway. We moved slowly, stealthily, covering only about twenty feet, when we heard the door slide open once more. All caution was forgotten as we hastened back to the cubicle. We reached it none too soon, for a quick peek indicated that Willo had once again entered the corridor. In each arm he carried an unconscious young woman, unwilling spectators, undoubtedly, of the day's blood orgy. I watched them for only a few seconds, realizing that Willo was walking in our direction. It occurred to me that this empty room belonged to the two women, and that—Willo was bringing them here! If he discovered us, we were as good as dead, for I doubted whether I would be able to overpower him.

I pushed Adara into the nearest corner and placed myself in front of her, resolved to at least make a fight of it. The heavy footfalls came closer, closer, until they were right outside. A shadow filled the room for an instant, and then was gone. Willo continued up the hallway, his destination someplace other than this. I lowered my weapons and breathed deeply, while Adara wrapped her arms around me from behind and laid her head on my back. We remained like this only briefly, when I realized that he would probably be returning the same way. We moved to another corner of the cubicle to prevent the giant sub-human from noticing us as he passed. I relied on the fact that his low intelligence would prevent him from performing any independent actions, that he would carry out only his given task.

Willo's destination must have been some distance away, for it was many minutes before we heard him again. Alerted, we placed our backs tightly against the wall and waited. Once more his heavy footsteps grew louder, until he was right outside our room, where—he stopped! Neither of us dared to breathe, and, despite the coolness of the chamber, the sweat poured profusely from my body. I could feel Adara's fingernails digging into my wrists, but was unable to make her stop.

What had caused the giant beast to halt where he did in the corridor was a mystery, but we were relieved when another instinct, probably his blind obedience to Ras-ek, sent him on his way. We listened to the diminishing thuds, daring at last to breathe. I moved quietly to the door and peered out, just in time to see Willo disappear down the stairs. Moments later the door slid shut, and the corridors of Sekkator were still. Willo had returned to the torture room below.

Fearing that he might again return, we held our position for many minutes. But the silence remained unbroken, convincing me that it was time to make our move. Choosing speed over stealth we hurried to the staircase, and after reassuring ourselves that the door to the Arena of Joy was closed, we began our ascent. The air grew cooler as we climbed, and the dim light from the torches below faded, until it became difficult to see even the next step. As we passed through an opening in the ceiling the darkness seemed to clutch at us, as though it were aware of our presence. I had been counting the steps as we ascended, but I stopped after reaching ninety.

The stairs finally ended, depositing us in a very narrow tunnel. At the end of this passage I could see a light, and it was toward this that we walked. I held on to Adara tightly, alternately sorry and glad that she was with me. She seemed to notice the vibration at the same time I did, and we stopped for a moment, our senses alert. We took five more steps, halting once again. Now there could be no doubt, for the

283

corridor seemed to tremble slightly. Unquestionably, we were approaching some inexplicable power source.

We emerged from the tunnel into a large room, the craggy stone walls giving the appearance of a cavern. The light here was not bright, but I was easily able to distinguish the contents of the room. There were human skeletons, hundreds of them, knee deep in some places. They surrounded the sole other object in the room, a large wooden table. On top of this lay the partly decomposed body of a man. It had—Oh, God!—I swear it had been chewed!

Adara wanted to gag, and it took every bit of will she could summon to prevent herself, for silence was imperative. I rushed her past the grisly feast through a portal that led to an adjoining chamber. The death room was quickly forgotten as we realized that we had found what we came for. In the middle of the chamber stood a large stone structure, this closely resembling a kiln. Ras-ek Varano lie supine on a slab of rock. He was completely naked, his body a ghostly white. His head and neck were within the mouth of this furnace, and every few seconds a brilliant flash of light radiated from its depths, nearly blinding us. It was obvious that this was the power source, for the vibrations were their strongest here.

While Adara stared in disgust at the still form, I tightened the grip on the haft of my knife and approached it. It was a small body, and it appeared to be very old. Without his turban I could see Ras-ek's head, a hairless travesty of misshapen lumps. The cauliflower-like ears were more deformed than I had thought. I stared at the helpless imbecile, wishing that Ter-ek, Lar-ek and the rest were there. If only Peter Collins could somehow know what I was about to do! I wished that all the people of Boranga could know that their freedom was about to become a reality.

Those few seconds that I spent in idle thought proved to cost me everything, for ere I could plunge the blade into that putrid heart, I heard Adara scream, and from the death chamber came Willo, growling and gurgling insanely. Adara froze in the beast's path, but he tossed her aside, his eyes only for me. To protect the Master was his only motivation for living, and he rose to the task. I ducked his charge none too gracefully, heaving my ax at his face as I did. My aim was poor, for the ax did nothing more than halve one of the enormous ears before it clattered to the floor. I ran after my valuable weapon and scooped it up, as the now infuriated Willo resumed his chase. As he ran, I threw my knife at him, trying to slow him down, but the agile creature was able to leap from its path. Before I could react again he was on top of me, lifting me high in the air and hurling me across the chamber. The fall stunned me momentarily, giving him enough time to reach me. I had retained the ax, but I was unable to use it, for Willo had placed his clubbed foot on my wrist. With an expression that approximated a smile, the hideous fellow leaned over and grabbed a handful of my hair. His face was only inches from mine, and I could smell his fetid breath.

Suddenly Willo leaped to his feet, shrieking loudly. He turned around, clutching at his back, and I could see the knife protruding from it, the blade that I had hurled at him only moments earlier. He staggered toward the frightened Adara, infuriated by her rash act. Freed, I leaped to my feet and drove the ax into his skull, barely denting it. Attacked from both sides, the mindless sub-human began to spin about wildly, not knowing what to do first. Adara circled around until she stood to the rear of me. With my beloved now temporarily out of danger I landed a blow to Willo's knee, which caused him to lose his balance and fall backward, driving the knife deeper into his back. Willo roared in pain, but the determined creature again rose to his feet and took up the pursuit. Without hesitation I motioned Adara into the other chamber, myself right at her heels, for I knew that his only thought now would be to tear us apart, regardless of what Ras-ek might have had in mind for us.

The sights of the death chamber bothered us not as we sought to elude our foe. I tipped over the table and its grisly occupant in an effort to slow Willo down. We hastened to the tunnel, and I ordered Adara through first. A quick glance back revealed Willo entering the chamber. The table delayed him little, for he simply detoured through the cairns of bones, which cracked under his heavy feet. I did not wait to see any more, but raced through the passage to the top of the spiral staircase, where Adara was waiting for me. We descended as quickly as the darkness would allow, but were no more than halfway down when the stairs shook, and I knew that many more hundreds of pounds of weight had been added to it. Aided by the dim light from below we quickened our pace, and were soon standing in the now familiar corridor. The short distance to the main doors was covered quickly, and with a minimum of effort we pulled open one of them about three feet. For the first time in many days we breathed the fresh air of Boranga. It was daylight, and even the depressing mesa on which Sekkator sat was a welcome sight. We should have run and never stopped, but something held me in that corridor.

"Ro-lan, why do you stop?" Adara screamed, realizing my delay. "We are free! Let us get away from this accursed place!"

"I must destroy Ras-ek," I told her. "He must not be allowed to continue these atrocities. The people of Boranga must be free!"

"But what about Willo?" she exclaimed. "He will not allow you near the Master's body. See, he comes!"

Willo reached the bottom of the stairs, staggering wildly, apparently nearer death than I had thought him to be. He took a few steps toward us, but I held my ground while Adara pulled at my arm. Willo finally stumbled and fell, panting like an animal as he lay there. With a supreme effort, he raised himself back up and returned to the base of the stairs. He clutched the railing with both hands and, with herculean strength, began to shake it. Before I realized what he was doing the staircase crumbled, toppling down with a crash and burying the beast. With his dying breath, this giant sub-human had destroyed the only means of reaching the Master, and as I stared upward I swore at the fates that had robbed me of my chance to rid Boranga of this monster.

Adara was well aware of my thoughts as we stood in the corridor of Sekkator that day, and she did her best to soothe me. We were freer that moment than we had been in weeks, but as long as Ras-ek lived, we could never be sure how long it would last. I must return to Var-Dor and make the others believe that the Master can be destroyed. If I failed in this, then I must return by myself and try to do it alone. I was obsessed with his destruction, but I could not help it for I had seen atrocities far beyond the human ken. Surely, reasonable men like Heran and Lar-ek would listen to me. Perhaps Denny would be waiting for me in Var-Dor. Yes, my good friend, Denny McVey. He would help me, as would Ter-ek. His Aleen was still among the Holy Ones, whether dead or alive I knew not. Ter-ek would . . .

My mind was rambling badly. I had to get away from here, and take Adara to some safe place. Her well-being was uppermost in my mind. I held her hand tightly and, with a final glance backward, we quitted the unholy Sekkator for the coolness of the Borangan day.

CHAPTER EIGHTEEN

DOWN THE OTONGO

The flight from Sekkator was undertaken with a minimum of planning, for the most important thing was to get as far away as possible in the shortest amount of time. I had no idea how long it took for Ras-ek's powers to be restored, nor was I anxious to find out. I prayed that we would be past the Other Side by the time it happened.

Adara and I started down the steep hill along the path that had first brought me to Sekkator, but the memory of what waited below caused us to leave the well-worn trail and begin angling down toward the southeast. Passage was rougher, and we both lost our footing a number of times during the descent, but I was convinced that it was the wise thing to do. Adara agreed with me for she had heard much of the Holy Ones, and had no desire to meet them.

Our descent took only a couple of hours, but the

precarious nature of it made it seem longer, and it was with a sigh of relief that we neared the bottom. Once again I gazed out over unevenly plowed fields of crops, and the sight of them brought back the nightmare of the Great Sacrifice. I estimated that we were a good few miles east of that field, but the similarity of the terrain served to remind me that caution would be highly advisable. These fields were planted by people, not by any supernatural power, and it was a distinct possibility that they could be nearby.

The bottom of the steep hill ended in a sheer drop of ten feet. I lowered myself as far down as my tenuous handhold would allow, falling the final yard with a jolt that served to reactivate all the aches in my body. Fortunately, I was able to help Adara down a bit more gently, and together we raced across the open fields until we reached a copse of fruit trees. Only then did I allow us the luxury of rest, though I doubt that we paused more than two minutes. We ate sparingly of the bountiful fruit, taking some with us to have at a later time.

As we walked through the beautiful orchards, I momentarily forgot where we were, for the color and life that was prevalent here appeared incongruous with the evil that surrounded it. What did these demented souls know of beauty, of life, or of love? What thoughts ran through their diseased brains as they watched strangers, friends, even those of their own families, suffering horrible deaths? Perhaps in their own sick way they were able to fulfill these emotions by the perpetration or witnessing of such acts. I shuddered at the idea, though something told me that I was not far from wrong.

Neither of us saw the man until he stood only a few yards in front of us, a broad smile across his face. I cursed myself for my apparent lack of alertness, but it struck me that Adara had not noticed him either. Likely he had emerged from behind a tree. He was a young man, no more than twenty or so, with no visible deformities. His handsome face indicated intelligence, while his broad chest and muscular arms denoted strength. I wondered if he did not belong here, but his words told me otherwise.

"Ah, Roland Summers," he replied cheerfully, walking toward us with both hands extended. "It's so good to see you again. We missed you the other night after the Great—"

He had no chance to say any more, for I leaped forward and caved in the side of his head with my ax. He crumpled in a heap, a dreamy smile frozen on his face. As I wiped the gore from the ax, I realized that I did not feel the slightest bit of remorse for what I had just done. Adara, however, was stunned by my sudden action, and she stared at me in disbelief, her hands covering her mouth to stifle the scream that was within her. She turned away from me as my eyes met hers.

"It had to be done, dear one," I told her insistently. "This fellow was one of them, and he would have had others upon us if I had merely chased him away."

"He was so young, Ro-lan!" she pleaded, as she turned around. "He greeted you in peace. How could you—?"

"He was a Holy One, Adara!" I snapped. "Don't you understand that? The Holy Ones are devils, all of

291

them! You know what they are capable of. As for his age, I would destroy one of their children if it stood in the path of our flight from this accursed place. I despise what I have become, but it seems to be the only way to stay alive here."

"I know that you did the right thing," Adara replied, now more composed. "But it is such a shock to witness. I'm sorry I reacted the way I did, Ro-lan. I will be stronger next time."

"Your reaction is the result of your humanity, Adara, and you must never lose this quality. To merely accept these violent acts with no compunction would make us no better than the degenerates who perpetrate their atrocities here. I pray that we never fall that low."

She kissed me softly on the cheek and I managed a smile, though it seemed harder to control my emotions. We resumed our eastward journey only after I had concealed the body of the young man behind some dense shrubs. Without any other encounters I felt sure that we could cover much ground, for I guessed that it was only late morning. The orchards provided us with ample cover, and this time I was careful not to allow us to be taken by surprise again. We hid behind trees at any hint of people, and in this way we were able to avoid at least half a dozen confrontations that would all have ended in the same way. That two of the people we saw were women made me even more glad for our stealth. It did slow us down considerably, but it was less dangerous and far more humane.

Hours later, we discovered that the landscape changed drastically. The leafy, abundant orchards were gone, replaced by numerous tall, dead trees. The ground, where no rocks dotted it, was hard and dusty. It was difficult to imagine that anything had ever grown here before. Visibility was less limited here, and a cursory scan told me that we were all alone in this mockery of a forest. We had not encountered anyone for the better part of an hour. I doubted that the Holy Ones would find reason to bring them this far east, but I nevertheless kept my eyes open, though the pace of our journey was brisker than before. The terrain varied little as I altered our direction southward. I knew that we would have to pass through the Vale of Fear eventually, but with the Master incapacitated I guessed that there would be little danger.

We had been traveling south for only a few miles when Adara motioned me to stop. She had heard something off to our left. Though inaudible to me, I indicated that she should walk toward the sound. We covered only a few yards when I too heard it, just beyond a dense clump of dead trees. I recognized the sound but it seemed too good to be true. As we emerged from the trees I saw it, and my heart pounded. In front of us was a river—a wide, swiftly-flowing river! What better means of escape from this place? For the first time in many weeks, I felt that we were being smiled upon. I lifted Adara high in the air and whooped wildly. She grinned questioningly at me, puzzled by my actions.

"Do you know what this means, my love?" I shouted happily. "The river flows south. By utilizing it, we will be able to journey as far away from here in a day as we could have in many days on foot. This *must* be the Otongo, for what other larger river is to be found on Boranga? See! Its headwater is high in the mountains to the north."

"But how will we travel on the river?" Adara questioned.

With a wave of my hand, I indicated the trees that we had just passed through. I returned to them and began my examination, selecting a few of the thinner, sturdier ones. After felling them with my ax, I trimmed the rotted bark from them. Adara, now caught up in my excitement, assisted me, and soon we had three durable logs of similar proportions. I managed to bind them together, albeit loosely, with the thin leather thongs that bound our sandals to our feet and ankles, discarding the now useless soles. We launched the makeshift raft with no ceremony, and the first leg of our voyage down the Otongo was under way.

The river ran wide for many miles, no less than forty feet across at any point. We had paddled with our hands until we were in the center, which appeared to be quite deep. Although at its mercy, the Otongo seemed content to carry us gently and swiftly along. We encountered no obstacles, and its only bends were gradual. I was more confident now than I had been before that we would escape from the Other Side, and I smiled happily at Adara as we kept watch on either bank.

We had just rounded a slight bend when I noticed a large object on the west bank. I had to look twice to make sure I was not imagining things, for the object was a two-masted sailing ship, embedded deeply in mud and standing nearly upright a couple of yards from the river. The stern of the vessel was facing us, enabling me to read the name. It was the *Sea Star*, Peter Collins' old schooner! When he had discovered it missing, he assumed that it had sunk. What it was doing here was hard to imagine, though I had a vague idea as to who was responsible.

Adara and I paddled furiously until we reached the bank. There, we pulled the raft up behind us. I became instantly alert as I realized that we were not the only ones here. From the river, the *Sea Star* had blocked our view of the man and the small girl but now they were clearly visible. They were on the ground near the bow of the vessel, the man in the throes of a seizure. He banged his head on the ground, frothing madly, while the child sat nearby and giggled. Somehow, he noticed our approach, and leaped to his feet. As he charged us, his head bleeding profusely, he shrieked loudly. I quickly dispatched him and he fell at my feet. My attention then turned to the little girl who was running toward Adara, an insane giggle coming from her lips. She was a pretty child, no more than seven or eight years old. With a few rapid steps I intercepted her and lifted her high in the air by the throat. I raised my ax as she struggled, but before I could carry out the execution, my hand was stayed. Looking into her wild eyes, I realized that this was only a child, a little girl. I glanced at Adara, who stood apart from me, determined not to interfere. Hoping that my action would not prove deadly, but glad that a spark of humanity still remained within me, I let the child go. She ran screaming and giggling into the woods, where she disappeared from our view.

"I couldn't do it, Adara," I stated helplessly. "No matter what she is, what she might turn out to be, I just couldn't kill that little girl. What would that have made me?"

"I would not have prevented you from doing it, my love," she answered, "but I am glad that you didn't. They all deserve to die, and perhaps they will some day, but I shudder to think of us as their executioners. Ro-lan, this is my grandfather's ship, is it not?"

"Yes, this is Peter's beloved *Sea Star*," I told her, "though how it turned up here is a mystery. Let's take a quick look at her, for I'm afraid that our little friend might return with others."

A close examination revealed that the once lovely schooner was a shell of her former self. Most of her wood had either been broken off or had rotted away, and the forward mast was cracked in half. Little remained of the furled sails, other than a few tattered rags. I explored the interior of the hull, only to discover that every removable item was gone. This ship had been given a thorough going over, most likely by the Holy Ones. The only useful item left was one small life boat, which had been battened down securely to the deck. The oars were gone, but that did not matter, for I was sure that the dinghy would serve us infinitely better than the makeshift raft.

Adara had remained on the ground while I examined the vessel. I leaned over the railing to summon her for assistance, but my words caught in my throat as I saw her. She stood near the bow of the *Sea Star*, her right hand touching, perhaps caressing, the rotted wood. A dreamy expression covered her face as tears rolled down her cheeks. This derelict of a ship represented the last link with the parents and grandmother she never knew and with the grandfather that she had loved. I was deeply moved by the scene, and I withdrew my head so that she might be alone with her memories for the moment.

Unfastening the dinghy proved to be of little challenge, and I had it free in only minutes. The wood was worn in spots, but no holes were evident, and I was sure that the small craft could be utilized. I dragged it along the deck as far as I could, but I knew that without help I would be unable to lower it to the ground. Though loath to interrupt my beloved's memories, so precious to her, I nonetheless was still aware of the child I had released, and the certainty that she would bring others. But before I could summon her, Adara's head appeared over the railing on the port side. Her eyes were red as she asked if I required help. As I pulled her onto the deck I avoided looking into her eyes, sparing her the necessity of an explanation.

Soon the dinghy rested on the edge of the river. I broke off a couple of sturdy planks from the ship to use as oars, and we departed only moments after releasing the raft into the river. Adara caught on quickly to the use of the oar, and we paddled hastily out into the center of the Otongo, where we were satisfied to let the current do the work. My beloved kept her eyes glued to the final resting place of the *Sea Star*, straining to keep from losing sight of it; but finally it was gone from our vision, and with a deep sigh she turned. From my position in the bow of the dinghy, I leaned back and placed my hand on her cheek as I smiled at her. She returned the smile, though I knew that her heart, her thoughts, were still back there on the bank of the river.

An hour or so after passing the wreck of the *Sea Star*, the Otongo veered off in an easterly direction, narrowing as it did. Soon the low mountain range to the east became visible through the overcast. To the south of us, not very far, a pall of darkness hovered. I was now certain that the Otongo would circumvent the Vale of Fear, most likely through the mountains. Minutes later I knew that I was right, for the river carried our tiny craft into a narrow gorge, and the ominous gloom disappeared from our sight.

The wall of mountains on either side of us rose to great heights, reaching into the clouds high above. Although an awesome sight, I spent little time gaping at it, for the flow of the current had increased significantly, the white water churning with foam. The tops of boulders dotted the river ahead of us, but it was the hidden rocks that I feared more than these. With Adara's help I was able to guide the craft safely past the outcroppings, and with luck still on our side we managed to avoid ramming others. Our only mishap was the scraping of the boat along the side of one jagged stone finger, resulting in the loss of one of the oars as we tried to push off.

Once again the river began to widen, and the current slowed down enough for us to relax our vigil. Only an occasional rock now protruded, these easily avoidable. The Otongo had turned and twisted many times, but I believed that we were now moving toward the southwest, and our subsequent emergence from the gorge confirmed this. The harsh, barren plains of Boranga now surrounded us on all sides, and in my mind I embraced them.

Adara and I had successfully escaped from the Other Side, from Sekkator, from Ras-ek Varano. A feeling of pride swelled within me as I realized what we had accomplished. I couldn't wait to see the expressions on the faces of those in Var-Dor when they realized that Adara had returned, that by her courage she had defied the Master and lived. Only the most cowardly of the Homarus would not wish to join in and put an end to this reign of terror.

We were kept busy for the rest of the day with maneuvering the dinghy, for the Otongo had begun to swerve erratically. The two of us took turns with the remaining oar, and this additional effort served to further tax our already fatigued bodies. By late afternoon, when we hauled the boat far up on the east bank of the river, we were exhausted. We dined on the remainder of the fruit that we had brought with us, washing down the meal with cold, brackish river water. Night had fallen swiftly while we dined, and afterward it proved but a matter of moments until we fell asleep on the hard ground. My sleep that night was dreamless, untroubled, though it was not destined to last.

"Roland Summers!" the hollow voice spoke.

"Yes?" I answered.

"I am so pleased to find you once again."

"Pleased?"

"You didn't think for a minute that you and your lovely woman could leave Sekkator for good, did you?"

"Sekkator?"

"Now you must return to Sekkator, Roland. I will even overlook your destruction of my dear Willo. Return to Sekkator, return, return . . ."

My eyes snapped open quickly, and I glanced with concern at Adara, but she appeared to be sleeping comfortably on the ground next to me. I shook her gently on the arm, and she looked questioningly at me as she rubbed the sleep from her eyes.

"Ro-lan, my darling, what is wrong?" she asked.

"Nothing is wrong," I replied. "It is nearly dawn, and I wished to get an early start. Why don't—no! Oh, no!"

"Ro-lan, what is it?"

"The boat! It's—*it's gone!*"

We raced to the spot where we had left the dinghy. No marks were in evidence, other than those made by us when we first dragged the boat ashore. It had simply vanished! In a gesture of futility I drew my ax and held it poised, while I cast glances into the crisp air around us. I knew now that I had not been dreaming, that we were once again in the gravest of danger.

"What is happening?" Adara pleaded. "Oh, please, tell me what is happening, Ro-lan!"

"I dread to even think of it, dear one. We must leave this place quickly. Follow me!"

With no further conversation, I grabbed Adara's hand and began running along the bank of the Otongo. If Ras-ek had indeed found us, then I could only guess that he was toying with us. I decided that it might prove easier for him to find us if we stayed

300

close to the river, so we turned eastward. My left leg throbbed mercilessly from an injury that I had incurred, and my head began to hurt once more. After only five minutes I realized that neither of us could maintain the pace, and I motioned for Adara to stop. The two of us dropped to the ground, breathless.

The first hints of daylight were visible when we heard the sound, and the feelings of despair, frustration that overwhelmed me were shared, I'm certain, by Adara. No more could I run, nor could I fight. To have come this far and lost was the final crushing blow. As the nimbus of evil heads swirled around us I stared resignedly at them, not even caring. Adara held tightly to my arm, a similar look of resignation on her face. When Ras-ek's full image appeared, we did not even move.

"Ah, my wicked, wicked children," he chortled. "I welcome you as honored guests, and this is how I am repayed. Were you not enraptured by the joys of the Other Side, by the pleasures of Sekkator?"

"How—how did you find us?" I asked, dully.

"Never would I have dreamed that you could reach the river, much less negotiate it this far. Had it not been for the dear little boat-keeper's daughter, I might have spent days searching for you. Who knows? Perhaps I would not have been able to find you. No matter, for we are together once again. We shall return to Sekkator, where you will learn of my true benevolence. Come! The Holy Ones await your arrival."

People have performed feats of strength in stressful situations that far exceeded their individual capabilities. It was in such an instance that I summoned what strength of will I might have had left. I rose to my feet, swatting blindly at the heads that encircled me. I strode defiantly toward the image of Ras-ek, my ax raised. He seemed to retreat as I neared him. I quickened my pace, but he was able to maintain a distance of a few yards between us.

"You will never take us back to that fiendish place!" I shouted, brandishing the ax. "You may kill us here, but not without a fight! Stand still, you devil!"

The image froze, enabling me to close the distance between us. I drove the full force of my body into the blow, but only succeeded in cutting a swath through empty air. The Master cackled madly as I wheeled around to face him again, his body shaking uncontrollably from fits of mirth.

"You never seem to learn, do you, Roland?" he mocked. "Maybe I won't take you back to Sekkator right away. I still find you most interesting. Perhaps another challenge would provide me with entertainment. Yes, that is what I shall do."

I seemed to be standing still while the whole world spun wildly around me. Adara, Ras-ek—everything became a blur. I was faintly aware of my ax, and that my hand was sore from the tight grip I had on it. When my vision cleared, I saw that I no longer stood on the barren plains of Boranga, but along the narrow ledge that encircled the underground lake of the Guardian. Less than ten feet away, I could see the head of the hideous reptile as it swiveled downward to investigate the morsel that had suddenly turned up in its lair. The morsel was Adara, my beloved Adara! She lay on her back screaming, her hand raised in front of her face in a futile gesture of defense. From within the cavern echoed laughter, insane peals of laughter.

The precarious ledge on which I stood was not easily negotiable, but I ignored this as I rapidly covered the short distance to where Adara lie. Tomo Raka's gaping, slavering jaws were almost upon her when I reached them, and in his desire for her soft flesh he apparently did not see me. I brought the ax down forcefully on his soft snout, retaining it with some difficulty as he pulled away, sputtering and roaring. He swiveled downward, disappearing in a froth of bubbles below the surface of the lake. Without the slightest hesitation I helped Adara to her feet and guided her carefully along the ledge. We moved as fast as the thin perch would allow, but the safety of the tunnel was still far off when the head emerged again less than twenty feet ahead, blocking our path. We changed direction, but the beast was able to close the distance quickly. I realized that the only chance was to fight him, so I ordered Adara to continue along the ledge while I remained. She refused, choosing instead to stand by my side.

Dripping jaws clattered grotesquely as the Guardian neared us. He seemed warier this time, the memory of the most recent blow still fresh in his tiny brain. Suddenly, I began to have trouble focusing on the beast. I rubbed my eyes in an effort to clear them, but to no avail. No longer was I able to maintain my balance on the ledge. I felt a hand grip mine tightly, just as the cavern began to spin. Adara was visible at my side, but all else was a blur. I recalled hearing that hideous laugh again before everything darkened.

*　　*　　*

I stood in the middle of a small clearing, surrounded on all sides by lush tropical vegetation. To my rear were hills, and behind them a tall range of mountains. I guessed that we were in the eastern forest of Boranga, though this particular place did not look familiar. Adara was just coming to, and I helped her to her feet as I pondered on the enigma of the Master's fiendish powers.

A crashing of foliage in front of us brought us both alert. From out of the forest emerged a satong, this one even larger than the two I had encountered during my journey with Ter-ek. The man-beast shrieked when it saw us, and without pause it raced toward us. Remembering the agility of these creatures, I knew I had no time to think; I charged straight at it and heaved my ax into its face. The weapon lodged deep in its skull, bringing the thing to the ground where it screamed and roared frenziedly. I did not know if the blow would prove fatal, nor did I plan to stay around and find out. Adara, who had nearly passed out from the sight of the monstrosity, joined me, and together we quitted the clearing for the hills. I hated to lose the ax, for I was now defenseless. For a moment I considered retrieving it after the satong died but, as I looked back, I saw two more of the things race from the foliage, and my idea quickly vanished.

We staggered blindly through the forest, finally emerging near the foot of the hills. Behind us we could hear the screams and roars of many satongs, all probably fighting over the body of their injured brother. The terrible clamor forced us to hasten into the hills, where we climbed for about fifteen minutes. We topped a ridge, nearly falling backward as we absorbed the sight that greeted us. The slopes were covered with satongs, scores of them! Many appeared to be feeding, for the air was filled with hissing and sucking noises, these most disgusting. Many of them showed no interest in our presence, but a few came toward us, and we hastened along the ridge to escape them. A quick glance back revealed that at least seven of them were descending to our level, anxious to take up the chase.

As we ran I considered the options, of which there were few. I was looking for a place above us that we could occupy and defend with stones. Though temporary, I did not believe that Ras-ek intended for us to be here that long . . . no! I must not consider that fiend's actions in our efforts to save ourselves. I had the feeling that he was tiring of the game, that our lives were very much in our own hands.

The man-beasts reached the bottom, and in our weakened condition I knew it would not be long before they overtook us. Suddenly, we were confronted with an opening in the side of the hills. The location appeared to be right; was it possible that this was—Peter's cave? Here was something that I doubted even Ras-ek could have anticipated. With the satongs only yards behind us, we entered the dark adit.

We traveled along the narrow tunnel, which penetrated deep into the hills. The ceiling of the cave was low, only inches above my head. Our stalkers had entered the cave on their hands and knees, but the narrowness of the walls eventually forced them to turn back. This surely was Peter's cave, for his description fit it perfectly, and the thought of what was on the other end of the tunnel caused our spirits to soar again. Once at sea he would be unable to find us, and we could formulate new plans for the future. With this hope, shared by both of us, we covered the distance through the lengthy cave uneventfully, finally reaching the seaward opening some hours later. It had been many years since the floor of this cavern had been trod upon, for Peter Collins' boat still rested there proudly, undisturbed.

Adara and I stood silently, hand in hand, and stared lovingly at the efforts of that incredible man. The boat was exactly as he had described it to me, even more than I had visualized, for it appeared to be a fine, seaworthy craft. It had taken him ten years and many hundreds of miles to complete, and now he was not here to share its maiden voyage with us. I regretted this more than anything.

"An interesting vessel, Roland Summers. Strange that I was unaware of its presence."

The voice that echoed through the cavern was Rasek's! Many hours had passed since last we heard him, and we had been lulled into a false sense of security. I should have known better. We spun around and saw the image of his evil face, this so large that it nearly filled the cavern.

"We have come too far for you to stop us now, you spawn of the Devil!" I screamed. "Adara, quickly! Get in!"

Adara ran to the boat and scrambled over the side. I started to push the vessel down the incline to the water that lapped gently through the large opening.

But I had moved it barely a few feet when my arms went numb, followed immediately by the rest of my body. I fell to the ground, helpless.

"I tire of this sport," Ras-ek snapped, "and I especially tire of you, Roland."

My body was lifted by invisible hands, and flung with great force against one of the stone walls. As I dropped to the hard floor, I realized that the paralysis had passed, and I nearly bit off my lip as the pain overwhelmed me. I was raised a second time and hurled against the other wall. Adara screamed, though this was drowned by the insane laughter of Ras-ek Varano. Back and forth between the two walls I was thrown, three, four, five times. My shattered body was finally deposited near the stern of the boat, where Adara, through a veil of tears, sought to assist me. I was barely conscious, unable to move.

"Adara, help—help me into the boat," I whispered, feebly.

She took hold of my arms, but the pain was unbearable, and I screamed. "Ro-lan, I can't! I can't!" she cried.

"Perhaps I might be of help," Ras-ek crowed. "After all, you will need a proper coffin for your funeral. Yes, a burial at sea would be fitting for you, since it was the sea that brought you here."

The invisible hand lifted my broken body up and deposited it on the floor of the boat, the force of the fall causing me to cry out once more. The vessel began to move down the slope to the waiting waves. I called meekly to Adara to get in with me.

"Ro-lan, I cannot move!" she screamed.

"Surely you do not wish to subject this lovely

creature to the perils of the sea, do you, Roland?" said Ras-ek, mockingly. "Oh, no; she will return to Sekkator with me. You would only die soon, and she would be all alone out there. How cruel of you, Roland, how cruel."

"Ro-lan, I cannot live without you!" Adara cried, her voice trembling. "I will kill myself, rather than return to Sekkator. Forgive me, my darling."

The vessel reached the water, and the tide began to take it slowly through the opening out to sea. From my position at the bottom of the boat, I was able to look up into the cavern. Adara stood riveted to her spot, while the turbaned fiend grinned wickedly behind her. My body cried out in pain, as I summoned whatever I had left in an effort to raise my head a few inches.

"My darling, never concede . . . to death," I implored. "I . . . will return for you . . . some day, somehow. You must . . . believe me. I . . . love you. Promise me . . . that you . . . will do . . . as . . . I . . . ask . . ."

"I-I promise, Ro-lan," she stammered. "I will wait for you, always."

"How charming. How touching," Ras-ek mocked. "Maybe I should not have injured you so severely. That way, if by some miracle you returned to your own world, you would have had to live with the thought that Adara was mine. For you, this would have been worse than death itself. A pity I didn't think of it sooner. Farewell, Roland Summers!"

I stared at Adara for as long as I could, but the torment of keeping my head raised was unbearable. The boat had drifted some distance away from the sea cliffs, but through the sound of the sea I could still hear Ras-ek laughing and, mingled with his laughter, was a dear voice, calling my name repeatedly. It grew fainter, fainter, until it was gone. I was all alone in my seagoing coffin.

The rest of what happened is vague in my mind. Ama, the fierce sun, beat down on me, but I cared not. I remember drifting for what seemed an eternity, but could have been no more than a day or so. My brain tried to tell the rest of my body that I was cold, though I could not imagine why. I recall strange, irrelevant thoughts that passed through my head. There was a car of some kind in an amusement park, and it hurtled faster and faster, finally ending up in a large room, one so brightly lit that it blinded me. Next I was on the carousel, atop a white stallion. He went around slowly at first, but soon began to spin faster. I could hear the calliope as I hung tightly to the horse's neck. The lights from the park burned brighter and brighter as they whizzed by, forcing me to shield my eyes. I felt euphorically dizzy, and then, nothing . . .

They told me that I was found early in the morning by a fishing boat, a few miles north of Kauai. The doctors said that it was a miracle I still lived. Nearly every bone in my body was broken, and there had been much internal bleeding. They worked hard to save me, and for this I am most grateful to them. It was only after hearing my story that they began to doubt my sanity. I know how I must have sounded to them, for even I still tend to doubt it myself at times.

I was placed under "observation," but after destroying some hospital equipment in a couple of abortive attempts to get out, they locked me up. I have no relatives, no one to take responsibility for me. They tried to contact Uncle Jack, but he had died. I am physically well now, but they will not release me until they're sure that I've been "helped."

Everything that I have written here is true. There is an island called Boranga, dominated by the enigmatic powers of a madman. Adara, my beloved, my wife, is real, a prisoner of the Master. Denny McVey, my best friend, remains there, his fate unknown. The satongs, the Holy Ones, everything was as I related it. If you are reading this, I beg of you: I must return to Boranga! Somehow, some way, I must find that warp again! My friends are there! My beloved is there! I have nothing here any more! Help me to find my way back! *Please!*

EPILOGUE

I placed the last page of Roland Summers' story down on the table, and for a few minutes I sat there, trying to absorb all that I had just read. Five years ago I would have believed anything that Roland had chosen to tell me, but I would be remiss to say that I was not incredulous regarding this tale. Whatever the case, one fact was for certain: Roland Summers needed help, and it appeared that I was the only one left who could help him.

The next morning I sent a wire to the Chief of Psychiatry at Pacific Hills Medical Center, informing him that I would be arriving in Honolulu the following morning. I spent the rest of the day at the office, taking the time between patients to rearrange my upcoming week's schedule. Dr. DeFillipe consented to handle the bulk of my work, and I was grateful to him. I packed my bags that night and retired early, for I had to catch a morning flight.

The long trip to Hawaii was uneventful, with clear

weather preventing any delays. I felt a thrill as I saw Diamond Head from the air for the first time in more than ten years. At the airport, I rented a car and drove straight to the hospital, not even bothering to check in at my hotel. After a short wait, I was ushered into the office of Dr. George Reynolds, a most genial man who, along with one of his staff, Dr. Larry Bellman, proceeded to give me a nearly thirty-minute briefing on their patient, Roland Summers. They were most thorough, and their concern was evident.

"You can see our problem, Dr. Morrison," Dr. Reynolds concluded. "After all these months of therapy, he still insists on sticking to his story. At times he's even fanatic about it."

"Do you feel that this constitutes him as a danger?" I inquired.

"To others, probably not," Dr. Bellman offered, "but to himself, yes. Here, we've been able to keep an eye on him but unsupervised, I would fear for him. He appeared to have no one who cared. You are the first to express an interest in him."

"His parents were close friends of mine. I have always thought highly of Roland. Would you consider releasing him to my care? My wife passed away a couple of years ago, and my daughters, both married, are living back east. I would enjoy having him around."

"Would you be able to spend an adequate amount of time with him?" Dr. Reynolds asked. "After all, you are a physician."

"When Edna passed away, I increased my work load considerably to keep myself from going crazy," I told them. "I could just as easily reduce it, and I would be more than happy to do it for Roland."

"I suggest you hold your decision until you've had a chance to see him," said Dr. Bellman.

"When will that be?" I asked.

"We can do that right now," said Dr. Reynolds.

The doctors led me to an elevator, which took us up to the fifth floor. We strode down the corridor to room 511, Dr. Bellman opening the locked door with one of many keys on a large ring. I saw him the moment we entered, sitting in a chair and staring out at the ocean through a barred window. He turned around slowly when he heard us enter. Physically, he looked the same as I remembered him, perhaps a bit thinner. He stood up when he saw me, and I noted two enigmatic flecks of crimson burning deep in his eyes. The image lasted for just a moment, and then was gone.

"Dr. Morrison, you came!" he said, happily pumping my hand. "I was beginning to believe that I was all alone in this world."

"Hello, Roland," I replied, smiling. "It's so good to see you."

"Roland, Dr. Morrison would like to take you out of here, back to California," said Dr. Reynolds. "Would you like that?"

Roland absorbed the doctor's statement for a few seconds, looking first at the two psychiatrists, then at me. He turned away from us and stared out the window again, his hands on the back of the chair. So tight was his grip, that the chair began to shake. His whole body began to quiver, as if he was fighting to gain control of himself. I glanced at Dr. Reynolds, who motioned me to remain where I was. When it finally passed he once again turned around, a meager smile on his face.

"I knew that I could count on you, Dr. Morrison." He turned to Dr. Reynolds. "When can I go?"

"We have a few matters to take care of first," Dr. Reynolds answered. "It should not take more than an hour or two."

We returned to Dr. Reynolds' office, leaving Roland to anticipate his pending freedom. A hastily called staff meeting commenced, and I was included. With everyone in agreement to Roland's immediate future, the paperwork was begun. In a little over an hour the preliminaries were concluded, and we returned to room 511. Roland had donned a pair of dungarees and a green pullover shirt to replace the drab grey of his hospital garments. The doctors accompanied us down to the lobby, where they said their farewells to the subdued Roland. I herded him into the car and started off for the hotel.

Roland remained silent as we drove along, apparently content to look out the window. I decided that he would talk when he wanted to, so I left him alone, opting to tune in some quiet music on the radio. He turned his head and smiled briefly as he heard the pleasing sounds.

A couple of miles further on we passed through a business district, and for the first time since we left the hospital, Roland spoke: "Dr. Morrison, you read of my experiences," he began. "Do you—? Never mind. I don't mean to put you on the spot so soon after getting out. Look! There's my bank. I still have some money deposited there. Could you pull over, please?"

"Are you sure it can't wait?" I asked.

"I would feel more comfortable with some cash in my pockets," he said.

I parked the car and offered to go in with him, but he told me that he would be brief. More than five minutes passed while I waited, and I began to grow concerned. I was about to get out of the car when Roland reappeared, an envelope in his hand.

"It took longer than I thought," he told me. "My bankbook had been lost when the *Queen* . . . well, I lost it."

The hotel room was more than adequate, the sight of the comfortable beds reminding me how tired I was from the long day. My greatest ambition at the moment was a cool shower and a short nap. I asked Roland if there was anything he wanted, but he assured me that he was fatigued from the excitement of his release, and that he merely wished to rest. He stretched out on one of the beds, and in a few minutes he was breathing deeply and evenly. Satisfied that he was well, I entered the shower.

All my life I have considered showers a pleasurable luxury, and for this reason I always tend to linger under them. That day was no exception, for it must have been at least twenty minutes before I emerged. When I did, I found that Roland was gone, and so were the car keys I had left on the dresser. In its place was the bank envelope, and a note. The note read:

Forgive me, Dr. Morrison, for the deception, but I had to do it. I hope that my disappearance will not cause you too much trouble. Whether you believe my story or not, I must try and get

315

back there. I have left some money to take care of any loose ends. Once again, I'm sorry.

Roland

I quickly called Dr. Reynolds, who was angered by the news. He told me to stand by the phone while he notified the proper authorities. I dried myself off and got dressed, all the time cursing myself for my lack of diligence. With nothing left to do, I sat on the terrace and stared at the ocean, waiting impatiently for Reynolds' call.

A long hour later, the psychiatrist called back. He had just heard from the police, and was able to piece the story together. Roland had driven to Honolulu Harbor, where he had stolen a medium-sized power boat. The owner of the vessel saw him take it, but by the time he reached the slip it was too late, for Roland was already headed out to sea. The man reported the theft to the police, who in turn notified the coast guard, and they were now searching for him. Dr. Reynolds had received permission to accompany one of the search vessels, and he wished me to go along.

In less than an hour we were out at sea, frantically scanning the horizon from our position on the bow of the small patrol boat. Dr. Reynolds had notified the authorities of Roland's condition, and the search was intensified to include helicopters and light aircraft. All day long the hunt continued, but to no avail. When darkness fell the search was called off, and we were advised to report back at dawn. I payed the harried boat owner more than enough to cover his loss, after extracting from him the promise not to

316

press any criminal charges should Roland be found.

The search continued for two more days, but was finally abandoned during the third day, this due to a series of violent squalls that hit the islands. The storm lasted for nearly forty-eight hours, causing severe damage along the shoreline. The coast guard people assured me that there would have been no way Roland could have survived the storm in so small a vessel. Though disheartened, I accepted their word.

On the day prior to my departure from Hawaii, I strode along the nearly deserted beach in front of the hotel at dusk. As I stared out on the calm sea, I thought to myself: What if, as impossible as it might seem, Roland's story was true? Was Adara still waiting for him, or had Ras-ek destroyed her, as he destroyed everything? Was Denny McVey still alive, or was Ter-ek unable to save him? How could the Master's cruel reign of terror be ended?

I prayed for Roland, prayed that somehow, somewhere, he was still alive. Be well, Roland Summers, wherever you are at this moment. I hope that you have found your Boranga.

DON'T MISS THESE BEST-SELLING HEROIC FANTASY FAVORITES!
EDITED BY ANDREW J. OFFUTT

SWORDS AGAINST DARKNESS (239, $1.95)
All-original tales of menace, high adventure and derring-do make up this anthology of heroic fantasy, featuring novelettes and stories by the great Robert E. Howard, Manly Wade Wellman, Poul Anderson, Ramsey Campbell, and many more.

SWORDS AGAINST DARKNESS II (293, $1.95)
Continuing the same outstanding success of the first, Volume II includes original, all-new novelettes and stories by best-selling authors Andre Norton, Andrew J. Offutt, Manly Wade Wellman, Tanith Lee and many others.

SWORDS AGAINST DARKNESS III (339, $1.95)
Here is Volume III in the highly successful SWORDS AGAINST DARKNESS anthologies, including first-time published short stories and novelettes by best-selling writers Ramsey Campbell, Manly Wade Wellman, Richard L. Tierney, Poul Anderson, plus 9 others!

SWORDS AGAINST DARKNESS IV (539, $2.25)
Fantasy masters new and established bring an unforgettable, all-new original collection of novelettes and short stories in this fourth volume featuring John Campbell Award Winner Orson Scott Card, Fantasy Award Winner Manly Wade Wellman, Poul Anderson, Tanith Lee, plus many many more.

SWORDS AGAINST DARKNESS V (550, $2.25)
All original, all-new tales of heroic fantasy, high adventure and sorcery make up this fabulous fifth collection featuring a dozen never-before-published novelettes by best-selling authors: Ramsey Campbell, Tanith Lee, Paul McGuire, Edward DeGeorge, Simon Green and many others.

Available wherever paperbacks are sold, or order direct from the Publisher. Send cover price plus 40¢ per copy for mailing and handling to Zebra Books, 21 East 40th Street, New York, N.Y. 10016. DO NOT SEND CASH!